ROKKA:
Braves of the Six Flowers

3

Illustration / MIYAGI

Dozzu

Nashetania

Can

I

come

save

you?

ROKKA: Braves of the Six Flowers

3

ISHIO YAMAGATA

ILLUSTRATION BY
MIYAGI

YEN ON

NEW YORK

ROKKA: Braves of the Six Flowers 3

ISHIO YAMAGATA

Translation by Jennifer Ward
Cover art by Miyagi

This book is a work of fiction. Names, characters, places, and incidents are the
product of the author's imagination or are used fictitiously. Any resemblance
to actual events, locales, or persons, living or dead, is coincidental.

ROKKA NO YUSHA
© 2011 by Ishio Yamagata, Miyagi
All rights reserved. First published in Japan in 2011 by SHUEISHA, Inc.
English translation rights arranged with SHUEISHA, Inc.
through Tuttle-Mori Agency, Inc., Tokyo.

English translation © 2017 by Yen Press, LLC

Yen On
1290 Avenue of the Americas
New York, NY 10104

Visit us at yenpress.com
facebook.com/yenpress
twitter.com/yenpress
yenpress.tumblr.com
instagram.com/yenpress

First Yen On Edition: December 2017

Yen On is an imprint of Yen Press, LLC.
The Yen On name and logo are trademarks of Yen Press, LLC.

The publisher is not responsible for websites (or their content)
that are not owned by the publisher.

Library of Congress Cataloging-in-Publication Data
Names: Yamagata, Ishio, author. | Miyagi, illustrator. | Ward, Jennifer (Jennifer J.), translator.
Title: Rokka : braves of the six flowers / Ishio Yamagata ; illustration by Miyagi ;
translation by Jennifer Ward.
Description: First Yen On edition. | New York, NY : Yen On, 2017–
Identifiers: LCCN 2017000469 | ISBN 9780316501415 (v. 1 : pbk.) |
ISBN 9780316556194 (v. 2 : pbk.) | ISBN 9780316556200 (v. 3 : pbk.)
Subjects: | CYAC: Heroes—Fiction. | Fantasy. | BISAC: FICTION / Fantasy / General.
Classification: LCC PZ7.1.Y35 Ro 2017 | DDC [Fic]—dc23
LC record available at https://lccn.loc.gov/2017000469

ISBN: 978-0-316-55620-0

10 9 8 7 6 5 4 3 2 1

LSC-C

Printed in the United States of America

CONTENTS

Adlet

Fremy

Rolonia

Mora

THE EVENTS THUS FAR

When the Evil God awakened from the depths of darkness, the Spirit of Fate chose six Braves and bestowed upon them the power to save humanity. The self-proclaimed "strongest man in the world," a boy named Adlet, was chosen as one of these Braves of the Six Flowers and headed out to battle to prevent the resurrection of the Evil God.

But when the Braves gathered to meet at the designated location, they found that, for some reason, there were seven of them. The Braves, realizing that one among them was the enemy, fell prey to suspicion and paranoia. However, with their leader, Adlet, their wits, and the powers of the Saints in their party, they slowly but surely solved these mysteries.

After a fierce battle with Tgurneu, one of the fiend commanders seeking to stop them, the Braves of the Six Flowers set off again, deep into the Howling Vilelands...

Illustration: Miyagi

Prologue

The Evil God and the Flower

From the putrid muck sprouted a single flower—and that was all.

The Weeping Hearth, where the Saint of the Single Flower once defeated the Evil God, was nothing but mud and the lone blossom.

Massive walls encompassed the westernmost point of the Howling Vilelands—location of the Evil God's resting place known as the Weeping Hearth. Erected by one of the fiend commanders, Cargikk, the bulwarks of unhewn rock formed two concentric circles. The radius of the outer ring was about three kilometers, while that of the inner stretched some five hundred meters. Despite their crude construction, they were larger and more solid than any defensive fortification that could be found in the human realms.

The area commonly called the Weeping Hearth actually referred to the small, solid red-black zone within the inner wall. Toxins oozing from the Evil God's body had seeped deep into the ground there. Without so much as a single blade of grass or any animal life, the dead land sprinkled with rocks made for a barren vista.

In that place, there was only sludge and a single flower.

"Aaadlet..."

An unsettling mass of sediment about the size of a horse's stable lay atop the lifeless earth. It squelched and writhed as if in terrible pain, black as coal, tinged with bloody crimson. Red tentacle-like limbs protruded from within. The five-meter-long appendages reached out, seemingly searching for something, but then, as if resigned, returned to the mud.

"Freeemy…Rolooonia…"

Near the center of the fetid mound was a pair of large lips that would rise to the surface, disappear, then emerge again, only to withdraw once more. The red, full, womanly lips wailed in a hoarse, feminine voice. The uncanny timbre, laced with hatred and bloodlust, called out the names of the Braves.

"Goldooof…Chaaaamo…Aaadlet…Haaans…Mooora… Chaaamo…Freeemy…Nashetaaania…" The mud writhed and droned on and on in that hate-filled voice.

This was the Evil God—the worst calamity ever to befall the human race, and progenitor of fiends.

Every few minutes, the muck would give birth to a strange creature. Each was about the size of a kitten, and no two looked exactly the same. One was a snake with innumerable eyes scattered across its body; another had the appearance of a monkey in the upper half, and that of a winged insect in the lower. Then came a dog with no legs or tail—just a head and a torso. After, a praying mantis with a head and nothing else. Some of them, like the seven monkeys' arms fused together, didn't even seem to be living creatures. The eerie organisms emerged from the corruption to wriggle, flounder, and squirm as if in existential despair for having been born so repulsive.

Following these births, the red tentacles would immediately snatch the eerie creatures, throttle them, and then return the deceased to their squalid beginnings. Birthing only to kill, murdering only to give life. The Evil God continued its meaningless cycle without end.

The thing imparted no sense of dignity, none of the beauty that wicked things possess, and none of the nobility begotten by a prolonged existence. Its form was ugly and foul and pitifully small. Barnah, the Brave of the Six Flowers who had fought the Evil God seven hundred years in the past, had described it as "so wretched it inspires despair."

Beside the Evil God bloomed a single flower—so small it could comfortably fit in a child's palm. Its six petals, pale purple, were not steeped in the Evil God's toxin. Softly, gently, as if nestling close to the abomination, the blossom sprouted from the ground. It was said the Saint of the Single Flower had planted it here a thousand years ago. But the true nature of this flower was not recorded in any documents or records. None aside from the Saint of the Single Flower knew if it had any power at all.

Three times humanity had fought the Evil God and defeated it. The first battle had been one thousand years ago, when the Saint of the Single Flower had sealed the deadly being in the Weeping Hearth.

The second battle had been seven hundred years ago. The Braves of the Six Flowers had kept Archfiend Zophrair in check while Heroic King Folmar and Bowmaster Barnah fought the Evil God. Their enemy had retaliated with its tentacles and toxins. Amid the suffocating stench, Folmar's sword sliced the sordid lump into pieces while Barnah's fiery arrow burned it. After an hour-long battle, the Evil God raised a hair-raising shriek and fell still.

The third battle had been three hundred years ago. More than a thousand fiends had flooded into the Weeping Hearth as the second generation of Braves charged the Evil God. With Marlie, the Saint of Blades, and Hayuha, the Saint of Time, holding enemy forces at bay, Merlania, the Saint of Thunder, activated a hieroformic gem. She had spent the past thirty years charging it purely for the sake of taking down the Evil God. Scores of lightning bolts streamed from the heavens, incinerating their quarry, and once more it became still.

The legends say that both times the Evil God fell, the Crests of the Six Flowers had shone brightly, and at the same time, all of the fiends had stopped in place and wailed at the sky. The grief-stricken moans of the fiends traveled far, beyond even the borders of the Howling Vilelands. According to the tales, although the Six Braves had only moments earlier been fighting for their lives, when they saw the fiends contorted in grief, they felt pity for their foes. And even when the surviving Braves departed the Howling Vilelands, the keening never ceased.

According to what some say, once the fight was over, the crest of each Brave began gradually fading, and after about six months they had disappeared entirely.

One of the Braves who had returned alive, Marlie, the Saint of Blades, had an analysis of their nemesis to share: The Evil God was the master of the fiends but did not give them any particular orders, and likewise, the fiends did not look to it for direction. The Evil God most likely lacked a conscious mind. If it did possess one, it was equal to that of an animal or even less. Nothing more than a manifestation of pure hate for humanity, with no purpose beyond wishing their death and destruction.

On the other hand, it was not unusual for fiends to be sentient. Some of them were even smarter than humans. The commanders giving orders to the rank and file belonged to that class of cognizance.

The monsters' allegiance to the Evil God was absolute. To a human it would be unthinkable to so fully serve a thing with no conscious will, but fiends were different. They devoted everything to their service of the Evil God and lived only to grant its desires.

Marlie wrote that loyalty to the Evil God was the meaning of the fiends' existence, and without it they could not be.

Marlie, the Saint of Blades was generally correct—with one exception.

One fiend did possess its own will, its own ambitions, and lived not for the Evil God but for itself. Its name was Dozzu. Around two centuries ago, it had left the Howling Vilelands for the realms of man. Over the course of two hundred years, it had laid its plans, making the preparations necessary to fulfill its ambitions before eventually returning to the Howling Vilelands. Close by Dozzu's side was the fiend's one and only comrade, a girl it had personally nurtured: Nashetania.

Chapter 1

Reunion

"I wish to hear all your thoughts," said Mora.

It had been fourteen days since the Evil God's awakening. After escaping Tgurneu's scheme, the group of seven had proceeded to the Bud of Eternity, the safe zone within the Howling Vilelands. There they waited for the severely injured Hans and Mora to heal.

There was hardly a fiend to be seen around the Bud of Eternity. They seemed to be lying in wait farther west, in a place called the Cut-Finger Forest. The vast woodland covered about two-fifths of the Howling Vilelands, and it was so named because a thousand years before, the Saint of the Single Flower lost a finger on her left hand in an attack there.

As they waited for the pair's wounds to heal, the group discussed various topics—first on the list being who might be the seventh. Each of them presented what clues they had found, and they reviewed their speculations and arguments many times over, but in the end they reached no conclusions. They couldn't even guess how the fake crest had been created.

They had discussed in further detail their fight within the Phantasmal Barrier. After finding out Nashetania's true identity, Adlet had passed out, so he asked his allies what had happened while he was unconscious. They told him Hans, Mora, and Chamo had chased Nashetania in circles, but near dawn she had escaped the barrier and disappeared. They considered why Nashetania had turned traitorous and how deeply the fiends had pervaded human affairs, but they found no answers there either.

However, Fremy had provided inside information about the fiends. Apparently among Tgurneu's subordinates were some known as "specialists." Rather than ordering them to evolve themselves to be stronger in battle, Tgurneu instructed them to focus exclusively on the unique abilities they each possessed. Certain fiends might specialize in pursuit, while others acquired the ability to invade the body of a Saint and block their powers. One was skilled at interrogating humans. Another fiend had an extremely powerful sense of smell; and there was the creature that had gained the ability to give birth to a child through intercourse with humans. Fremy wasn't informed as to the powers of every single one of these specialized weapons, but she told the party all she knew about their abilities and appearances.

After that, the group discussion continued to several other points. By the time the night ended, they had exhausted their supply of talking material. But then suddenly Mora asked for their opinions on a certain matter.

"What do you want to know, Mora?" asked Adlet.

"I suggest each of us share right now whom we suspect," she replied.

"I told you before, we're not going to throw accusations around."

"And I understand that. But telling us not to have suspicions won't change the reality that we do. Knowing everyone else's misgivings could help us avoid false accusations, don't you agree?"

The suggestion made Adlet uneasy. But Fremy said softly, "I don't think it's a bad idea."

"*Meow-hee*, I don't think there's meowch point though," said Hans.

"Of course, we will kill no one until we find definitive proof," assured Mora. "This is ultimately just for possible reference in the future."

"Well…I guess we don't have much choice," said Adlet, deflating.

"I suspect Goldof." Fremy was the first to speak. "He served Nashetania. He's the most obvious suspect."

"Oh? Chamo suspects *you*, Fremy," Chamo cut in. "It's so obvious. You were our enemy until just a little while ago. Chamo hasn't forgotten that fight, you know."

"I'm sure. Anyone else?" Fremy seemed unbothered by Chamo's remarks.

"...Speaking frankly, I suspect Goldof as well," Mora said next. "His service to Nashetania doesn't prove he's the seventh. However, I sense nothing that suggests he's truly devoted to our victory."

Goldof silently listened to the three speak. With listless eyes, he gazed vacantly at the ground, hunched over where he sat. He had been like that ever since they had arrived at the Howling Vilelands.

"Goldof, if you aren't the seventh, should you not contribute more to the group? You must show us with your words and your attitude that you're not the traitor. It can't be pleasant to be suspected like this." But Mora's concern didn't reach him. His heart was still closed to her words, if he even heard them at all.

When Adlet had first met Goldof, he had been far different. He'd been a strong, loyal young knight, slightly arrogant on occasion—or that was the impression Adlet had gotten, anyway. But once Nashetania had left them, it was as if he'd become an entirely different person.

"What do you think, Goldof?" asked Adlet. But the youth kept his silence.

Chamo raised her hand again. "Yeah, so Fremy's suspicious and all, but Chamo thinks Rolonia's weird, too."

"*Eeep!*" Rolonia, who had been listening quietly thus far, yelped with a hint of hysteria. "Wh-wh-why...might that be?"

"Hmm, well...'cause who knows what you're really thinking, you know? It's just fishy."

"I...I see...I-I'm sorry. I'll, um...try harder," Rolonia said, trembling like a leaf.

"Oh, but maybe it really is Fremy, after all. Yeah, my money's on Fremy," Chamo declared flippantly.

Mora sighed. "What about you, Hans?" she asked.

Hans put a hand on his chin, considering for a moment. "Me...? I've got my doubts about Adlet an' Chamo, *meow.*" All present, aside from Goldof, looked at Hans with surprise. "I'm not thinkin' about who's fishy.

What's important to me is who we'd have to worry about most if they was the seventh. If one of us is the seventh, the most dangerous'd be Adlet and next'd be Chamo. That's why I suspect 'em."

Adlet was a bit impressed. *That's one way to think about it.*

"So what about mew, Rolonia?" Hans passed the question on to her. Rolonia examined the faces around her, seemingly reluctant to speaking.

"Just say it," Fremy advised her. "Chamo just said she doesn't know what you're really thinking, didn't she?"

Very quietly, Rolonia said, "I suspect…Goldof. It's…for the same reasons as Lady Mora."

Three of the five so far had chosen Goldof. The situation didn't bode well for him, whether he was a real Brave or the impostor. But still he showed no sign that any of this had affected him.

"What about you, Adlet?" asked Fremy.

"I won't say. I'm the leader. If I announce who I suspect, it'll damage trust," Adlet said flatly.

"Well, meowbe that's fer the best," said Hans.

All eyes turned to the final member, Goldof. He raised his head, and his empty gaze wandered over the others.

"Goldof," said Hans. "Whaddaya think? You're listenin' to our talk, ain'tcha, *meow*?"

"…I've been listening," Goldof said after a pause.

"So who d'ya suspect, *meow*?"

"…Nobody." His declaration confused them all. Should this have been taken as a confession that he was the seventh? "I don't…care who's the seventh. I don't care…at all."

"Goldof. That attitude is the very reason Rolonia and I are suspicious of you." Mora was finally getting angry. "Why will you not think about who the seventh might be? Why will you not tell us what you know about Nashetania? Do you really want to protect the world?!"

"…Protect…the world?" Just for a moment, life returned to Goldof's eyes. He looked at his palms and then clenched his fists. "Yeah…Mora… I'll…protect the world. I have to…protect it…I'll…protect the world…

That was why I…" His fists began trembling with a strange creaking sound. His grip was so tight the bones in his hands were grinding together.

"That's right, Goldof. You'll keep everyone safe. Are you with us again?" Mora put her hand over Goldof's, but he coldly shook her off. Then, once his head dropped down again, he wouldn't reply no matter what the others tried.

"Well, that was pointless," said Fremy.

"So it seems. I'm sorry," Mora apologized.

"Enough about this," said Hans. "I care meowr about Tgurneu."

"Right," Fremy said. "The Cut-Finger Forest is ahead of us. Tgurneu is probably waiting to ambush us there."

Even once the conversation turned to other matters, Adlet kept watching Goldof. *I'll protect the world.* For some reason, Goldof's claim had not felt promising to him. In all honesty, though Adlet hadn't said so, he suspected Goldof, too—he just didn't seem to be a part of the group.

Even amid the paranoia smothering the party, they'd still been building a sense of unity. Hans, Adlet acknowledged, was sharp and skilled. Despite his remarks just now, Adlet knew the assassin trusted him. Chamo was a handful, but Adlet had discovered she was surprisingly tractable sometimes, and even cute. Mora had betrayed them once, but her desire to protect her family and her allies was real. He was glad to have Rolonia with them, since she trusted him from the bottom of her heart and would always back him up. Fremy was always at odds with him, but still, in his eyes, she was the most important of all.

But Goldof was different. Adlet had simply been unable to communicate with him. There was nothing inside him that Adlet could understand; sometimes the young knight seemed like an alien beast to him. He still had no idea who Goldof Auora really was.

It was the fifteenth day after the Evil God's awakening. Hans and Mora were all patched up, and Mora's broken armor had been repaired. The party set out once more, late at night this time, while Fremy's bullets and Chamo's slave-fiends killing all the enemies observing the Bud of Eternity before the troupe made their way to the vast forest.

They all covered themselves with black cloaks courtesy of Adlet, keeping low to the ground as they advanced. Melting into the darkness of night, they forged ever westward.

They weren't thinking about killing Tgurneu, nor uncovering the seventh. They only concealed themselves and evaded potential battles.

"Any enemies behind us, Mora?" Adlet called from the front of the group.

"No," Mora replied while bringing up the rear. She was walking backward, her fists raised and facing away from the group. With Hans watching their right and Fremy watching their left, the seven crept forward.

An earthworm wriggled up to their feet. Chamo plucked it up, bringing the worm's mouth region up to her ear. "It says about three hundred meters ahead, the enemy made a fence. There's whole ton of fiends in front of it."

"I see," said Adlet. "Fremy, how big is this fence?"

"It's nearly thirty kilometers across," she replied. "I don't think it's possible to go around it. Mora could probably break it, but there's a mechanism that sets off a loud noise if you come near it."

"Do you know how the alarm works?" Adlet asked.

"It's a clapper made of string and wood. If your foot catches on the string, the clappers smack together to make noise."

"*Meow-hee*, is that it? I could get past that, easy-peasy."

Adlet put a hand to his jaw and considered for a while. Then he gathered the group around him to explain the plan. "First we retreat back about one kilometer. Fremy, you plant a bomb in the ground. After one hour you blow it up. Meanwhile, we'll be moving north."

"So a diversion," said Mora.

Adlet nodded. "When the bomb goes off, the fiends should all go toward it. Then Chamo's slave-fiends will attack the fence. This is also a distraction. We'll head south toward the blockade. Fremy will snipe the remaining guards, and Hans and I will break the clapper. Mora, you smash us a way through as quietly as you can."

"Understood," said Mora.

"And please," he finished, "don't let the fiends—or Tgurneu—find you."

The party moved into action. Soundlessly, they advanced as Fremy's bomb and Chamo's slave-fiends sowed confusion among the enemy. Fremy attacked a weakly guarded area, while Adlet, Hans, and Mora burst through the fence. Then, before the fiends on watch could return to their positions, the Braves quickly slipped through to the west.

"So...it's all going smoothly, huh, Addy?" Rolonia said, walking beside Adlet.

"For now." He happened to glance up at the sky peeking through the gaps in the forest canopy. The stars had already faded, and the black of night was slowly giving way to gray. "Tgurneu's probably lost track of us. If it did have a hold on what we're doing, there'd be more fiends waiting for us here."

"Y-yes...I'm sure you're right."

"Anyway, our party needs to keep a low profile. We're gonna run as hard as we can away from Tgurneu until we're out of this forest, past the ravine, and reach the Weeping Hearth." After listening to Adlet's explanation, Rolonia nodded. It seemed the rest of the group didn't even need to be told. They were not going to fight Tgurneu, and they wouldn't let it figure out where they were. The top priority was making a beeline straight for the Weeping Hearth. That was the plan.

"Have you noticed, Adlet...?" Fremy said abruptly.

"Noticed what?"

"I've heard some fighting behind us, a few times now. The sound is too faint, so I couldn't tell who's involved."

As they marched, Adlet listened closely. The stirring of the trees, his companions' footsteps, and also fiends' cries, or so he thought. "You're right. There's a battle going on back there. But who, and with whom?"

"You want Chamo to go check it out? It'll take a little while," said Chamo.

Adlet shook his head. "I'm curious, but our time is more important. We'll leave it and move on."

Fremy and Chamo nodded, and the seven proceeded farther west. Adlet looked over his shoulder, but the fence was already out of sight.

About an hour after Adlet's party passed the blockade, a fiend came to examine the damaged fence. "Hmm. So they've broken through here, too. Oh, dear." The creature had a yeti's body and the head of a crow, and in its hand was a large fig. The yeti-fiend—Tgurneu—sighed and said, "It seems their plan is to do everything they can to avoid me."

Around him were throngs of fiends, clamoring until their voices were hoarse. The superior fiends, those that could speak, were giving out orders to their subordinates to hurry and find the Braves of the Six Flowers.

"What do you think, Number Eighteen?"

Beside Tgurneu was a snake-fiend, slender enough to grip in one hand but more than ten meters long. Two arms, thin as twine, grew from its trunk about fifty centimeters from its head. "They're terrible cowards. Not worth fearing at all," it sneered. This fiend was one of Tgurneu's specialists, considered unique even among its followers—the eighteenth specialist, to be exact. It had evolved itself according to Tgurneu's instructions to develop its exceptional powers.

"*You're* the one not worth fearing," Tgurneu scoffed, kicking Number Eighteen lightly. "What would you do if you were in their position? What would be your priority?"

"I would consider discovering the seventh to be the most important," said Number Eighteen.

Tgurneu sighed. "The worst choice you could think of. The way things stand now, they have no means of ferreting out the impostor, and I doubt they've even found any clues that could lead them to the answer. What course do you believe they should take in such a situation?"

"Üm…"

"Wait until the seventh makes a mistake. That would be my strategy, if I were them. Any other ideas?"

"Perhaps they could prioritize defeating you, Cömmander Tgurneu."

"That would be an amateur play. Killing me, if they could, would indeed bring them much closer to victory. But they would have to sacrifice something valuable for it. Do you know what?"

"W-wëll…"

Tgurneu didn't wait for Number Eighteen to reply. "*Time.* There are only fourteen more days until the Evil God's revival. If they fail to reach the Weeping Hearth before then, we win. If the Six Braves had targeted me, I would've devoted all my resources to stall for time. As long as I remained alive, those precious days and hours would slip away."

"…"

"Now do you understand what the best choice available to them is? It's to run from us, ignore me, and head straight for the Weeping Hearth. As long as I don't know where they are, even I have only so many options available." Tgurneu's beak moved. It seemed the fiend was smiling. "Not bad, Adlet. It seems you're capable of simple reasoning, after all."

"…I have a propósition, Commander Tgurneu. Why don't we order the sevénth to tell us where the Braves of the Six Flowers are?"

Tgurneu's shoulders slumped in utter exasperation. "Any further foolishness from you and I'll squash you," it threatened, raising one foot over Number Eighteen.

The snake-fiend placed its thin, twine-like arms on the ground and bowed its head in apology.

"Well, no matter. Let's take it easy. You may conduct a search attempt to lure them out. We have so many ways to play with them."

For two days after departing from the Bud of Eternity, Adlet's party continued its flight through the Cut-Finger Forest.

Fremy guided them through the intricate and complex growths as Chamo's slave-fiends hunted around for nearby enemies and unguarded areas. Mora's power of mountain echo was useful in disorienting enemies, while Adlet and Hans put their heads together to deduce the enemy's next ploy. When bad luck brought them into contact with the fiends, they fought with everything they had to kill them all before Tgurneu could learn about their position.

To completely kill a fiend, you had to find the core and smash it, since an intact body would revive again a few years later. But they didn't have the time for that now. They tossed aside the corpses and pressed forward.

The Cut-Finger Forest was vast. No matter how great the enemy numbers, they couldn't hope to guard the whole thing. For two days, Adlet's party went undetected. As the night ended, the eastern sky swathed in red, the group neared the perimeter of the forest.

"There was no sign of fiends beyond the woods. I think we can relax and move on," said Fremy when she returned from scouting ahead.

"None behind us, either. Guess we've totally gotten away," said Chamo.

"Tgurneu probably thinks we're farther neowrth. I think we can keep goin' this way," said Hans.

"So that's one barrier down, huh?" said Adlet.

They all shared smiles and shook hands. Adlet offered his hand to Fremy, but she looked away, arms crossed. Equally stubborn, Adlet kept his hand extended. In the end, she reluctantly hooked her fingertips on his and gave him a weak shake. After that, Rolonia and Mora tried to get a handshake, too. Though she regarded the pair sourly, Fremy accepted the gesture. Hans's offer was refused.

"The seventh still hasn't taken action yet, though, have they?" said Fremy. As the party had proceeded through the forest, they had constantly observed each other for signs that they would attack under cover of night or help the enemy find them or covertly contact Tgurneu. But nobody had done anything suspicious.

"We don't have to rush to find them," said Adlet. "The seventh is bound to do something eventually. We just have to keep our eyes open to make sure we catch it."

"I hope you're right," Fremy replied.

Adlet's gaze happened to land on Goldof at the fringes of the group. They had not shared a handshake yet. When he offered, surprisingly enough, Goldof accepted it willingly.

"You've done well, too. Let's keep on fighting," said Adlet, but Goldof didn't meet his eyes or reply.

During their advance through the woods, Adlet had kept a particularly close eye on Goldof. The knight had followed instructions faithfully and had done nothing at all suspicious. But Adlet still had no idea what he was thinking. Was that soulless attitude an act, or was it real? He couldn't tell.

"It's time to go, Adlet," Fremy prompted him. "Once we're through the forest, the ravine is next. Don't let your guard down."

"S-sure. Got it," Adlet responded and started walking. But Goldof's behavior wouldn't leave his thoughts. What was he thinking? What was Nashetania to him now? Even after they emerged from the forest, pressing on westward, he had no answers.

Adlet was totally unaware of the situation that had already begun to unfold. In a corner of the Cut-Finger Forest, an unimaginable scene was occurring.

As the party escaped the woods, Tgurneu was reclining in a hammock with a book and a large fig on its chest.

An eagle-fiend descended from the sky. "I have a rèport, Commander Tgurneu."

"Chamo's slave-fiends attacked and killed the specialist tracking the Six Braves. You've basically lost the trail and the scent and presently have no clues at all to their whereabouts. Am I wrong?" Tgurneu answered with mild irritation, eyes still closed.

"Y-yës, Commander."

Tgurneu withdrew a map from above its hammock and examined it. "Now, then, I wonder where they went. Are they still in the northern section of the forest, or have they already arrived at the ravine...?" It mulled over the map for a while.

"...Commander Tgurneu, your ordérs?"

"They've already left the forest. Leave half the troops there and send the other half to the ravine. We can make that our next playground. Let's flank them when they're vulnerable, right when they're crossing."

"Verÿ well, Commander." Right as the eagle-fiend was about to fly off, Tgurneu reached out to grab its leg. "What iš it, Commander?"

Tgurneu didn't reply but instead glanced around. Its inexpressive crow's head revealed none of its thoughts. "I take back what I just said. Summon the pawns to me."

"Uh…why, Cómmander?"

"The enemy."

The eagle-fiend flew off immediately. Tgurneu dropped from its hammock, bit into the fig, and then picked up a club on the ground, squeezing it tight.

Nearby was the sound of a disturbance—like someone running.

They must have walked for about five hours after leaving the forest. The sun was already high in the sky. No fiends attacked the seven during their advance due westward. They had now covered two-fifths of the Howling Vilelands.

After crossing the plains, they were confronted with their next obstacle.

"*Meooow!* That's huge! I've never seen nothin' so big!" Hans cried out when he saw it, sounding delighted for some reason. Its massive size left Adlet speechless, and Mora, Rolonia, and Chamo's eyes were wide with shock.

What lay in their path was a ravine.

It had to be nearly a hundred meters deep and at least a hundred and fifty wide, cutting straight north to south. Looking in either direction, they couldn't even see the ends. The cliff was a vertical drop of smooth rock with no visible handholds. A boiling river lined the bottom, venting thick steam all the way up to where the seven stood and raising the ambient temperature by five degrees. Adlet had never seen such an enormous canyon in his life. Three days earlier, at the Bud of Eternity, Fremy had told him about this place, but it was far beyond what he had envisioned.

"I can't believe it. Fiends carved out this whole thing?" said Rolonia, beside Adlet.

"The fiends have been preparing for their battle with the Braves of the Six Flowers for three hundred years," said Fremy. "Digging a ravine like this is nothing to them."

The colossal valley before them had not existed when the Saint of the

Single Flower battled the Evil God, or when past generations of Braves had answered their calling. It was called Cargikk's Canyon. The biggest moat in the world, it had been made by the fiend commander Cargikk. According to Fremy, the ravine divided the Howling Vilelands clean in two, and to reach the Weeping Hearth required a successful crossing.

But the sight of the great ravine transfixed all of them. Eventually, Mora glumly posed the question. "How will we cross it? Tgurneu will eventually notice our departure from the forest. The fiends will flood in, and we'll be surrounded."

"It won't take us long to find a way. It'll all work out," Adlet said, pulling out a rope from the iron box on his back. He gave one end to Mora and climbed down the cliff face. But about seventy meters down, the rising steam became too suffocating, and he immediately scrambled back up to the top.

"It's no use, Adlet," Fremy said curtly. "Even with a Saint's power, getting across this thing isn't easy."

"Isn't there a bridge, Fremy?" he asked.

"There is," she replied. "One at the northern end and another at the southern end. But I don't think either one is an option. Cargikk's minions are waiting for us there, and the bridges are set up to immediately self-destruct if we ever get close to crossing."

"Hey, Fremy. Aren't there any secret paths? Like some way to get across safely without the bridges?" asked Chamo.

"There'd be no need, would there?" Fremy retorted. "Since the fiends always use the bridges."

"'S'pose you're right..." Chamo crossed her arms and puzzled over the problem.

The rest of them tried to devise a way across the ravine, too, but no great plans were forthcoming.

"Rolonia's whip...wouldn't reach, I guess," said Adlet.

Rolonia gave him a regretful nod. She had soaked the weapon with her own blood so she could manipulate it at will. But even with her powers, it wouldn't work for a bridge. Her whip was only about thirty meters long. Even if they used Adlet's rope to add to its length, it wouldn't reach the other side.

"Do any of yer pets fly, Chamo?" asked Hans.

"If they did, we wouldn't be worrying over this. Do you think Chamo is stupid, catboy?" she replied testily.

"If Athlay were here, she could have made us a bridge of ice," Mora lamented, frustrated. The Saint of Ice had been well-known as a candidate for Brave but Fremy, the former Brave-killer, had assassinated her. Athlay had been dead.

"The reason I killed Athlay of Ice first was to prevent you from getting past this ravine. Tgurneu's orders," Fremy said bluntly.

After that the seven continued to discuss their options for a bit longer, but the only conclusion they reached was that the ravine was insurmountable. Digging a moat to prevent the enemy's attack was such a simple and straightforward idea, but such banal stratagems really did tend to cause the most trouble. Standard tactics became standard precisely because they were effective. Cargikk could turn out to be an even tougher enemy than Tgurneu.

"Anyway, standing around talking won't get us anywhere," said Adlet. "We'll split into three groups to look for a way across. Find us something we can work with, no matter how trivial. Hans and Mora, you go north. Me, Rolonia, and Goldof will go south. Chamo and Fremy, you stay here and guard our backs."

"This is a more troublesome obstacle than I expected," said Mora.

With a nonchalant expression, Adlet replied, "This Cargikk guy is shaping up to be a pretty tough opponent, too. If you guys didn't bring the strongest man in the world along, you wouldn't have a chance."

"Oho, *meow*, it's been a while since we heard your *strongest man in the world* spiel," Hans said with a sarcastic smile.

"'Cause everyone knows it's a fact by now, so I don't need to go out of my way to say it."

"You're the only one who believes that stuff, Adlet," Chamo retorted with some annoyance.

"I-I believe it. I believe Addy is the strongest man in the world," said Rolonia, trying to be considerate and wondering if he would get angry.

"I believe so, too," agreed Mora. "Adlet may indeed be the strongest in the world, in a way."

"Not 'in a way,'" protested Adlet. "I *am* the strongest man in the world."

Fremy coldly interjected, "You announce you're the strongest man in the world whenever you're feeling anxious, don't you?"

She'd hit the nail on the head. Suddenly, he didn't know what to say.

"*Meow-hee*, so his incompetence is what made ya fall fer him, then?" asked Hans.

"No," Fremy said flatly.

"*Hrmeow-meow-meow.* Then just what about him do ya find so attractive?"

"…You're terribly obnoxious, aren't you?"

Mora cut into their increasingly acerbic exchange. "We have no time. Let's just go and find a way to deal with this ravine. Come, Hans," she said, dragging the man northward.

Adlet was about to head south with Rolonia and Goldof when Fremy called out to a member of the trio. "Rolonia."

"Y-yes? What is it?" She had been startled at the sudden mention.

Fremy leaned in close and whispered something into her ear. Rolonia nodded and ran up to Adlet.

"What did she say to you?" he asked as they set off at a run.

For some reason, Rolonia hesitated. "U-um…she told me to make sure to keep you safe." When Adlet looked back, he saw Fremy watching him. Embarrassed, Adlet continued south.

"Fremy is a nice person, isn't she?" said Rolonia.

She is, thought Adlet, and he nodded. A little while ago, he'd started getting the feeling that Fremy and Rolonia had become friends. Had Rolonia gotten attached to Fremy, or was it the other way around?

Meanwhile, about twenty kilometers south of Adlet's party, fifty-odd fiends were gathered together. They had just emerged from the Cut-Finger Forest into a barren land covered with jagged rocks.

Steam rose from beneath the boulders, and geysers erupted up around them. The fiends called this region the lava zone. A magma-heated water vein ran dozens of meters underneath the surface of the area.

One of the fiends there was a massive amphibian with stone-plated skin and a large mouth. Occasionally, a strange-smelling vapor wafted from its body. A monkey-fiend was present, too, human-size but painfully thin. Its fur rustled incessantly, never coming to rest.

And in the center of them all sat a downright adorable creature. It was small and odd-looking, like a cross between a squirrel and a dog.

"The preparations are complete, Nashetania," the cute fiend said quietly. Its name was Dozzu. This was the traitor who had rebelled against the Evil God and left the Howling Vilelands, and one of the three commanders governing the fiends. "We will determine our fate today, right here. Nashetania, no matter what comes, let us never give up and always keep on fighting." Dozzu spoke very softly, so as to be heard only by the girl sitting beside him.

"Are you worried about me, Dozzu?" Nashetania asked, and then she smiled. "Relax. I'm not scared of anything. Our victory is clear."

"...Nashetania."

"Goldof is with us, so we have nothing to be afraid of."

Dozzu nodded silently.

"Then let us fight for our ambitions."

"For the sake of humanity and fiendkind's future."

"And for our fallen comrades," Nashetania said, standing and patting the dust off her bottom. "All right, everyone. It's time for us to kill Chamo Rosso."

And with those words, the wheels began rapidly turning. Nashetania smiled as she watched the fiends around her.

"Hey, Addy...Goldof..." After about ten minutes, Rolonia called to the other two as the two men stared down the cliff.

"Did you find something?" asked Adlet. His voice held an edge of impatience. No matter how much they searched, no leads were turning up.

"No, I haven't, but...don't you think this is odd?" she asked.

"What's odd?"

"Why are there no fiends around?"

Now that she mentioned it, Adlet scanned the area nearby. Tgurneu should have noticed by now that they were out of the forest. Even if Tgurneu hadn't figured it out, it should have at least posted a scout to the ravine. It was quite odd they hadn't encountered a single fiend so far.

Adlet took out the signal flare Fremy had given him. The plan was that if anything unusual happened, Fremy would blow it up from afar to summon Adlet, Rolonia, and Goldof. "I guess this means that Fremy's and Hans's groups haven't run into any fights, either."

"That's weird, too…huh?" Rolonia pointed up at the distant sky. Above, a gigantic moth-fiend was flying toward them from deeper in the Howling Vilelands. Apparently unaware of them, it was streaking full-speed toward the southeast. "There was another fiend flying in that direction a little while ago, too."

"Strange." Adlet looked to the southeast, puzzled. He could guess that fiends were gathering, but he didn't know why. Tgurneu must have predicted that the Six Braves would head to the ravine. Was there any reason to ignore their party and amass fiends in some unrelated location?

That was when it happened—Goldof started staggering off toward the southeast.

"What's wrong, Goldof?" Rolonia called out to him. But the boy didn't stop. Slow at first, gradually picking up speed, he distanced himself from the two of them.

Confused, Adlet followed. Something was peculiar about Goldof. Adlet chased him down—the young knight was running now—and grabbed his shoulder. "Hey, don't just run off. We're not doing anything over that way right now."

The moment Adlet realized his wrist had been grabbed, he was flipping head over heels. Before he could grasp what had just happened, his back hit the ground, and he had an unobstructed view of the blue sky.

"Addy!"

It was only when Rolonia called his name that he realized he'd been thrown.

"What the hell are you doing, Goldof?" Adlet wrenched himself free and rolled to his feet.

"...Her Highness...is in danger..."

"What happened? Did something happen to the princess? Did something happen to Nashetania?" But Goldof didn't reply to Adlet's question. He just kept striding rapidly to the southeast. "Wait, Goldof. Explain to me! What's going on with Nashetania?"

"Her Highness is in danger...I'm going...to save her..."

"What are you thinking? Nashetania is the enemy!" Adlet circled around to block his path. Goldof's fist immediately plunged into Adlet's gut, driving the breath from his lungs. Adlet's legs buckled, and his knees hit the ground.

"Goldof! What are you doing?!" Rolonia cried, running up to Adlet.

The boy turned around and said to them, "Adlet...Rolonia...I'm... going...to save...her."

"W-why now, all of a sudden?!" Adlet couldn't speak, so Rolonia asked for him.

"Listen...up. Just...listen. Don't...get in my way. I'm going to... save...her." Goldof had been like a dead man ever since they had reached the Howling Vilelands, but now light had returned to his eyes. Deep behind his dark irises lurked a glittering flame. "I'm...going...alone. Don't...follow me."

"Wait, please, Goldof! What happened?!" Rolonia yelled after him.

"The situation...has changed. If you get in my way...I can't let you live."

"C-can't let us...live?" she stuttered fearfully.

That was when Adlet noticed something surprising. Tears were falling from Goldof's eyes. He was looking in the direction that the fiend had disappeared, crying without a sound.

By the time Adlet was on his feet again, Goldof had already turned away from them and set off at a run again. When Adlet tried to follow, Rolonia stopped him. "You can't go alone. Right now, he's...not in his right mind." With a fearsome speed that was surprisingly for his large frame, Goldof headed southeast. Adlet and Rolonia could only watch his receding back as he left.

Half an hour later, the six were sprinting across the plains after Goldof.

"What is going on here?" Fremy demanded. The others, who had learned about the situation from Adlet and Rolonia, all expressed similar bafflement. Adlet didn't know what it meant, either.

"Maybe he just finally went insane?" suggested Hans.

Frankly, Adlet thought that was the most likely explanation, too. Goldof's behavior was incomprehensible. He knew that the knight felt deeply for Nashetania. And now that she had sided with the fiends, it was only natural for Goldof to want her back on their side. Was that what he had meant by "going to save her"? But Adlet couldn't figure out why he'd run off to do that *now*.

Farther down the road, the party discovered the bodies of some fiends. There were three. Adlet approached them, examining their wounds.

"Was this Goldof's work?" asked Mora. As far as Adlet could tell from the wounds, it most likely was. Something heavy and sharp had killed all three fiends in a single blow. Strangely, after they died, each one had had its stomach ripped open.

"It's like someone shoved a hand into their stomachs and stirred everything around," said Adlet. "Goldof is looking for something."

"Maybe he's trying to save Nashetania," Fremy suggested.

"…Saving Nashetania by ripping open fiends' stomachs? How would that work?" The probability that Goldof's sanity was slipping rose even further.

They continued after their missing comrade. "What's ahead?" Mora asked as they pressed forward.

"A little farther and we'll be back in the forest," said Fremy. "Beyond that is the lava zone. There's a magma chamber underground with active geysers everywhere. It's a dangerous place."

"That idiot…What is he trying to do in a place like that?" Adlet muttered while Fremy came to a halt. The others stopped with her. "What is it, Fremy?" But when Adlet met her eyes, he knew what she was going to say.

"We shouldn't follow him."

"What?"

"We have to assume that the lava zone is packed with fiends. Goldof is trying to lure us in. I don't know what kind of trap Tgurneu and Nashetania have laid for us, but to continue would be suicide."

"You're saying that Goldof is the seventh?" said Adlet.

"I can't say for certain. But this is extremely suspicious."

"B-but, Fremy," Rolonia timidly protested, "he may have fallen into some kind of trap himself. Maybe Nashetania tricked him and lured him there…"

"What do you mean?" asked Fremy.

"He loves her, doesn't he? If someone told him that Nashetania was in danger, I think he would go save her. The enemy might have lied to him to lure him into the lava zone."

"That doesn't make sense," countered Fremy. "How would Nashetania have tricked him and lured him in? Neither you nor Adlet saw or heard anything, right?"

"Well…I…"

She had a point. Chamo turned to the now-silent Rolonia and said, "Ohhh? Didn't *you* suspect Goldof? Why're you trying to defend him, then?"

"U-um…I…"

After a moment's thought, Fremy spoke again. "You're sharp, Chamo. Now that you've pointed that out, I've come to see a different possibility: Rolonia has tricked Goldof and sent him off to the lava zone. Now she's having us chase Goldof to lead us all there. It's not entirely unlikely."

Rolonia was stunned, unable to say anything as her lips opened and closed.

"No more baseless speculations. Let's leave that aside—we must reach a conclusion now on what to do about Goldof. Adlet, what do we do next?" asked Mora.

But Adlet couldn't decide. It seemed virtually certain enemies were lying in wait for them, and it was true that Goldof had been acting suspiciously. In his hesitation, he looked at Hans for wisdom.

But Hans shook his head. "You decide,' *meow*. Someone who don't make decisions ain't a leader." He was right. Adlet was ashamed of himself for trying to leave this to someone else.

"Frankly, I'm suspicious of Goldof, too," he finally said. "And just abandoning him right now...Well, it wouldn't totally be out of the question. But..." He stopped, agonizing for a moment. "I saw Goldof's eyes. You can't fake that kind of look. He's sincerely trying to save Nashetania; I know that for a fact. At the very least, he's not trying to trick us."

Rolonia nodded in response. "So?"

"I think there's still a possibility that Goldof isn't the seventh. And as long as that possibility remains, we can't abandon him. If we give up on helping and protecting our allies, we're done for."

With cold anger filling her eyes, Fremy replied, "Fine. We'll suppose that Goldof isn't the seventh. And let's say that Goldof has gone off to try to save Nashetania. But Nashetania is our enemy. If Goldof is going to save her, then he's not on our side. He's just a traitor. Why are you going to go save a traitor?"

"He hasn't betrayed us. He was in love with her. Wanting to protect the one you love isn't betrayal."

"...Are you seriously going to go save Goldof?" Fremy demanded. Adlet nodded. Furious, she grabbed him by the collar. "Stop screwing around!"

"F-Fremy..." Rolonia was upset.

"You're naive!" said Fremy. "Goldof is either the seventh, a traitor, or a lunatic! It's one of those three! Why do we have to throw ourselves into danger in order to save him?!"

"*Meow.* Yer yellin', Fremy." But she didn't even hear Hans's attempt to calm her down.

"I won't abandon an ally. I've made my decision, and I'm not changing it," Adlet said, and he pried off Fremy's hands.

"Then I can't go with you," she said.

Then Rolonia said, "Fremy, I think Addy is right."

"Why?"

"I'm hopelessly anxious right now," Rolonia explained. "I have no idea what kind of traps are waiting for us, and I could fall under suspicion of being the seventh at any time. And even so, we have to fight."

"So?"

"But Addy will never abandon me. He'll trust me to the very end. That peace of mind is what helps me fight, even if I can just barely manage it. I can join this battle because I believe Addy won't betray me. And it's not just me—I think all of us feel that way." The group fell silent.

"Fremy, you should yield this once," said Mora. "I understand your feelings, but…let's trust in Adlet."

"We made the decision to let him lead. Say what ya want, but there's no helping it neow." Hans smiled and started walking.

Fremy looked down, shoulders slumped. "Adlet, I…" She started to say something but then held her tongue. Adlet could tell she'd been terribly hurt, but he couldn't find any words to comfort her.

One hour later, the six stepped into the lava zone, watchful of their surroundings. The ground was covered in craggy, dark gray rocks. Some of them were red hot, and Adlet could feel the heat through the soles of his shoes. Occasionally, steam would spew out from cracks between the rocks. The stench of the sulfur was strong enough to bring a grimace to Adlet's face. The land was utterly lifeless, without a single insect or plant to be seen.

Adlet didn't know anything about the area. Neither the Saint of the Single Flower nor past Braves had visited this place. Even Fremy said that she'd only passed close by here a handful of times.

"…Not a fan of this terrain," Adlet muttered. Rows of steep, rocky mounds between five and twenty meters high rose before them. Almost nothing was level. The hills were irregular, making visibility especially poor. Even from a higher vantage point, he couldn't make a proper mental map of the topography. It was the perfect place to launch an ambush.

"This doesn't appear to be naturally occurring," said Adlet.

Fremy replied, "I heard it was originally a big volcano. When Cargikk made that ravine, it diverted the lava from here to there."

At the top of a nearby rock hill, Hans pointed off in the distance. "*Hrmeow.* There's fiend corpses over there, too. Guess Goldof made it pretty far into the lava zone." They all headed in the direction he had indicated.

The bodies were in a similar state to ones they had found in the forest. They had been impaled, killed instantly, and then their stomachs had been sliced open.

"What is Goldof doing?" Mora grumbled. They continued on.

After about thirty minutes of walking, they crossed a string of small but steep hills. Between the hills, they discovered yet more corpses. Adlet had expected an ambush in the lava zone, but all they had encountered were dead bodies and no living fiends at all. There was no indication they would be attacked, either.

"No one's here. Maybe it is a trap," Chamo suggested.

Goldof couldn't have killed them all, Adlet thought.

When they walked even farther, a large, trapezoidal hill, about thirty meters high, came into view. When they climbed to the top, they found it was hollowed out in the center, forming a flat pit with a radius of about seventy meters.

When Adlet peered down into the cavity, he gulped. "What on earth...?" Inside were piles of bodies—more than two hundred. The group rushed down the slope into the pit.

"Goldof couldn't have done this all alone, could he?" said Rolonia.

"Of course not," Adlet answered. "If he could kill this many on his own, he wouldn't be human." He surveyed the bodies. Most had met their end from teeth and claws, but some had died by fire or acid. The wounds were still fresh, as if they had died only a few hours ago. "Were the fiends killing each other?" he murmured. The ground had been dug up in spots, and shards of shattered rock were strewn about. It told the story of a fierce struggle.

Fremy examined the faces of some of the fiends and said, "The majority were of Tgurneu's faction, but quite a few of Cargikk's faction are here, too. We should definitely interpret this to be a falling-out among fiends." Fremy had told them before that their enemies had a complex and antagonistic relationship. According to her, the fiends were divided into three factions: the largest, Cargikk's; the second biggest power, Tgurneu's; and hidden within both those groups, the servants of the traitor fiend, Dozzu, or so it was said.

"Did Cargikk and Tgurneu fight?" asked Adlet.

"…I don't know," Fremy replied. "It's true that Cargikk and Tgurneu do clash, but I can't imagine they'd be so stupid as to fight right in the middle of the battle with the Braves of the Six Flowers."

"So then it's that Dozzu critter?" said Hans. "Not like I neow anythin' about that one, though."

"Did Dozzu have enough followers to cause an insurrection like this? It's hard for me to imagine that." Fremy seemed to be contemplating the possibilities.

Adlet could tell that something they knew nothing about was going on somewhere. But would these events work to their advantage or not? And how was Goldof involved? "Anyway, if fiends are killing one another, that's good news for us. But let's leave this for now and find Goldof," he said, and that was when a voice came from behind them.

"Oh, my. Have you come looking for Goldof?"

The moment Adlet heard that voice, he reflexively dropped his iron box and drew his sword. The others, aside from Rolonia, all raised their weapons, too. There was no way any of them could forget that high, soft voice or its polite and refined tone.

"I thought for sure you had come to kill me." At the top of the rim of the pit was a girl. She was sitting calmly on a fiend's body as she gazed down upon them, clad in a magnificent set of black-and-white armor with a helmet designed to resemble rabbit's ears.

When had she shown up? Just three seconds ago the place had been totally abandoned.

"It's been a long time, Braves of the Six Flowers."

Adlet had known they would encounter her again eventually. It was the first impostor, who only four days earlier they had battled with for their lives: Nashetania.

Chapter 2

The
Blade Gem

Three days earlier, at the Bud of Eternity, Adlet had asked his allies a question.

"Hey, after I passed out in the Phantasmal Barrier, what the heck happened?"

After the battle, Adlet, badly wounded, had immediately fallen unconscious. He functionally had no recollection of what had happened between that time and when he had woken up the next morning.

The group had retold in turns to Adlet and Rolonia the events of that night. Hans, Mora, Chamo, and Goldof had followed Nashetania. She had run all over the area, evading their pursuit the entire night. Immediately after being revealed as the impostor, she had deactivated the Phantasmal Barrier, but Mora said that it had remained in effect until the mist dispersed.

Hans and Chamo explained that they'd wounded Nashetania more than once, and a few times they had even been certain they'd finished her off. But still, she had gotten away.

"Nashetania uses some kinda weird power. You think you've got her, and then she'll disappear just like that. Chamo thought she was dead, but then there was nobody," said Chamo.

"I've seen that power, too," said Adlet. He remembered that after Nashetania had been exposed, Mora had smashed her head in. But then she'd immediately disappeared, and the real Nashetania appeared far away. It really was a mysterious ability, and not one that normally belonged to the Saint of Blades.

"I don't know how, but it seems Nashetania has the powers of a fiend. I think that's a stealth-fiend's ability," said Fremy.

A stealth-fiend. Adlet had never heard of that type, and he had studied at the foot of the fiend specialist, Atreau Spiker. He was not unfamiliar with the enemy's abilities and biology.

"Stealth types are incredibly rare," explained Fremy. "I doubt there are more than five among all the fiends in existence. I've only heard of them—I've never actually seen one in person."

"So what is this power?" asked Adlet.

"In a word, it's like hypnosis." Fremy explained that stealth-fiends released a vapor from their bodies that drugged their enemies while simultaneously emitting a unique sound wave. Inhaling the drug and hearing the sound would addle your perceptions, blinding you to the stealth-fiend's presence. She then pointed out that Nashetania's powers were unique even among stealth-fiends, since she could make you hallucinate her presence.

"…That's an incredible power." Adlet broke into a cold sweat. If Nashetania were to approach them in stealth and catch them by surprise, they wouldn't stand a chance.

But Hans smiled and waved away Adlet's worries. *"Meow-hee.* From what I can see, it's not that meowerful."

"What do you mean?" asked Adlet.

"I've seen the princess's stealth power a few times. She can probably hide herself for ten seconds at meowst. What's more, once she's used it, she can't use it again for another five minutes. And this is just a guess, but…I think she can only use that stealth ability when she's runnin' away."

Fremy's eyes widened. "Quite the astute analysis. That's basically it." She supplemented Hans's explanation, clarifying that the stealth ability was exhausting and it was not possible to attack while using it. At most, Nashetania could only run. This was true of all stealth-fiends.

"Now that you mention it," said Adlet, "my master said that there were a handful of fiends out there that could use hypnotism. But he also said the effects were only momentary."

"...I've been wondering for a while," said Fremy, "who is this Atreau Spiker? How did he come to know so much about fiend biology?"

"I dunno. I asked him plenty of times, but he wouldn't tell me anything," Adlet replied, and Fremy lowered her eyes in thought.

"Atreau Spiker isn't important. What *is* important is: Is there a way to trump this skill?" Mora asked.

Fremy replied, "When a stealth-fiend uses their power, they're surrounded by a sweet scent. You should be able to tell if the ability is active based on the smell."

"So if she does use her power, what should we do?" asked Adlet.

"You can break the hypnosis by focusing your senses, staring hard, and causing yourself pain. A good bite to your tongue should be enough. That's how you can beat it."

"All right. So if you smell something funny, stare hard and bite your tongue."

"That's right."

I'm really glad she's with us, thought Adlet. Nashetania's stealth ability wasn't that formidable. But still, if they'd had to fight her without knowing how her powers worked, it could have spelled disaster. But as with any ability, once you knew the trick to it, it wasn't anything to be afraid of.

The moment Nashetania was done greeting them, there was a gunshot. A blade sprouted from the ground to deflect Fremy's bullet, and it ricocheted away.

"You're quite the violent person, aren't you, Fremy?" Nashetania said. After blocking the shot, she calmly jumped down from her perch atop the dead fiend. Fremy was reloading, but Adlet stopped her.

"Is that...Nashetania?" Rolonia asked from behind him.

"Nice to meet you. So you're Rolonia? I'm sure we'll be seeing more of each other." Nashetania put a hand on her chest and bowed, and Rolonia lowered her head in return.

"What happened to Goldof?" Adlet asked.

Nashetania pointed south. "He's about two kilometers that way. Once he's finished a little errand there, I think he'll come back here."

"And what is this little errand?" Adlet asked.

"That's a secret." Nashetania put her finger mischievously to her lips, acting just like she had back when Adlet had first met her in his jail cell.

Adlet glanced at the back of his hand. All six of the flower petals were there. If Goldof was a real Brave, then at the very least, he wasn't dead. If he was the seventh, that was another story, though. "Did you use him to lure us out here?"

"Heavens, no. I just wanted him to help me out with something. I didn't imagine that all of you would come running after him," Nashetania said.

She was clearly lying, and Adlet was certain this was a trap. Obviously, Nashetania was about to pull something. Adlet eyed their surroundings in an attempt to figure out her ploy. "How did you ask him to come help you?" he probed.

"Our hearts are connected. I don't have to tell him anything. All I have to do is wish for it, and he'll come to me from anywhere."

"What're you talking about? You betrayed him." Chamo's accusation didn't seem to bother Nashetania.

"Is Goldof the seventh?" Adlet asked.

"How cruel of you to say that, Adlet," Nashetania said. "To suspect my dear Goldof! He's a genuine Brave of the Six Flowers. And this guarantee is coming from me, so there's no question about it."

Did she show up here just to tease us? Her nonchalant attitude was getting under his skin. "By the way, we're going to kill you now."

"Oh dear, I'm so scared."

"When is your precious Goldof going to come running?"

Nashetania giggled. "*Save me*, Goldof! I'm over *heeere*! They're going to *kill* meee!"

Adlet scowled at her weak attempt at a joke. He shot a look to Fremy and Hans beside him. The two of them nodded, and he gave the order.

"Kill her."

Fire burst from Fremy's gun, and Hans darted straight toward Nashetania while Adlet turned around. It was just as he'd expected. Thirty fiends were now on the slope with red-hot boulders at the ready, about to throw.

"I'll get behind her!" Adlet yelled as he pulled a flash bomb from his pouch and hurled it. The powerful light overwhelmed the fiends, but they still launched the scorching rocks. His attack had ruined their aim, though, and the Braves dodged easily.

But then one of the fiend corpses moved. A tentacle reached out from the ground toward Adlet's neck.

"Watch out!" Rolonia cried, and her whip sliced through it just barely in time. Strange-smelling blood spurted from the tentacle, and the fiend wailed. One after another, the apparent corpses began rising to attack.

"Rolonia! Mora! You help me slow down these guys!" Adlet yelled. A blade stabbed up at him from the ground, but Rolonia's whip broke it off.

"*Hrmeow-meow!* You leave the princess to me!" Hans called as he rocketed through the air for a swipe at Nashetania. In response, she summoned another wave of steel from the rock below.

"I've got your back, Hans!" said Fremy, and she threw a bomb and fired a shot at Nashetania. The former impostor rolled away from both attacks. Hans and Fremy were stronger than her. Two-on-one, there was no reason they could lose.

"Be careful of her stealth meowers, Fremy!" said Hans.

"You don't have to tell me that."

Nashetania ran from them both. With the hilt of her slim sword, she blocked Fremy's shots while keeping Hans at bay with her conjured blades.

"You need Chamo's help?" the youngest Brave asked, having already vomited up her slave-fiends.

But Adlet shook his head. "Nashetania must be planning something. You keep an eye on the situation and be ready for the next attack, Chamo."

"Gotcha."

The melee continued for a few minutes after that. Fremy and Hans fought Nashetania, while Adlet, Mora, and Rolonia held back the fiends flooding in to support her. Chamo cautiously observed the area under the watch of her slave-fiends. The situation was clearly to the Braves' advantage, as there was no indication of incoming enemy reinforcements.

Adlet slammed his sword down on the crown of a charging fiend. When it recoiled, Rolonia whipped it to shreds, until blood spurted from it like a fountain and it was dead.

There were about thirty fiends. It was more than a few, but with these numbers, the Braves could certainly keep them at bay. If fighting continued like this, they would beat Nashetania.

"…No way…Is this it?" Adlet muttered as they fought. He couldn't imagine that this was the full extent of what Nashetania had planned. Her scheme back in the Phantasmal Barrier had been so meticulous, he found it hard to believe she would challenge them to a battle like this without something more.

"*Meow-ha!*" Hans's sword swept toward Nashetania. Frantically, she blocked it with her signature Saint technique. One of the fiends slipped past Adlet's team to guard Nashetania, and somehow she managed to slip away after nearly being cornered.

"I'm not letting you get away," Fremy said as her bullet pierced Nashetania's leg.

The princess grimaced. "I'm sorry! Come save me quick, guys, okay? *Eek!*" She no longer looked so composed. But that didn't make Adlet relax at all. Nashetania clearly had something lying in wait. Was there another ambush? Or would she use Goldof as a hostage? Or maybe Tgurneu was going to appear and come after them?

"Hey, Adlet." Chamo, still spectating, spoke up. "Can I just kill Nashetania now?"

"…All right. Do it!" Adlet made the decision. This was probably some kind of trap. But beating the enemy in front of them was more important than worrying about that.

That was when it happened. A fiend slipped past Rolonia's whip and Mora's fists to rush over to Nashetania: a giant lizard-type fiend with rocky skin. Nashetania dodged a slice from Hans and leaped astride the stone lizard-fiend, which never broke its pace. Was it going to carry Nashetania and escape?

"Where ya goin', *meow?!*"

The stone lizard-fiend was not moving terribly fast. Hans chased after Nashetania and tried to leap on its back, too, but a moth-fiend swooped in to knock him off. Fremy shot at Nashetania's back, but the moth blocked the attack with its body. With the bullet buried in its chest, the moth-fiend fell to the ground in a shower of fluids.

But as this was going on, Chamo's slave-fiends had circled around to block Nashetania's way. Ten slave-fiends all in a row attacked in unison. *They got her,* Adlet thought, but the moment he was certain she was done, Nashetania replied to Hans's question.

"Where am I going? I'm running away." As the slave-fiends leaped at her, Nashetania smiled boldly. "Since I've done what I came to do, after all."

All the slave-fiends suddenly stopped. No blades had pierced them. Nothing had attacked them. *What happened?* Adlet wondered, and while he searched for the cause, the fiends took full advantage. A lion-fiend swiped at his neck from behind. He ducked and whipped around, throwing a poison needle into the creature's face.

Nashetania took the opportunity to escape the crowd of slave-fiends surrounding her and flee. "Let's go! Hurry, hurry!" She hit the stone lizard-fiend's back, and it kept thudding along. Nashetania repelled a shot from Fremy with a blade, while another of her fiends rushed in to hinder Hans's pursuit. Rolonia and Mora's opponents had repositioned to serve as a rearguard for Nashetania's flight, preventing Fremy and Hans from chasing after her.

For a moment Adlet hesitated, wondering if they should try to follow. But they had something more important to deal with. "What happened, Chamo?!" he cried, running up to her.

She didn't seem right, clutching her stomach with an expression of shock. She stared at her hands and her body and muttered, "…Huh? What…?"

Then she covered her mouth. The next moment, blood began pouring from between her fingers. She collapsed without even a cry, and as she did, all of her slave-fiends immediately rushed back into her mouth. Adlet couldn't see any visible; he had no idea what had hit her.

"Chamo!" Mora cried as she and Rolonia rushed to the fallen girl. Mora held the young Brave while Rolonia tried to stop the bleeding. But when they attempted to treat her, they were left speechless and confused. They couldn't find any wounds.

"…What's wrong, Chamo?" asked Adlet.

Trembling, the girl held her hands over her mouth. It had to be the first time ever that she'd been afraid for her life. "There's…swords… inside…my stomach…" She gasped, and then she vomited up another gush of blood.

Fremy and Hans tried to pursue Nashetania, but the fiends fended them off, and Nashetania gradually widened her lead. Then she was past the slope and out of sight.

Nashetania knew exactly what had happened to Chamo—of course she did. She was the one who had meticulously, painstakingly set the trap for her in the first place.

Some Saints possessed a certain ability: They could imbue an object with their abilities to create tools with special powers. These tools were generally referred to as hieroforms. The Saint of the Single Flower, who had devised the original Crest of the Six Flowers, had been the most powerful creator of hieroforms in history. In more recent times, Mora of Mountains and Willone of Salt were known to often utilize this skill. Chamo and Rolonia could not do it at all, and Fremy did not seem very proficient at it, either. The typical target objects for this infusion of power were stakes inscribed with hieroglyphs, or written texts, or any sort of gem. It was said that giving a crest power, as the Saint of the Single Flower had, was an extremely advanced technique.

Publicly, Nashetania hadn't been able to create hieroforms—but that was a lie. If her capabilities were widely known, she wouldn't have been able to fulfill her role in this scheme.

About two years earlier, Nashetania had left Piena to visit All Heavens Temple. More than twenty servants accompanied her: guards, a coachman for each carriage, maids to handle her meals and clothes, and even someone to care for Nashetania's pets. At the time, acting Temple Elder Willone, who had been managing the shrine, seemed quite displeased by the flaunting of luxury.

"It's unusual for you to come all the way to the temple, Princess," said Willone. "What brings you here?" Nashetania had normally trained in Piena with Goldof and the knights. She rarely left the country.

"Same as always. Just a whim," she'd replied, evading the question.

That day at All Heavens Temple, they were practicing battling fiends. The Saints fought Chamo Rosso's "pets" on the temple training grounds. Slug-fiends, water-snake-fiends, and more attacked without mercy, and Athlay, the Saint of Ice, Liennril, the Saint of Fire, and other skilled warriors pummeled their opponents with their techniques. The training session was just like real battle. Not all the blood on the ground belonged to the slave-fiends.

"…Wow," said Nashetania in awe when she'd seen the spectacle. "So the girl in the middle is Chamo? She's so cute. I'm sure she'll be really pretty when she grows up."

Willone was taken aback by Nashetania's happy-go-lucky grin. "… Um, Princess, if you came here without knowing what was going on, maybe you should reconsider. Chamo isn't a bad kid, but she's somewhat… atypical."

"Oh, really? Well, that's a little unsettling. But don't you worry about me."

"Please, just try not to get yourself hurt."

"If I avoid ever getting hurt, I wouldn't learn anything, Willone," said Nashetania, and she tossed aside her dress. Underneath, she wore simple training clothes. "I can't wait any longer. Nashetania, Saint of Blades, joins the fray!"

"Ah! H-hey! Hold on!" Willone had attempted to restrain her, but it was in vain. Nashetania leaped into the arena, slicing into slave-fiends with swords growing out of the ground.

"Huh? A newcomer, huh? Hey, Willone, is that one of the Saints I'm allowed to kill?" Chamo asked, and she vomited up more slave-fiends.

"No! Absolutely not! And there aren't *any* Saints you're allowed to kill!" Willone dashed into the arena to protect the princess.

Nashetania was smiling, summoning blades as she began the clash against Chamo. "Wow! This is really amazing! So this is what it's like to fight fiends!"

"They're not fiends," said Chamo. "They're my pets."

Nashetania kept on fighting for half an hour or more, grinning all the while. By this point in time, the plan to kill the Braves of the Six Flowers within the Phantasmal Barrier was already under way. Nashetania had come to the temple to analyze Chamo's fighting abilities, since she was bound to end up in combat with the girl eventually. While Nashetania played the tomboy princess who enjoyed the battle, privately, she thought Chamo was a monster.

"You're pretty strong, sword lady," said Chamo. "I dunno you. Who are you?"

"My name is Nashetania. Pleased to make your acquaintance." Her head and body drenched in blood, Nashetania smiled.

"This whole thing has been a pain in the butt, but Chamo's glad to be here. Guess it'll be more fun than I thought."

"Really? I'm enjoying myself, too." *Coming here to reconnoiter was the right choice,* thought Nashetania. Forget one-on-one—even if she ganged up on Chamo with Goldof, she wasn't sure she could win. She would prefer to leave Chamo to the real Braves, but that scheme might not go smoothly. She would have to put that thing inside her after all.

Before coming, Nashetania had packed her power into a very tiny fragment of diamond. If she silently prayed for the diamond to activate—and certain requirements were fulfilled—then dozens of blades would burst from it. She didn't have it on her at the time of the temple visit, however.

"Princess, please be more careful! I can't take responsibility if you get hurt!" Willone was practically tearing her hair out in one corner of the arena.

Nashetania ignored her, yelling, "Let's go, Chamo! Keep it coming, please!"

"Are you sure, Princess? You might die," the girl replied.

Nashetania's body was marred here and there with acidic burns, hot wounds, and bites. She had fallen and twisted her arm, possibly fracturing something. "Someone who aspires to be a Brave of the Six Flowers cannot retreat from something like this."

"Then I won't hold back," said Chamo.

Nashetania glanced toward the arena's audience seats. Her maids and guards were all white as sheets. Beside them there was a cage containing her pets. Nashetania had three cats, two dogs, and two squirrels, and she took them along with her wherever she went. The creatures were trembling in fear inside their cage.

Then one of the dogs began flailing around. The cage broke open, and all the animals scampered away. Watching out of the corner of her eye, Nashetania gave the tiniest snicker.

And then she thought, *I'm counting on you, Dozzu.*

"...Ngh!" The strike from the snake's tail knocked Nashetania's sword from her hands. Willone panicked and cut in between her and Chamo. "Hold on. Chamo, Princess, let's leave it at that. If this keeps up, someone is gonna die."

Nashetania picked up her sword and pointed it at Chamo. "We're not going to stop, Willone."

"Come on, Princess—"

"I want to become stronger. I can't protect the people, my father, or anyone at all unless I get stronger. I can't allow myself to be afraid of a little girl."

Chamo reacted to Nashetania's provocation. "...Just a little girl, huh?"

Nashetania pretended she hadn't heard that and continued. "I want to fight stronger opponents. This still isn't enough."

"Is that right, Princess?" There was a flash of anger behind Chamo's smile. "Sorry, Chamo shouldn't have gone so easy on you. Let's fight for serious." She plunged her foxtail down her throat, and every one of her slave-fiends was unleashed into the arena.

Willone yelled, "Stop, Chamo!" and grappled with Nashetania as her pillars of salt sprang up one after another to block the attacks. Athlay of Ice and Liennril of Fire helped keep the slave-fiends at bay.

"What are you doing, Willone?!" Nashetania demanded. "This is rude!"

"Shut up, Princess Numbskull! You've exhausted my patience!" Willone fled the scene with the struggling Nashetania in her arms. The slave-fiends circled around them as if to say, *We're not letting you get away,* and descended upon the both of them.

"I can watch this no longer! Stop the princess!"

Nashetania's knight guards jumped into the fray then, too. In the midst of the chaos in the arena, the princess secretly smiled to herself.

Fifteen minutes later, the chaos in the arena had settled. Nashetania had been made to sit on the ground, where her maids were giving her an earful. On the other side of the arena, Chamo and Willone were yelling at each other.

Nashetania looked at her pets' cage and said, "Hey, Porta and Powna aren't in there." Two of them, one cat and one dog, weren't in there. The maids paused their lecturing and started a hunt for the two missing animals. They found the cat immediately, trembling at the edge of the audience seating, but the dog was gone.

"A dog? Okay. I'll look for it," Willone reassured the princess after she told her and Chamo about it. They searched the arena.

"Wait, maybe…" Chamo shoved her foxtail down her throat and hocked up a giant slug. She whacked it on the back a few times, and with a gloopy sound, something came up from the back of its throat.

"Eek! Eeeeek! Porta! Porta!" Nashetania scooped the dog up in her arms. It was a funny-looking animal with a rotund little face and body, almost like a cross between a dog and a squirrel. Its fur tips had been digested, but it didn't seem to be in mortal peril.

"When did you swallow that?" Chamo scolded her slave-fiend. "Hey now, you're not allowed to eat weird stuff."

"Porta! Hold on, Porta!" Nashetania called the dog's name over and over. Watching, Willone held her head in her hands.

No one but Nashetania knew that during the chaos, the dog had scampered about the arena in apparent fright, and then, when it was sure that no one was looking, it had jumped down the slug-fiend's throat. The dog had been carrying a very tiny diamond in its mouth. Once it was inside the slug slave-fiend, it had embedded the gem in the creature's flesh.

The dog's name was Porta, but that was just an alias it used to hide itself in the human realm. Its real name was Dozzu, and it was one of the three commanders that ruled over the fiends.

"...It was a success, Nashetania," Dozzu told her quietly. None but Nashetania could hear.

"Thanks. I knew you'd do it, Dozzu," she replied, smiling.

The slug's nerves were dull, so it probably wouldn't notice the gem stuck inside it. In other words, Chamo would have no way of knowing it was in there. If the proper conditions were met and Nashetania prayed, the gem would unleash its power. Dozens of blades would slice the interior of the slug's stomach. And what's more, if Chamo had the slave-fiend inside her at the time, the blades would damage her organs.

There were two conditions for its activation: Nashetania had to be near her target, and Chamo had to attack Nashetania first. But the gem wasn't that powerful. Once the two were more than a kilometer apart, it would lose effect. This was because Nashetania had yet to mature as a Saint.

But there were only two ways to cancel the blade gem. Namely, Nashetania could annul it herself, or it would happen naturally if she died. While she had been running around inside the Phantasmal Barrier, she had deliberately chosen not to activate it. There wouldn't have been any point. It was better to reserve her trump card.

Nashetania estimated that once the blade gem was triggered, it would take about three hours for Chamo to die.

"...*Guh...guh...gwaaaagh...*"

Chamo's moans of pain were the only sounds in the corpse-strewn lava zone. She was desperately trying to vomit up the blade gem. All that came from her mouth was saliva and blood. No blade gem and no fiends.

"Chamo...Please, keep trying," Rolonia urged her.

Mora and Rolonia's fervent attempts at treatment had been ineffective. Chamo's stomach was so unique, normal treatment didn't work. All Mora could do was to pour energy into her body to shore up her vitality.

"So...we have no choice but to kill Nashetania, after all," Adlet murmured.

Mora had used her powers to give them a general understanding of the nature of the gem. It would take about three hours for it to kill Chamo, and if Nashetania moved far enough away, it would lose effect. The radius of the gem's effect was around one kilometer and there were only two ways to nullify it: Either Nashetania had to cancel it, or they had to kill her to save Chamo.

Mora was still chanting in the divine tongue, to further analyze the gem stuck in Chamo's stomach. Hans and Fremy were chasing after the culprit. If they lost sight of her, saving Chamo would become infinitely harder. Adlet anxiously awaited their return.

"Auntie...Chamo's not gonna die, right?" the girl asked weakly.

Mora grasped her small hand and encouraged her. "How can you say that, Chamo? We're all with you, aren't we? Do you think we would let you die so easily?"

"...Ah-ha-ha...You're right...yeah."

Nashetania got us good, thought Adlet. Judging from her behavior, she hadn't planted the gem during the Phantasmal Barrier incident. She'd done it long before the Evil God's awakening. Adlet should have foreseen this;

he'd known she'd been preparing for this fight over the course of many years.

That was when Hans returned from his pursuit of Nashetania.

"What's the word, Hans?" asked Adlet.

"*Meow.* I lost sight of her once, but we found her." He seemed somewhat rattled. He was fully aware just how important Chamo was. "She's about a kilomewter away from here, just hangin' around. The damn woman gathered about thirty fiends, and now she's just sittin' in the middle of 'em and smilin'. I didn't see no other fiends, though."

"And where's Fremy?"

"She's watchin' the princess from a little ways away. Fremy ain't dumb enough to fight her alone."

"I'm worried," said Adlet. "And about Fremy, too."

"There was neowthin' else to worry about. I didn't catch sight of Tgurneu, neither…or Goldof," said Hans.

Adlet scowled. But now it was clear—Mora's analysis was right, and Nashetania couldn't get too far from Chamo. Mora's estimate of one kilometer for the area of effect also seemed accurate. "First, we get Chamo away from here and cancel the gem's effects. Mora, can you move her?" Adlet asked.

But Mora shook her head sadly. "She's just barely clinging to life. I don't know what would happen should we move her."

"There's no other way. Nashetania needs to die, after all." Adlet hurried to replenish his weapons from his iron box. "Me, Rolonia, and Fremy will go kill Nashetania. Hans and Mora, you stay here and protect Chamo." Adlet chose to leave Hans, whose combat skills he trusted most, right by Chamo. This was because he was still worried about Tgurneu, who had yet to show up.

"All right," said Hans. "I'll leave the princess to mew guys."

"And, Mora," Adlet continued, "call Goldof one more time with your mountain echo."

Mora nodded. She took a deep breath and amplified her voice. **"GOLDOF! WHERE ARE YOU?! I'VE CALLED YOU MANY**

TIMES! NASHETANIA HAS NEARLY KILLED CHAMO! RETURN TO US AND HELP SAVE HER!"

When Chamo had first fallen, Mora had called Goldof over and over with her powers, explaining the situation to him. But yet again, her voice echoed throughout the lava zone in vain.

"He still won't return," the oldest Saint said.

"...Addy, what will we do about Goldof?" Rolonia asked.

Adlet had no answers. First of all, he didn't know if Goldof was even a real Brave or not. Was he the seventh, and had he lured Chamo here to kill her? If so, Adlet was forced to assume that the next time they encountered him would be in a skirmish. But there was still the possibility that Nashetania was deceiving and using him. Perhaps the fact that he had yet to return meant he was in trouble.

"We'll deal with him later," said Adlet. It was too much to think about. He'd make the simple decisions first. "Sorry. Goldof is going to have to get through this on his own. Right now, let's just focus on saving Chamo. Let's go." He took Rolonia and dashed off northward.

The rocky hills of the volcanic region made running difficult. Adlet and Rolonia jumped over ditches and dodged geysers of hot steam as they pushed northward. After about five minutes of running, they heard gunshots. Fremy was battling fiends.

They arrived at the rendezvous point Hans had indicated. Fremy had taken up a position at the summit of a rock mound, shooting down at the fiends attacking her from below. "Nashetania ran west! Follow her!" she yelled.

Adlet didn't hesitate. He turned away from her and headed west. Scanning around from the top of the highest peak in the area, he could see something moving in the shadow of a mound about three hundred meters away. "You're not getting away!" he said, breaking into a sprint to give chase. He found Nashetania among the twenty fiends speeding across the rock hills. She was riding the back of a wolf-type, glancing behind her as she fled.

When Adlet descended the rock hill, two fiends rushed up from below to attack him. A spider-fiend spewed thread at him, while a big snake-fiend spat fire. Adlet sprang backward, but the rock beneath him crumbled where he landed, sending him tumbling down the slope.

"What are you doing, idiot?!" Fremy swiftly sniped the spider.

"Sorry." Adlet gave her a quick apology as he scrambled to his feet, dodging an attack from the snake-fiend before slicing its head off. The uneven footing of the volcanic terrain made this bout particularly challenging. It restricted the agility characteristic of his fighting style.

"Addy! Incoming!" Rolonia cried. Another fiend approached him from the west.

"You take it, Rolonia!" Adlet said, and he darted past the enemy to pursue Nashetania. She was probably sending her forces out a little at a time just to slow them down while she and her fiends focused on escaping.

Rolonia pulled out her whip. When a fiend's claws were almost to her neck, her shriek ripped through the lava zone. "Don'tmoveyourottendirtyvileverminI'llstopyourbreathI'llstopyourheart!" In an instant, her whip had slashed bloody, gushing ribbons into the fiend.

The three of them kept on sprinting after the swarm, closing the distance bit by bit.

Adlet ran side by side with Fremy and apologized. "I'm sorry, Fremy."

"?"

"If I'd listened to you and been more cautious, things wouldn't have ended up like this."

"Don't be stupid. What's the point of apologizing to me?" she replied, sounding uncomfortable. "Don't worry about it. I'm not angry, and I don't care."

Adlet nodded and kept his pace.

He realized that Nashetania was running in an arc. She was drawing a half-moon with a one-kilometer radius, the pit where Chamo lay at its center. Adlet had originally been heading north, but now he was already turned in the opposite direction. Just as Mora had sensed, Nashetania couldn't move more than a kilometer away.

They were now within a hundred meters of their target. Fremy manifested a bomb in her palm and plugged it into the barrel of her gun. She fired, and the explosive fell ten meters off from Nashetania's side. Adlet made a simple sling with some rope to launch another bomb at the fleeing traitor.

"Is her plan just to keep running like this until Chamo dies?" Fremy asked as the chase continued.

"Maybe. But at this rate, we'll catch up!" Rolonia replied.

She was right—if they kept bombarding Nashetania to slow her down while they pursued her, they would eventually catch her. Against just Nashetania and twenty-odd fiends, the three of them were sure to win.

"Something's fishy, Adlet," said Fremy.

"Yeah, I think so, too," he agreed. They halted their assault, slowed down, and ran just fast enough as to not let Nashetania slip away entirely.

"What's wrong? We're not going to fight them?" Rolonia was confused.

Nashetania would know that she could not evade them forever just by running around the one-kilometer circle, and there was no way she could keep defending herself with just twenty fiends. If that was all, then she practically showed up just to get herself killed. But Nashetania had to have something else up her sleeve, maybe a special means of getting away. As they continued tailing her, Adlet pondered what the trick might be.

Fremy had clearly noticed, too, and tried to puzzle out what Nashetania was thinking. "This feels like a diversion to me, Adlet."

"Yeah," he agreed. "Is she waiting to be attacked?"

"...Maybe to spring the same kind of trap as the one she pulled on Chamo," Fremy suggested.

But Adlet didn't think that was possible. On the way to the Howling Vilelands, he had journeyed together with Nashetania for eleven days. Once he had discovered that she was the impostor, he had reinspected himself and all his equipment, thinking she might have placed something on him during that time. But he'd found nothing odd. At the very least, she hadn't set any traps on his person. Fremy and Nashetania had been in contact for only one day. It seemed unlikely that Nashetania would have had the time to sneak something on her, and this was the first time she had ever met Rolonia. Adlet figured that Chamo was the only one who had been loaded with a blade gem.

"Would there be any other reason for Nashetania to be such an obvious idiot?" asked Fremy.

That was when it hit him. "Fremy, have you been watching Nashetania this whole time?"

"No, I lost track of her a number of times…Oh. A transforming-type fiend?"

Adlet nodded.

Rolonia said, "Huh? What do you mean?"

"I mean that the Nashetania we're chasing right now might be a fake, a transforming-type fiend in disguise," Adlet clarified.

Some fiends could transform into any shape they wanted, and there were more than a few of them. Adlet had encountered one such creature himself during the Phantasmal Barrier fight. A shape-shifter wouldn't be able to transform into Adlet or Hans. In order to create the perfect replica of someone, the fiend needed either that person's cooperation or access to their corpse. So one could have easily disguised itself as Nashetania.

"At the very least, the Nashetania we fought was the real one—she used the power of blades and activated Chamo's blade gem. But there's no guarantee that one over there is the real thing."

"Hans and I did lose sight of Nashetania," said Fremy. "She had enough time to make the switch."

"I understand," said Rolonia. "So that's what's going on. But how can we tell which is the real one?"

"If we see her using the power of blades, we'll know she's the real one," said Adlet. "We've also got another sure-fire way to know what she really is. Don't we, Rolonia?"

"What do you mean?" Rolonia, behind him, tilted her head in thought.

So she hasn't realized it?

The three of them sped up their chase after Nashetania. They were already only about thirty meters away from her and her pack of fiends. Still astride the wolf-fiend, she looked back at them. She was apparently expecting Fremy to shoot, so Adlet figured he could surprise her. What he needed to watch out for was Nashetania's stealth ability—but he already knew how to counteract that, too.

"Let's go!" Adlet yelled.

Instantly, Rolonia's whip wound around him. She planted her feet and lifted him into the air. "Be careful, Addy!" she cried, throwing him. As he hurtled through the air, arcing down toward Nashetania's wolf-fiend, he drew a small knife. Attached to the handle was a fine chain that wrapped around Adlet's arm.

"Eek!" Nashetania blocked the knife with her left arm. As blood poured from her left wrist, a cute yelp escaped her. Dozens of blades sliced up from the ground toward Adlet as he flew. He blocked them with his sword and the iron plates fitted into his boots. The blades scored him with tiny cuts before he landed on the wolf-fiend's back.

"Watch out, Adlet!" Fremy yelled. Nashetania stabbed at his throat. Adlet blocked her sword with an armored shoulder as he pulled out a secret tool—a tiny, poison-filled bottle. She smacked it away with her weapon, but Adlet had anticipated that she'd avoid it. The bottle was just a decoy, and the real attack came from his own sword.

"...Ngh!" Nashetania ducked. He was so close to knocking her off the fiend's back. But then the wolf-fiend twisted, bucking Adlet off.

"This is our chance! We'll take him out, all together!" Nashetania cried, holding her wounded left arm. Fiends surged toward where Adlet had fallen on the ground.

But Fremy fired off a round in his defense, and Rolonia wrapped her whip around his hand. Once he was holding on, Rolonia heaved him up with an "Up we go!" like she was reeling in a fish. Adlet kept the fiends at bay with a smoke bomb during his retreat.

"We bungled that one. Well, no matter. Let's run!" Nashetania said to the fiends that were about to pursue Adlet. They obeyed her orders and guarded her as she fled.

"We blew it," said Fremy.

Adlet had been left lying on the ground after Rolonia had reeled him in, and Fremy helped him up. They'd been so close, and Nashetania had gotten away, but it hadn't been in vain. Adlet showed Rolonia his tiny, bloodstained knife. "Do your thing, Rolonia."

"...Oh, *that's* what you meant."

He handed the knife to her and immediately set off again. They couldn't lose sight of Nashetania and her entourage.

As they ran, Rolonia licked the blood off the knife blade. As the Saint of Spilled Blood, she possessed the ability to analyze blood by taste. Never slowing down, she rolled the liquid around in her mouth for a time.

"...So Rolonia?" Fremy asked.

"I've never tasted Nashetania's blood before, but...this is from a female in her teens. A powerful Saint. It seems she's exhausted, but generally in good health, and she's had a very affluent lifestyle. I think it's safe to say this is Nashetania's blood."

"So we're chasing the real one, then, huh?" said Adlet. They were lagging behind again, about a hundred meters back. He could see that she was observing them closely from the wolf-fiend's back. "Though we knew she was the real thing once she used the power of blades, anyway. But it's good to be doubly sure."

"Did you learn anything else, Rolonia?"

"Well...though this is human blood, it tastes like a fiend. It's really abnormal. It's mixed with the blood of a fiend with strong restorative capabilities...and the blood of another with great physical strength...and the blood of some fiend I can't understand at all. I don't have the slightest idea how such blood would come to exist." Rolonia continued, panting.

"Great, Rolonia. Even that much is enough," said Adlet, and he grinned. He didn't know what Nashetania was plotting. But the real one was only a hundred meters away—they knew that for sure. They couldn't let this opportunity slip from their grasp. "We're gonna run as fast as we can to finish her off. Don't let your guard down," he said. Fremy's eyes turned grim, and Rolonia swallowed.

Fremy fired a shot to slow the fiends down while Adlet tossed a grenade. Bit by bit, the pursuers neared their prey. The enemy forces numbered fewer now, too—the three of them would be more than a match for the fiends.

"Fremy, you and me are gonna blast them with every explosive we have," said Adlet. "Then all three of us will charge in. You hold off the fiends. Rolonia, you use your whip to break Nashetania's blades. Leave finishing her off to me. Got it?" Rolonia readied her whip while Fremy created bombs in her hands. Adlet pulled tools from pouches at his waist for his final preparations.

"Please, come on! Can't you run any faster?!" Nashetania cried, smacking the rear of the wolf-fiend under her. Was her panic an act, or was it real? Adlet couldn't tell.

"Once she's over that mountain, go for her." But right as the words left his mouth, something flew toward them from a long way away. He heard it ripping through the air. When Adlet skidded to a stop, a spear was stuck in the ground right in front of him.

"!"

All three of them turned to look toward the source of the missile. It was the opposite direction from where Chamo lay in the pit.

When the hell did he get here? No—maybe he's been close for a while. They had been so focused on chasing Nashetania, they hadn't been keeping an eye on their surroundings. "He's here." Adlet scowled. He couldn't say he was happy to see the man was safe. Goldof Auora was looking down on them from the top of a rock mound.

"Why did you throw your spear at us, Goldof?" Rolonia murmured.

He didn't say anything, only watching them in silence.

Nashetania took advantage of the pause to put some more distance between them, and Fremy dashed after her. Goldof savagely gave chase himself.

"Rolonia! Stop him!" Adlet yelled. There was no more time for hesitation. He drew his sword and ran at Goldof, hardening his resolve to attack. Goldof would have heard Mora's mountain echo; he should know that Nashetania had attacked Chamo and that their ally's life was on the line. But he was still trying to protect Nashetania. Adlet had no choice but to consider him their enemy.

Fremy pitched a bomb at Goldof. He protected his face with his hands and made a running jump to one side to avoid the blast. Despite his heavy armor, he was agile enough to put Adlet to shame. Once he was on his feet again, he resumed his charge at Fremy.

"Oh no, you don't!" From the side, Adlet threw a poison needle at him. Goldof dodged it without looking up or stopping, but as he did, Fremy fired a bullet into his chest. He was launched backward, head over heels. But his thick armor protected him from the bullet, and the shot wasn't enough to kill him.

"Fremy! Rolonia!" Adlet yelled to the pair. "You follow Nashetania! Let me handle Goldof!" Their target was racing away from them.

But when the two girls tried to chase her, Goldof spoke for the first time. "...I can't let you go." He was on his feet and bolting for Fremy again.

Adlet pulled out a tear-gas canister and lobbed it at him. Goldof covered his eyes and mouth with his hands, dashing out of the smoke. It wasn't enough to slow him down.

With a roar, Adlet leaped toward the running Goldof, slamming his sword down onto his shoulder. Goldof blocked the strike with a gauntlet and gripped both Adlet's arms to throw him backwards. Then he completely barred Rolonia from further pursuit by seizing her armor and flinging her down. She tumbled along the ground, heavy armor and all.

"Ngh!"

Adlet and Rolonia both stood up at the same time. He had gotten careless because Goldof didn't have his spear—but the boy was formidable in unarmed combat, too.

"Fremy! Don't worry about us! You can't lose sight of Nashetania!" Adlet yelled.

Fremy nodded and rejoined the chase.

Goldof muttered something unintelligible and tried to sprint off after Fremy, but Adlet and Rolonia stood in his way.

"You…handle Fremy!" Goldof yelled loudly. Who was he talking to? Nashetania, or a third ally? He spread his arms and hunched low, turning back to Adlet and Rolonia. It looked like he was going to see this fight through to the end.

"Wait, please, Goldof!" Rolonia said, sounding frightened as she readied her whip.

"…You're in the way," Goldof said, and Rolonia shrank back a step.

"Why, Goldof?" Adlet said as he briefly retreated to pull Goldof's spear out from where it was stuck in the ground. He sheathed his sword and raised the spear instead. It was heavy and unwieldy, but it wasn't unusable. "You get what's going on, don't you? Chamo is about to die. We have no choice but to kill Nashetania to save her. Didn't you hear Mora's mountain echo?"

"Please stop, Goldof! We have to defeat Nashetania. We have no choice if we want save Chamo," said Rolonia. But it had no effect on Goldof's battle-ready stance.

"Goldof, talk to us," said Adlet. "Who tricked you? And how?"

"It's the same as what happened with Mora, right?" Rolonia chimed in. "You've been coerced to fight us somehow, right? Haven't you?"

But Goldof softly replied, "I can't let you…go beyond this point."

"Goldof…" Adlet began.

"If you want to get past me…you have to…kill me first."

At the sight of Goldof's eyes, a shiver of fear ran down Adlet's spine. Until now, he had not given up on the chance that Goldof was still on their side. But the moment Adlet saw that look, those beliefs evaporated. Goldof intended to kill him—and Fremy and Rolonia. All of them.

"Rolonia…you have to do that thing."

"That thing?"

"Where you wail, *die, die*! That thing you do when you fight for real."

"Addy…"

"We're going to kill Goldof."

Rolonia's eyes widened, and then she nodded wordlessly. As she did, Goldof lowered his center of gravity and charged straight for Adlet.

Yelling with everything he had, Adlet thrust out the spear. Just moving it made his arms tired, and he gained a new and personal appreciation for Goldof's unusual ability to whip the weapon around like a feather. Right before the spear would have connected, Goldof stopped. The spearhead was only a centimeter from his nose. Goldof immediately reached out to the haft. Adlet kicked him in the stomach to try to keep the weapon away from him.

"Urg!" Though Adlet had been the one to kick, he was the one who was repulsed. The shock ripped through his ankle, like he'd just slammed into a boulder.

Goldof grabbed at him, trying to catch him while he was vulnerable, but Adlet swept at his feet with the spear. The knight's greaves took the strike.

"Diediedietraitoryougottadieorthesunwon'trisetomorrow!" Suddenly, Rolonia's screeching resounded around them as her whip undulated like a snake. Goldof shifted, hunching over and covering his face with his hands. She lashed him over and over, with sharp, metallic clangs.

"!" Rolonia was shocked. Her whip, imbued with the power of the Saint of Spilled Blood, could wring blood from any enemy it touched. But she couldn't draw a single drop from Goldof. He blocked every strike with his armor.

"Rolonia! Don't stop! Rip off his armor!" Adlet yelled, thrusting the spear again. Goldof jumped, and the lance thudded impotently into the ground.

Goldof thwarted all their attacks. Rolonia's whip landed hit after hit, but his armor blocked every one, and she failed to reach his blood. It wasn't due to the quality his armor—it was his reflexes that were truly fearsome. Rolonia was aiming very precisely for the gaps in Goldof's defenses, but he warded off everything with only slight adjustments.

"Ngh!" Still intercepting her strikes, Goldof reached out to seize his spear. If Adlet gave him the slightest opportunity, Goldof would snatch it back. But if Adlet stopped attacking, Goldof was likely to target Rolonia instead.

"Adlet," Goldof said, blocking Rolonia's whip. "Don't kill…Her Highness."

"Enough of your bullshit!" Adlet yelled, stabbing out the spear. He was going for Goldof's armor. If he could just rip off one plate, then Rolonia could finish him off with her whip.

"Whywhywhywon'tyoudieyouwon'tdiedon'ttouchAddydon'ttouch-Fremydon'ttouchChamoDIEEE!" Rolonia screamed. Then the trajectory of her whip changed. It flailed in circles around Goldof, trying to ensnare him.

This is bad, thought Adlet. *She's getting anxious.*

"Her Highness…" Goldof began. Right when the whip was about to catch him, he leaped high, his large frame soaring just like Hans's as he slipped through the tiniest gap in the whip's path. When he landed, he charged for Adlet. The red-haired Brave whirled Goldof's spear around frantically, but he was a moment too late. What hit Goldof's shoulder was not the spearpoint, but the haft. Goldof's large hand grasped the weapon.

Adlet instantly judged that he couldn't hope to best Goldof in a wrestling match, and so he released the spear. Then, too fast for the eye to see, he pulled out a pain needle from a pouch at his waist. If he could stab Goldof with it, it would cause intense pain; no matter how tough Goldof was, he would be out of commission for a few seconds.

Adlet tried to aim for Goldof's hand with the needle right as it grabbed the spear—and that was when he noticed.

"!" Goldof wasn't going for the spear. He was going for the needle. Goldof released the spear and seized Adlet's hand. Squeezing with unnatural strength, he forced Adlet to drop the needle, then quickly snatched it out of the air between two fingers and threw it.

"Rolonia!" There was no way Adlet's cry would be fast enough.

Rolonia screamed and pressed a hand to her cheek, crumpling to the ground.

I have to protect her, he thought, pulling out a smoke bomb.

But Goldof immediately snatched back his spear, and then, out of the blue, said something very unexpected. "Listen…the enemy…isn't the princess… It's Fremy." Then he thrust the blunt end of his spear into Adlet's stomach.

After making sure Adlet was down, he turned away from the pair and escaped.

"…Damn it." Adlet couldn't chase after him. He couldn't even move. Even if it were an option, leaving Rolonia was not. Somehow, he struggled to his feet and went over to pull the needle from Rolonia's cheek.

"I-I'm okay, Addy." Rolonia engaged her power as Saint of Spilled Blood to bleed the wound on her cheek. It looked like that was enough to get all the poison out.

They chased Goldof for a while, but he was too fast. Adlet and Rolonia lagged farther and farther behind. Goldof was running along that same one-kilometer-radius arc. After about a quarter way around the circle, they lost sight of him.

Then, from far away, they heard gunshots. Fremy was fighting—and the sounds were coming from the very direction Goldof had run. "This is bad," said Adlet. "At this rate, Fremy'll be fighting two-on-one."

The two of them sped along over rock hills and the depressions between them. They could still hear Fremy's gunshots.

"Fremy!" Adlet called. Standing at the top of a rock hill, he finally caught sight of her. She was in a narrow valley, at the center of a circle of fiends. Goldof didn't seem to be anywhere nearby. "We're joining in!"

There were about fifteen enemies. Surrounded, Fremy was dodging this way and that as she squared off against the fiends. Close-quarters combat was her greatest weakness.

"Fremy! Watch out!" he shouted.

She had lost her balance. Adlet readied his sword, holding it tight, and aimed. He twisted the hilt to launch the blade, the recoil knocking him backward. The sword impaled a fiend's face, and Fremy took advantage of the opening it created to slip out of the ring and approach Adlet and Rolonia.

"I'llkillyouDIEI'llkillKILLyouifyoutouchFremyI'llkillyoushow-meyourGUTSyourottenfiends!" Rolonia wailed as she swung her whip around. The fiends were advancing toward her and Adlet. The two of them gave up on chasing Goldof and fought the coming enemies instead.

Fifteen minutes later, the enemy corpses lay at their feet. Of course, Nashetania was nowhere around, and neither was Goldof. Moments earlier, they had seen a flash of light in the direction the princess had gone and heard a noise like thunder. Now, both the sound and light were gone.

"There you are. So this is where you landed," Adlet said, picking up the blade. Compressing the spring in his sword hilt, he clicked it back into place.

"…You saved me there. That was close," Fremy said, and she breathed a heavy sigh.

"What happened with Goldof?" asked Rolonia. "He ran off in this direction."

"He passed by me earlier, running after Nashetania. I would have liked to kill him, but the fiends were blocking my way, and I couldn't get around. And there was also a tiny fiend following Nashetania."

"A tiny fiend? I wonder what that was."

"I don't know. It was nothing I've ever seen before."

"Really? Well, I'm glad you're safe, Fremy." Rolonia breathed a sigh of relief.

Fremy gave Adlet a reproachful look. "You let both Nashetania and Goldof get away," she said, arms crossed. "Unfortunately, Adlet, every one of your ideas has been a failure."

"…Yeah." He looked down.

He had insisted that Goldof had merely been deceived by Nashetania, and so they had followed him to the lava zone. As a result, they'd played right into Nashetania's hands, and Chamo was on the brink of death. Then, just moments ago when they had encountered Goldof, Adlet had hesitated to kill him. If been ready to kill the knight from the start, maybe things wouldn't have ended up this way.

"I blew it. Goldof is not on our side." Adlet remembered what they had discussed three days before, at the Bud of Eternity. Fremy and Mora had told him that they suspected Goldof. He should have taken that more seriously. His naive beliefs about keeping faith in his allies were the root cause of this whole mess.

"There's no point in stressing over it now," said Fremy. "I never believed your decisions would be perfect in the first place."

Cutting as ever, thought Adlet.

"B-but…it's still possible that Goldof has been tricked," said Rolonia.

"What do you mean?" asked Fremy.

"He told us that our enemy isn't the princess, but you, right?"

When Fremy heard that, her eyebrows twitched. "You're saying that I'm the enemy?"

"That's not what I mean!" Rolonia insisted.

Adlet understood what she was trying to say, so he supplemented for her. "In other words, someone's tricked Goldof. He's being made to believe that you're the enemy, Fremy, and he thinks that he has to kill you in order to save Chamo, and that's why he came to try to stop us. That's what you're saying, right, Rolonia?"

Rolonia nodded vigorously.

But Adlet shook his head. "No way." He rubbed his stomach. "He was fighting me like he didn't care if I died. I could tell."

"If Goldof believes that I'm the enemy, then why did he run right by me?" Fremy added.

"…W-well, um…" Rolonia couldn't think of what to say.

"Anyway, we need to hurry." Fremy cut off the conversation. "It's already been almost an hour since Nashetania activated the blade gem. There's just a little over two hours left, and Tgurneu could come to the lava zone with its whole army at any moment."

She was right—they had no time. If Tgurneu attacked them at that very instant, it was over. They would have no options but to try to move Chamo, even if it was hopeless, and run for it.

"Now that Nashetania has Goldof protecting her, she'll be harder to defeat," Fremy continued. "But still, the three of us should be able to do it. First, we have to find where Nashetania ran off to. Once we've done that, then we can talk."

Adlet and Rolonia nodded, and they began running over the rock hills.

"We *are* at a disadvantage," Fremy said. "But identifying the seventh is a major victory for us. Now if we can just save Chamo, our victory will be in sight."

Rolonia nodded. "You're right—we know who the seventh is now."

But Adlet didn't reply.

"What's wrong, Adlet?" asked Fremy.

He wasn't fully convinced. A number of questions rose in his mind. If Goldof was the seventh, he could have done it another way. For example, back in the Phantasmal Barrier, he could have killed Mora or Fremy or something and then pinned the deed on Adlet. So why hadn't he?

And there was another question: Why hadn't Nashetania shown up during their fight in the Ravine of Spitten Blood? If the enemy had carried out their scheme for Mora and the blade gem trap at the same time, then the Braves would have been unable to manage it all. Why was the enemy executing only one plot at a time? Why hadn't Goldof done anything so far, and why was he making his move now?

And not only that—there was another more important problem. What was Tgurneu up to? It should know by this point that the Six Braves were in the lava zone. So why hadn't it come to attack? Something was fishy. Behind the scenes, something was happening, and he couldn't even get a clue as to what was really going on.

"Rolonia," said Fremy, "you go tell Mora and Hans what's going on. Though I don't think it's likely, Goldof and Nashetania might attack them."

"Yes, understood," said Rolonia.

"We're going to keep chasing down Nashetania. If you find her, set this off. We'll come to you immediately," Fremy said, handing her a signal flare. Rolonia nodded and ran back toward Chamo.

"Snap out of it, Adlet. You're the leader, aren't you? Give the orders," said Fremy.

"O-oh…yeah. Sorry. I was thinking."

"I see. Let's go."

Adlet followed her. His mind was still on Goldof. The young knight's expression of shock when they had all found out that Nashetania was the seventh. His cast of despair as they'd progressed through the Howling Vilelands. That odd look on his face when he'd said he was going to go save Nashetania. Could someone really fake those things?

Adlet didn't know. He didn't understand Goldof. He was either an extraordinarily skilled actor or something else entirely.

In the rocky geothermal wasteland, there was no trail to track a person by. Adlet and Fremy decided to head for the spot where they'd seen that flash of light moments ago. Moving in a clockwise motion with Chamo at the center, they proceeded for about ninety degrees. Walking along, they searched carefully for Nashetania, overlooking no ditch or tiny pit or rock hill's shadow. It took time, but they didn't have much choice.

"I'm almost certain that Nashetania can't move farther than a kilometer away from Chamo. The circle's not terribly big. We're bound to find her," said Fremy.

They climbed a slightly more elevated rock hill to find a circular pit about twenty meters across. Smoke wafted from its center. "What's that?" Adlet said, approaching the smoke. There, in the middle, were the corpses of two fiends. Both had turned to ash. One was a snake, and the other seemed to be a human type. When he touched one of them with his hand, it was hot enough to make him yelp. They must have been fried only a few minutes ago. There were no signs the finds had been drenched in oil and set alight or showered with flames. This was probably from a lightning strike.

"What *is* this?" Fremy murmured. Upon closer inspection, the area around the fiends was scorched, too. They also found a few holes in the ground.

"...Nashetania was here," muttered Adlet. When she summoned blades from the earth, her attacks made pits shaped like this. "She fought someone here. There was also a fiend that can use lightning attacks—though I couldn't say if it was her friend or foe."

"I wonder who she fought. Was this the work of Cargikk's faction, too?" Fremy tilted her head. Now that she mentioned it, they still hadn't solved the mystery behind the pile of bodies in that pit where Chamo was.

"If it fought with Nashetania, then does that mean it's on our side?" wondered Adlet. "No, that can't be. There's no way we'd have any allies in the Howling Vilelands."

"Let's think about it later. Finding Nashetania is our top priority."

The two of them left the bodies and continued their search. They had about two hours left.

When they emerged from the pit, they found Rolonia running across the rocky hills. She noticed them and came near.

"How are Chamo and the others?" asked Adlet.

"They're safe," Rolonia replied. "But...a bunch of fiends from the forest are lurking nearby. It doesn't look like they're going to attack. They seem to be keeping a close watch."

That was weird. Why was Nashetania attacking in half measures like that?

"You didn't fight?" asked Fremy.

"Hans said, 'Don't worry about us; just go look for Nashetania.' He and Lady Mora were both...pretty anxious." Rolonia looked despondent. "But I do have one piece of good news. It sounds like Lady Mora can extend the time Chamo can hold on by just a little bit."

"How much?" asked Adlet.

"...About half an hour."

It was good news, but Adlet couldn't bring himself to feel glad. Chamo was still in danger. Besides, if Tgurneu brought its full forces to bear, that extra time would be meaningless. "Let's hurry. That's the only thing we can do right now," he said.

Maybe there was something going on in another place, and maybe there were factors they couldn't see, but they didn't have the time to ruminate on it. They would find Nashetania and kill her. They couldn't afford to focus on anything else.

Half an hour later, Adlet was crossing the lava zone by himself. He climbed a rock hill and scanned the area nearby, keeping his body low, and then he moved to another hill and searched again. He concentrated so as not to overlook a single shadow and listened intently for any sign of another being. Cautiously, slowly, he proceeded clockwise.

Fremy and Rolonia were not with him. Fremy was circling around counterclockwise, while Rolonia was searching closer to Chamo. They would surely be able to find Nashetania, no matter which way she had run.

Splitting up like this was dangerous, but considering the circumstances, they had no other choice. The plan was that if any of them found Nashetania or Goldof, they would immediately set off their signal flare to call the others. But Adlet had received no contact from the other two.

"!" Adlet heard a sound behind him and dashed toward it. But all he found at the bottom of the ditch were some steam and a tiny puddle of hot water. Realizing that the noise was only the discharge of a geyser, he clicked his tongue quietly.

Afterwards, he discovered two fiends. They were heading for the pit where Chamo lay. Adlet thought about killing them, but he changed his mind. Fighting the enemy was Hans and Mora's job. He ignored them and continued the hunt for Nashetania.

"Adlet!" A voice called to him from just ahead, and there was Fremy.

He didn't even have to ask, *Did you find Nashetania?* They'd already determined to call each other with a blast if they were successful. He approached Fremy and saw her expression was bitter. "You didn't just miss her, did you?" he asked.

"Hardly. Were you really not able to find her?"

As they spoke, Rolonia came running up to them, too. Seeing their faces, she immediately caught on that they had failed. They couldn't have overlooked Nashetania, not in this situation. They had searched every possible place she could have hidden.

It didn't take long to figure out why they couldn't find Goldof, though. This meant he had run outside the gem's area of effect. But Nashetania had to be within the area they had searched.

"Why can't we find her?" said Fremy. "It's just a one-kilometer radius."

"This makes me think she's got to be hiding somewhere, but…was there anywhere she could've hidden?" Adlet asked, recalling the area's topography. There was no such place.

"Maybe…Lady Mora's analysis was wrong?" said Rolonia.

"Impossible," said Fremy. "Mora is an incredibly talented Saint. I doubt she would ever misidentify the potency of a hieroform."

"But…maybe there's some way Nashetania could confuse her?" Rolonia suggested.

"If so, Mora would know it. Besides, Nashetania has only been a Saint for three years. I highly doubt she could use such a high-level technique."

As the other two discussed, Adlet happened to catch sight of something strange. There was a fiend standing on top of a rock hill just a little ways away, waving an object in its right hand.

"…A white flag?" he murmured.

The fiend had a crow's head and a yeti's body. An old rag was wrapped around its waist, and it held a club. The bludgeon was wrapped with a piece of white cloth, and its owner was waving its impromptu white flag around as it slowly approached the trio.

"An enemy." Fremy drew her gun and aimed at the yeti-fiend. The yeti-fiend flailed the white flag around, raising its hands to plead, *Don't shoot!*

Rolonia cut in front of Fremy and said, "Please wait, Fremy. That's a white flag."

"What's that?"

She doesn't know what that is? Adlet thought, a little shocked. Fremy was ignorant about the strangest things from time to time. "It's a sign on the battlefield that says you don't want to fight. You didn't know that?"

"Humans use such strange devices."

While they were talking, the yeti-fiend approached the bottom of the small rock hill where the three of them stood. About ten meters away, it stopped. The three of them kept their hands on their weapons, watching it.

"Hello," the yeti-fiend said. It was not a voice they recognized, but its inflection was familiar. The pronunciation was smooth and refined, unlike the somewhat strange pronunciation typical of regular fiends. "Thank you for not shooting. Privately, I was quite nervous when Fremy drew her gun."

"...Who are you?" asked Adlet.

The yeti-fiend shrugged. "I think if you see this, you might know," it said, and reached under its waistcloth. From within, it pulled out a large fig.

"!" Adlet and Fremy both moved at once. He aimed for the fiend's hand with a poison needle, while she shot the fig. The bullet pulverized it in a spray of fruity fragments.

"Unfortunately for you, this is just a fig. My main body's location is a secret."

"...Tgurneu," Adlet called the yeti-fiend's name. No—the name of the one controlling it.

"It looks like you folks have figured out what I really am, after all," it replied. "That's quite the accomplishment. What gave me away? Fremy was with me for eighteen years, and she never realized."

"What do you want?"

Fremy loaded the next bullet and aimed for Tgurneu's head. Her finger was already on the trigger, and she appeared ready to shoot the fiend dead.

"Wait, wait, wait, Fremy. I'm not here to fight. I want to talk."

"I don't," she retorted.

"Wait! Adlet, please stop Fremy," Tgurneu said.

Adlet didn't. Just like his ally, he was looking for the chance to kill Tgurneu. He had no reason to let the fiend live.

"I have a proposal, Adlet," it said.

Rolonia, too, was readying her whip, inching closer to Tgurneu. The commander had both arms up as it retreated backward, truly a pathetic sight.

But they all froze at its next words. "Why don't we work together to defeat Nashetania?"

"...What?" Adlet asked without thinking.

Seemingly surprised, Tgurneu said, "Huh? You haven't figured it out? I thought with a little effort, you'd be able to put it together. Nashetania and I are not on the same side."

"What do you mean?" Fremy demanded.

When Tgurneu saw her lower her gun, its beak trembled. It was hard to tell, but it seemed the fiend was laughing. "Nashetania is not my assassin. Dozzu is the one behind her—the disgraceful traitor to fiends. She is both yours and my enemy."

"...No way," Adlet muttered. He couldn't manage any other reaction.

"By the way, you three. What happened to your greetings?" Tgurneu said, beak shuddering in laughter.

Chapter 3

The Braves
Stray from
the Course

"…Blah…bleaaaagh!"

Chamo vomited blood again. One hand on her back, Mora sent her power streaming into her. The energy of the mountain was a force of healing, capable of restoring Chamo's vitality. But that couldn't suppress the blade gem itself.

About an hour and a half had passed since Nashetania had first activated it. In the pit, with fiends' corpses scattered around them, Mora waited impatiently for Adlet and the others to return with good news. The youngest Brave was withering before her eyes, her face pale and her eyes hollow. She clung to Mora like a trembling infant. All the older Saint could do was embrace the young girl and keep pouring life into her.

"Mya-mreow!"

The circular crater sloped down to where Mora and Chamo were in its center. Above them, Hans was fighting fiends.

Once he'd finished off all three of them, he returned to the pit. "I basically cleaned up the area, *meow*." He'd already killed nearly twenty, but there wasn't so much as a scratch on him, nor did he seem at all tired.

"Hans, you should go, too, after all. Join up with Adlet and defeat Nashetania," Mora said to him.

Not long earlier, Rolonia had returned alone. According to her, they now knew for sure Goldof was the enemy, and they had lost sight of Nashetania. Then she'd immediately left again to continue the search.

"The situation is unfavorable," said Mora. "Adlet's party alone will have difficulty defeating Nashetania. They need your strength."

But Hans shook his head. "*Meow. If* I coulda gone, I woulda gone a long time ago," he said, and pointed toward the Cut-Finger Forest. "We're bein' watched. If Chamo ain't defended, they'll come kill her straightaway. Can you fight 'em and keep Chamo alive at the same time, Mora?"

She couldn't. It would be impossible for her to fight while doling out life force. "...Curse them." Mora ground her teeth. The wait felt long—and even longer when an ally's death was nigh. Hans's expression was grim, too.

Then, in Mora's arms, Chamo moaned, "...Catboy...Auntie...sorry."

"Don't speak, Chamo. You'll exhaust your energy," said Mora.

Blood bubbles frothing from her mouth, the girl continued. "Chamo got careless... It was Chamo's fault... At this rate...Chamo's gonna be totally useless..."

Hans approached her as tears fell from her eyes. Hands wet with fiends' blood, he tousled her hair. "Don't talk big to me. Just shut up and sleep, kid."

"Chamo...is not a kid."

"Looks to me like mew've still got some kick in ya. Don't ya get weak, now," Hans said, smiling so kindly it surprised Mora. "You leave it to us. We're not gonna let that stupid woman beat us."

Chamo nodded obediently and closed her eyes. But Mora could tell that Hans was uneasy. Could Adlet and the others really defeat Nashetania on their own?

Adlet, Fremy, and Rolonia had no choice but to comply with Tgurneu's demand for polite greetings. Adlet gave the fiend a casual bow, which only angered it ("You call that a greeting?").

Why was this fiend so fixated on greetings? Adlet couldn't make heads or tails of it.

"…It seems now you're willing to hear what I have to say," Tgurneu said, nodding in satisfaction.

Adlet tried to calm his pounding heart. His throat was dry, his blood seethed, and his breathing was labored.

Once, long, long ago, Tgurneu had showed up in his village in just this way. It had exchanged words with the peaceful villagers and was all smiles, as if to befriend them. And then, in one night, it had enthralled the whole village, destroying Adlet's home.

The image rising in his mind now was especially vivid: the villagers, his family until that day, executing his sister, then capturing and killing the friend who had run away together with him. That day, Adlet's everything held dear shattered.

"Addy." Rolonia gently brushed the back of his hand. Her touch helped him regain his composure. Though the creature before them was the enemy of those he loved, now was not the time to fight it. He had to save Chamo, and he had to determine the veracity of Tgurneu's proposal.

"Are you all right, Adlet?" asked Tgurneu.

"Don't worry about me. The strongest man in the world is always calm," Adlet said, smiling. He looked at Fremy beside him. Her eyes were wide with anger, too, but she remained calm. *I should take a page from her book*, he thought.

"Is that so? Good. More importantly, let's talk about Nashetania. Unfortunately, I don't know where she is, either," Tgurneu said with some displeasure. "Have you figured out anything—even the smallest clue? Do you have leads about her current location?"

"Hold on," said Adlet. "Don't get ahead of yourself. Explain what's going on first. Why are you chasing Nashetania?"

Tgurneu drooped as if to say, *What a pain.* "Fremy, have you made sure to tell him about myself, Cargikk, and Dozzu?" it said. Fremy nodded. She had told them that the fiends were divided into three factions: Tgurneu's, Cargikk's, and Dozzu's, and the groups were not on good terms with each other. Tgurneu and Cargikk had differing opinions on what the fiends ought to be. Dozzu was known as the traitor to its kind, and the other two wanted it dead.

"As I said before, Nashetania is Dozzu's pawn," Tgurneu began. "About two hundred years ago, Dozzu betrayed us. He took his pawns and left the Howling Vilelands, concealing himself among humans. Cargikk and I sent our followers into the human realms to hunt him down while we went on killing the remaining members of Dozzu's faction in the Howling Vilelands. We believed that we had eliminated them all."

"...But you thought wrong. Is that what you're saying?" said Adlet.

"We were naive. They were still operating in places outside of my sphere of influence. He obtained a fake crest through different means from myself and infiltrated the royal palace of Piena to win over Nashetania. Then he gave Nashetania the fake crest and had her infiltrate your group."

It was too sudden. Adlet couldn't believe it.

"Meanwhile, I had also acquired a fake crest," Tgurneu continued. "I gave it to a human pawn and had them infiltrate your group. Quite the coincidence. Dozzu and I had been plotting the exact same strategy, and neither of us knew it."

Would a fluke like that really happen? Adlet wondered.

"I was astonished to hear of what happened within the Phantasmal Barrier. Because, you see, there was an impostor Brave I knew nothing of who was trying to kill you all of her own accord. I'm ashamed to say it was only after that battle that I realized Dozzu was behind it." Tgurneu went on. "I had also sent pawns into the Kingdom of Piena, and they had informed me of Nashetania's weaknesses, her habits, and her nature. I thought she would eventually be chosen as one of the Braves of the Six Flowers, and moreover, I thought if I did well, I might be able to use her like I did Mora. But I didn't have the slightest clue that she and Dozzu were working together."

"...I don't believe you," said Fremy.

Tgurneu set its white flag on the ground and crossed its arms. "Frankly, I can't believe it, either. Two fiends plotting the same scheme? Is such a coincidence even possible? Nashetania becoming a fiend's minion seems like nothing more than a joke to me. But there it is."

"Do you believe this story, Adlet?" Fremy asked him.

Adlet didn't reply. He just prompted Tgurneu to continue. This was hard to believe for him, too. But his desire to hear what the fiend had to say won over. "Go on, Tgurneu. We'll decide afterward whether or not to work with you," he said.

Tgurneu gave a bored shrug. "To be blunt, you and I are ultimately enemies. Frankly, I don't want to cooperate."

"Then we're in agreement, for once. I feel the same way," said Adlet.

"But I see Dozzu and Nashetania as far more powerful than your little troop. My priority is to kill him and his cohort, even if it ends up benefiting you, too."

"What did you say?" Adlet bristled. The fiend's remarks were humiliating.

"Is it so surprising? You Braves haven't presented any plausible threat at all to me thus far," Tgurneu said.

Anger flared in Fremy's eyes.

It continued. "Dozzu's reach extends further than I'd imagined. He's hidden large numbers of followers among both my pawns and Cargikk's. You've been seeing many fiend corpses, haven't you?"

Adlet nodded. He couldn't even count how many were in the pit with Chamo.

"While you and I were fighting over that matter with Mora and playing tag in the forest, Dozzu was steadily preparing to act. This morning, he began his operation. His faction came to attack us all at once. They destroyed nearly all the pawns I had in the Cut-Finger Forest, and there's no sign reinforcements will arrive. Right now I don't even know which among my followers belong to Dozzu's faction." Sadly, Tgurneu lamented, "I've ended up all alone."

If so, this would be an ideal situation for killing Tgurneu. Adlet even considered taking it out right then. But he suspected that it was all a lie. Tgurneu might well just be pretending to be alone to lure them into a trap.

"So what's your plan now?" asked Adlet.

What Tgurneu said next was very difficult to believe. "What else? Kill Nashetania and save Chamo."

"Save Chamo?"

As Adlet's party responded with confusion, Tgurneu explained. "I do have a reason to propose this—a reason I can't have Dozzu killing Chamo right now."

"...Which is?" prompted Adlet.

"Cargikk, Dozzu, and I have a contest to see who can kill the most Braves of the Six Flowers. The first one who kills three of the six wins, and the winner will make the remaining two submit to him, becoming the sole ruler of all fiends."

"A *contest?*"

"Two hundred years ago, we made a contract through the Saint of Words. The contract was simple: The first to kill or cripple three of the Six Braves would become the leader of all fiendkind. The remaining two would swear allegiance to the victor in perpetuity. Any who defied those terms would die. Obviously, if Nashetania kills all of you, that would mean points for Dozzu. Furthermore, if Dozzu's scheme causes a falling-out among your group and results in a death, that would also be a point for him."

Rolonia moaned. "A game...points...It's just like..."

Tgurneu's beak shook, and it sneered. "You're quick on the uptake, Rolonia. You're exactly right. This battle is not between you and me. It's a contest for the seat of leadership between myself, Cargikk, and Dozzu. Your party is nothing more than a pawn in our game."

"That's bullshit," said Adlet. Fremy was trembling in rage, while Rolonia's eyes widened in shock. Adlet's humiliation was deepening.

"Is that enough to convince you?" said Tgurneu. "This is the reason I will side with you. To be clear, the situation at present is overwhelmingly in Dozzu's favor. At this rate, Chamo will die. Dozzu probably also has a plan to kill the rest of you. It seems to me like you have no choice besides joining forces with me."

"What will we do, Addy? Are we really going to...?" Rolonia trailed off.

"I'll promise you this," said Tgurneu. "I will not attack any of you until Dozzu is dead. I've also ordered the seventh I sent to you to do everything in their power to save her. I haven't *actually* accomplished anything to obstruct you so far, have I?"

"Who are those fiends waiting to kill Chamo?" asked Fremy.

"Those are from Dozzu's faction. Though until yesterday, they were mine."

"...Give us a little time to think about it," said Adlet. He doubted that Tgurneu's entire story was the truth. But at the same time, he didn't think it was all fabricated, either. Only a fool would craft a lie that was pure falsehood from beginning to end. Lies were most effective when quietly slipped in among truths. Part of what Tgurneu was saying must have been true. But how much was false, and how much wasn't? That, Adlet couldn't determine.

"One thing about this doesn't make sense, Tgurneu," Fremy said. "Why did you enter a contract that stipulates the one who can kill three of the Braves becomes the ruler of all fiends? Aren't you and Cargikk and Dozzu enemies?"

Her question ruffled Tgurneu, just a bit. It looked away from her and said, "...An error of youth, I suppose. I was foolish back then. Never would I have guessed Dozzu would play as dirty as he has."

"Don't evade my question."

"It would be a long story, Fremy. I don't think you or I have that much time left."

"...True." In any other situation, they would have liked to press Tgurneu for detail. But at this point, the fiend was right.

"Come, what will you do? Decide, Adlet." Tgurneu urged him for a response.

Silently, the boy mulled it over. Was it really true that the traitor Dozzu opposed the other fiends? If not, that would mean that Fremy had lied to them, which was a possibility Adlet refused to even consider. She was an important ally.

There was a chance the fiend they called Dozzu didn't actually exist. So far, they hadn't seen Dozzu, not even once. Tgurneu could have produced a fictional enemy and then pretended to be on their side in order to approach them. That option could hold water.

But they had just seen those fiends' corpses, and they'd also witnessed signs that Nashetania had fought someone besides the Braves. It was pretty clear that their enemies were experiencing some internal conflict, and chances were high that this traitor Dozzu was real. So what about Nashetania? Was it true that she wasn't Tgurneu's, but Dozzu's?

"If you're slow to decide, Adlet, your chances at victory will escape you," said Tgurneu.

"Shut up, Tgurneu," said Fremy. "Do you want to die here and now?"

Adlet considered further. There was a clear contradiction in what Tgurneu had told them: Goldof. Nashetania and Tgurneu's seventh were on opposite sides, and the fiend commander had said that the seventh was doing everything they could to save Chamo. So then what was Goldof?

After a long silence, Adlet spoke. "I think your idea of working together is not a bad one, Tgurneu."

"You're joking, right, Addy?"

"Don't be stupid!"

Rolonia and Fremy were both shocked. Adlet ignored them and continued. "But you still haven't told me the most important part. Is Goldof one of yours?"

"Yes, that's the problem, isn't it?" Tgurneu stroked its beak. "I only know one thing about him. Goldof is not the seventh I sent you. That is all."

"...In other words?"

"I don't know who Goldof really is, either. I used to think that he was one of the real Braves of the Six Flowers. But Goldof was Nashetania's loyal retainer, so why didn't she reveal the truth to him? That part is a mystery to me." Tgurneu paused for a moment. "I can think of three possibilities. The first is that he is a second impostor, sent by Dozzu. If he is, then we don't know where the remaining Brave is, do we? The second possibility is that he is a real Brave, and Dozzu is controlling him somehow. I believe that's most likely."

That's not it, thought Adlet. When they'd fought, the look in Goldof's eyes had not been that of a man being controlled. He was fighting of his own will and making his own judgments.

"The third possibility is that he's a real Brave who betrayed you in order to protect Nashetania," Tgurneu continued.

"That wouldn't happen," said Adlet. No Brave of the Six Flowers would betray the cause. You had to have an unwavering desire to defeat the Evil God, even if it meant your life, in order to be chosen.

"You think it's impossible? Mora betrayed you once."

"But she—"

"You should be more suspicious. Our battle has been nothing but the impossible," said Tgurneu.

Unable to reply, Adlet fell silent.

"In any case," Tgurneu continued, "it's safe to consider that Goldof is the one who holds the key to this fight. Who is he, and whose will does he act on?"

"…Goldof said he would protect the princess," said Fremy.

Tgurneu's beak shook. Apparently, that was a derisive laugh. "Both you and I have been quite confounded. Hans and Mora are occupied and unable to leave that pit. That imbecile Cargikk is showing no sign of action now, of all times. What on earth does Goldof think he's protecting Nashetania from?"

"Tgurneu, do you have any clues as to where she's hiding?" Adlet asked.

The fiend shook its head. "My pawns were watching both her and Goldof. After your fight, Nashetania convened with Goldof, and then Dozzu."

"What kind of fiend is Dozzu?" asked Fremy.

"Dozzu has the power to manipulate lightning and shape-shift at will. His current form is rather odd, like a cross between a dog and a squirrel. I haven't seen him in person for two hundred years, but I'm certain that was him—Dozzu is the only fiend out there that can control lightning."

"And?"

"They were in a pit about one kilometer east of here. My pawns followed them, but before I knew it, two of them were dead and one had fled. Then a few minutes later, Goldof emerged from the pit alone and headed off farther east. My subordinate peeked inside the pit one more time but told me there was no hint or sign of Nashetania."

"Do you have any idea how Nashetania is hiding?" asked Adlet.

"It's hard to say, but…"

Uneasy, Rolonia watched the conversation between Adlet and Tgurneu become more involved. Her eyes accused her ally. *Are you seriously going to work with Tgurneu?*

"She's probably not using a fiend's power," said the fiend.

"What do you mean?" asked Adlet.

"Four-thousand-odd pawns serve me, and I've never seen a fiend with the ability to make a human vanish without a trace. No, I doubt such a fiend could exist. You agree, don't you, Fremy?"

Fremy didn't reply, but she didn't deny it, either.

"So you're saying she's using a Saint's power to hide?" said Adlet. "That couldn't be. Nashetania is the Saint of Blades. There's nothing she could do with that power to make herself disappear."

"And therein lies the problem," said Tgurneu.

The two fell silent. Wordlessly, Fremy asked Adlet, *How long are you going to keep talking? You're not going to kill it?*

"Wait," Adlet whispered.

"…I've heard that four hundred years ago, the King of Piena had Saints make him some special hieroforms," said Tgurneu. "They were passed down through generations of kings, and it's said that they were bestowed to vassals recognized for their talent and loyalty. Unfortunately, I've not been able to discern who holds which hieroform or what kind of powers they might have. Perhaps one of those has the power to conceal a person, and Goldof or Nashetania is using it."

A hieroform was a tool that contained a Spirit's power. Mora would know something about that.

"Do you have any proof?" asked Adlet.

"No. But I can't think of any other possibilities." Tgurneu suddenly began striding away. "We can't waste time standing here talking. Let's search for Nashetania." Adlet followed Tgurneu, and Rolonia trailed after him.

"So what's your plan?" asked Adlet.

"First, we'll head to the place where my pawns last sighted Nashetania. We'll look for clues there."

Sounding upset, Rolonia protested. "Are you serious? Addy, are you actually going to work together with Tgurneu?"

"Don't worry. Just be quiet and follow me," Adlet said over his shoulder.

The meaning in Rolonia's expression was clear. *I can't believe this!*

But Fremy kept her composure. *I'd expect nothing less,* thought Adlet. She understood what he was thinking, even if he didn't say a word.

"If there are no clues there, then we'll look for Goldof. He has to know something about Nashetania's location. And then—" Right in the middle of Tgurneu's sentence, something rolled to its feet. Fremy's bomb. The instant before it exploded, Adlet leaped and drew his sword.

The attack took Tgurneu by surprise, and it couldn't defend itself. All it could do was protect its face with its hands and jump away. As the blast hurled the fiend backward, Adlet swung his sword at it. "Now that you've told us everything, our business with you is done," he said.

"You maggots!" Tgurneu blocked Adlet's sword with one arm. The blade sliced halfway into the limb and then stopped; the fiend's muscle was frighteningly hard and elastic. Tgurneu threw a punch at the boy's stomach. Adlet whipped around to circle behind his enemy, wrapping both hands around its neck and squeezing.

Without missing a beat, Fremy shot Tgurneu in the chest. It fell to the ground, taking Adlet with it as he restrained the fiend. Adlet was certain now—this Tgurneu was far weaker than the one they had fought in the Ravine of Spitten Blood. "Rolonia! Go right! Circle it!"

"O-okay!"

Fremy and Rolonia ran to either side of Tgurneu. Tgurneu tried to shake Adlet off, yelling, "Don't be stupid, Adlet! Don't you get that I'm telling the truth?!"

Adlet smirked. "Even if I did suppose all of that was true, that's still no reason for us to let you live."

"...You'll regret this."

Fremy shot its knee, shattering it, while Rolonia whipped blood from its body. The moment Tgurneu stopped moving, Adlet revealed the ace up his sleeve, his weapon that could kill any fiend in one stab: the Saint's Spike. He found the fig that was Tgurneu's true form and prepared to pierce it when—

The fiend's body did something peculiar. Suddenly, its neck stretched and tore off with a loud rip.

"!"

The decapitated yeti tumbled weakly to the ground, while the crow's head grew wings. The head rose into the air with unbelievable speed.

"Fremy! Shoot it down!" Adlet yelled. Holding the Saint's Spike in his left hand, he threw poison needles with his right. Fremy fired a shot. The crow's head dodged the bullet, but a few of Adlet's needles hit the target. Still, even as the crow's head lost its balance in the air, it flapped on desperately to escape.

"The head is its main body!" Adlet yelled, hurling the Saint's Spike. Tgurneu just barely managed to avoid the deadly missile whizzing past its wing.

"S-someone, come to me! Stop the Braves!" Tgurneu yelled. But no one was there to reply. "Damn it, no one's coming?! You incompetents!"

It was now too far away for Adlet's needles to reach. Fremy kept up the attack, and a number of her shots grazed their mark, but none were good enough to bring it down. Tgurneu continued on, disappearing into the distant sky.

"...Damn it!" Eyes still on the sky, Adlet punched the ground. Steam rose from his fist thanks to the heat of the earth. They had missed their best chance to kill Tgurneu.

Now that it was over, he went to go pick up the Saint's Spike he'd thrown. These were his strongest weapons, and he had only three left. He had to take care of them.

"I'm relieved. I thought you really would join forces with Tgurneu," Rolonia said once Adlet had returned with the Saint's Spike in hand. She seemed reassured.

"Of course I wouldn't. The enemy of my enemy isn't my friend."

"Somehow, though, it seems more pathetic than I imagined." Rolonia gazed off in the direction Tgurneu had gone.

"That's an act. It'll casually do that sort of thing to make us let our guard down," said Fremy. "So what do you think about what Tgurneu said, Adlet?"

"I don't know. It felt like a pack of lies, but I also get the impression that some of it was true. At the very least, though, it was not actually going to cooperate with us. It was looking for an opportunity to kill us."

"Yeah...I picked up on that, too," Rolonia agreed with a nod.

"It's not even worth considering," said Fremy. "Everything that comes out of Tgurneu's mouth is lies. The impostors are Nashetania and Goldof, and the mastermind behind it is Tgurneu. It came to us with an offer to work together to make us let down our guard. Dozzu doesn't have anything to do with it."

"That would be the natural assumption, wouldn't it?" said Rolonia.

"There's no way that two different fiends would separately come up with the exact same plan," said Fremy.

"No," said Adlet. "If Tgurneu were just coming to kill us, it wouldn't have had to approach us all alone. It'd just have to send its whole army here. At the very least, there was some reason that Tgurneu couldn't order its minions to do it. Much of what it said just might be true."

"But how much?" Rolonia asked. Adlet was silent.

It was clear a complex situation was forming within the fiends' ranks. But who was against who, and why? Was Nashetania really Dozzu's assassin, or was she working for Tgurneu after all? Who was Goldof? Was he Tgurneu's follower or Dozzu's? Or was he actually a real Brave? Their plight was nothing but unknowns.

But they weren't going to win this through hesitation. Adlet had to figure out what to prioritize and what to leave until later and then act. "We'll kill Nashetania and save Chamo. That should help us figure out what's true."

Fremy and Rolonia nodded. The trio climbed up the rock hill and started running once more.

Adlet, Fremy, and Rolonia resumed searching for Nashetania. First, they went to the spot where Nashetania had disappeared, according to Tgurneu. It was the same place Adlet and Fremy had checked out once already. There were two fiends' corpses, burned up by lightning, along with evidence that Nashetania had summoned her blades. But nothing else. The three of them carefully searched the ground and surveyed the area but didn't discover anything that seemed like it might be a clue. Rolonia licked the earth but couldn't detect anything from the blood of the scorched fiends.

"There's nothing here. It's just these fiends' bodies," Fremy said grumpily.

"Tgurneu was just trying to trick us, after all," said Rolonia. "It has to be that."

What the fiend had said rose in the back of Adlet's head. *Not a fiend's power.* Tgurneu had suggested that what hid Nashetania was the power of a hieroform belonging to Goldof. Should he believe that?

"Let's split into two groups," he said. "I'll try asking Mora about hieroforms and what kinds have been passed down in the royal family of Piena. If they did have any, I'll ask what methods we could use to break them. You two, search any places she might be hiding."

"But there's nowhere…" said Rolonia.

"Underground, I suppose," said Fremy. "There isn't anything else."

"How can we search underground? If we could use Chamo's power…"

"It's okay, Rolonia. I'll find her," said Fremy, and she created a bomb in her palm. The object was oddly shaped, like a thin spike. She tossed it, and it landed upright in a crack in the rock. After a loud boom, the explosive had gouged out a section of the hill. "If she's hidden underground, that's convenient for me. I'll scour the area with my bombs. I'll bury her alive and then torture her to death."

"Hold on," said Adlet. "There aren't any other possibilities?"

"Well..." said Fremy, "Rolonia said that there were fiends lurking near Chamo, didn't she? She could be in one of their stomachs."

Nashetania had used the technique of hiding inside a fiend's belly back in the Phantasmal Barrier—though it hadn't been herself but Leura, Saint of Sun.

"Let's kill all the fiends within the gem's area of effect and tear open their stomachs," Fremy suggested. "Is there anywhere else she could have hidden?"

The three of them kept thinking. Nashetania's modus operandi was to do the unthinkable. Adlet doubted it'd be that easy to figure out what her plan was. So they suggested various ideas. She could have grabbed a flying fiend to hover a kilometer high or used the power of a transforming-type fiend to turn into rock. Maybe she was underground, maybe inside a fiend's stomach, or maybe she'd used a hieroform's power. They couldn't think of anything else.

"Enough thinking," said Fremy. "It's time for action. If anything occurs to anyone, they can bring it up then."

Adlet agreed. "Yeah. First, search everything underground, and while you're at it, kill every nearby fiend and rip open its stomach. I leave that to you."

"Yes, I'll handle that part. One hour is enough to cover this area." Fremy summoned bombs into her hands again and lobbed them at the rock hill before them. With a roar, the hill crumbled, clouds of dust rising in the air. Steam spurted out, enveloping the area in hot air.

"Rolonia," said Fremy, "use your whip to probe the earth. If you find anything, tell me right away."

"O-okay!"

With the two of them on the job, things should go fine. If Nashetania was hidden underground, they'd surely be able to find her. Adlet decided to look into the hieroform that Goldof might possess.

There was only a little over two hours until Chamo would die. They had to hurry.

The lava zone suddenly erupted with booms. Adlet arrived at the pit, incessant explosive roars accompanying him.

Twenty-odd fiends lurked around in groups of about five. They didn't fight or run; they just watched what was happening with Chamo and the others. Hans was in the pit, fighting some of them. Mora's arms were wrapped around Chamo, protecting her from attacks. Adlet joined Hans, and together they drove away the onslaught. When the fiends had scattered like so many baby spiders, Adlet gave a simple explanation of the current situation.

"You're saying…Tgurneu would be our ally?"

"Against Dozzu, he says. This is gettin' meowr and meowr confusin'. But is all that true?"

Mora's head dropped into her hands as Hans puzzled it over.

"More importantly, about that hieroform. Do you know anything about it, Mora?" asked Adlet.

"The power to conceal someone could be none other than the power of illusion. But…" Mora shook her head, her expression somber. "When a hieroform is created, we are required to keep records of it at All Heavens Temple, and we always do. Hieroforms have been given to the King of Piena in the past, but none with the power to conceal. One that could hide anyone might be used for a plethora of evil deeds—assassinations or espionage."

"So was Tgurneu lying, after all?" asked Adlet.

"*Neow.* Not necessarily," said Hans. "Holy Saints are humans, too. They can be lured by coin or bend to political authority. Meowbe even love could be a motivation. I wouldn't be surprised if somethin' like that was kept secret from All Heavens Temple." Mora didn't deny it.

This again? thought Adlet. All the information they had accumulated suggested potential answers, but there was no hard evidence. "So if Nashetania or Goldof has a hieroform, is there a way to break through the spell?"

"...There is." Mora was holding Chamo against her chest, stroking her back. She lay the girl on the ground and stood before Adlet. "When a hieroform is used, the dregs of its power remain. It is possible to sense these. This technique has been passed down through successive generations of temple elders. I can grant the ability to you, though only for a short time." Mora glanced at Chamo. "It will take time. Chamo, hold on until it's done."

Curled up on her side, the young Saint lifted her head just slightly and nodded. *I'm okay.*

Mora closed her eyes and began intoning the sacred tongue. After about ten minutes, she put her hands on Adlet's face, still chanting. When she touched her thumbs to his eyes, it felt like something hot was pouring into him.

"...Did it work?"

Mora staggered, but then immediately returned to Chamo and held her again, putting a hand to her back to send energy into her.

"So *meow*?" Hans asked.

Adlet could now see things he hadn't been able to before. He could see a light in Chamo's stomach—that had to be the power of the blade hieroform that Nashetania had put there. He saw the same thing on the back of his hand and on Mora's back where her Crest of the Six Flowers was. That was the power of the Saint of the Single Flower.

"In places where you see a shining light, there is a hieroform being used. If you see a faint haze, that means one was activated there not long ago. The effect only lasts for about three hours, though..." Halfway through Mora's explanation, she grimaced, putting a hand to her forehead. She was wearing herself out. "...And it's merely a borrowed power. You won't be able to detect everything perfectly. Most likely, you won't be able to see any remnants of weaker power."

"That's not encouragin', *meow*," Hans remarked.

"However," she continued, "you are sure to see any hieroform powerful enough to make someone disappear. Go, Adlet. We have no time."

"Hold on. You never looked at Goldof with that meower of yours?"

"I have, but I couldn't see anything. Ultimately, this power is only effective when a hieroform is in use."

Hans drooped.

"I'm gonna go back to searching for Nashetania," said Adlet. "You guys handle things here. If you see any fiends, be sure to kill them and rip open their stomachs. She might be hiding inside."

"Understood. Now go, Adlet. Hurry," Mora urged.

But before Adlet left, he went to Chamo. Complexion pale, she was curled up against Mora's chest. Her entire demeanor had turned utterly haggard in only a few hours. It was heartbreaking. "I'll catch Nashetania," he said. "Don't you worry."

"Eh-he-he… That's…right…yeah…Chamo is just fine."

"…"

"Why're you…looking so…worried? Chamo's strong. So…it'll be fine."

Adlet silently stroked her head and then rushed out of the pit.

Adlet kept on running through the lava zone. The rock beneath him was trembling from Fremy's cannonade. He climbed to a high point to scan the area with the power Mora had given him, but he didn't find anything. Despairing, Adlet continued to run. He ascended and descended the rock hills, going up and down and up and down again. During his search, he encountered Fremy and Rolonia, who were still bombarding the ground.

"Addy! How are things going with you?" Rolonia called to him.

"Mora gave me the power to search for hieroforms! You can leave that part to me!" Adlet shouted back.

"You're in the way, Adlet!" Fremy was about to throw a bomb near his feet. Flustered, Adlet scooted away.

He proceeded through the parts of the region that Fremy had already demolished. Now that the lines of rock hills had crumbled, the field of view was much more open. With each step, shattered rock crumbled under his feet, making the footing especially difficult to run on.

They had rearranged the terrain so dramatically, anyone attempting to hole up underground would not stand a chance. Even if Nashetania had been able to withstand the explosion, it was highly unlikely that she could stay hidden. And even if she was lucky enough to stay hidden, there should still be some kind of sign of her presence. Nashetania wouldn't have been able to dig dozens of meters deep to take cover, either. She'd hit magma or the underground water vein.

Adlet kept his pace, and then finally, he found his goal. When he concentrated on his eyes, within the drifting steam and smoke, he could pick out a faint haze of light. This light was far less distinct than what he'd seen in Chamo's stomach. Someone had used a hieroform here in the past.

He approached the shining vapor. This was where they had found the fiends that had died by lightning strike. Tgurneu had told them that Goldof, Nashetania, and Dozzu had disappeared on this spot.

Adlet looked around, but he couldn't find a place where the light shone any brighter. There was no hieroform currently in use nearby, nor were there any other signs of a previous activation. Adlet dug up the ground and closely inspected the whole area, but he didn't find Nashetania or any clues. But he knew one thing for sure now. Either Goldof or Nashetania had some kind of hieroform, and they had set it off.

He left the area to search further for Nashetania. There was no way they'd fail to find her. He was certain. If Nashetania had set up a hiding spot where she would never be discovered, she would have gone there immediately after activating the blade gem. But she had fought them briefly and then disappeared. In other words, in the middle of their fight, she had given up on running, which had forced her to conceal herself. So Adlet figured there must be a way to find her.

But he'd already searched more than two-thirds of the gem's area of effect, and Fremy and Rolonia had already blown two-thirds of the circle to pieces. Whether Nashetania was lurking underground or using the power of a hieroform to hide, they had to uncover her soon.

Maybe she was moving around to different hiding spots, then? No, that was impossible. They would have found something like traces of a hieroform that had been used or an underground path.

Don't panic, Adlet thought as he continued his search. The clock was ticking.

Meanwhile, Fremy and Rolonia were in Chamo's pit. They were driving bombs into the trapezoid-shaped hill, blasting the ground little by little. Magma was pouring up from underground through a big hole they'd created. There was no sign of any fiends around—Rolonia, Fremy, and Hans had killed them all.

"Not here, either?" Fremy muttered as she looked up. They'd searched through every cavity dotting this area, but they didn't find Nashetania, and neither did they find any signs that she'd dug a hole here.

Mora watched over her allies, in deep distress as she continued administering life support to the girl in her arms. Chamo already lacked the strength to pretend she was all right. Now even Mora didn't know when the girl might die.

"Fremy," said Hans, "any more searchin' underground is a waste of time. Nashetania ain't there."

"...But there's still places we haven't searched," Fremy said. "Maybe we overlooked her. Or she hid underground and then used some other kind of technique."

Hans shook his head. "Forget it. If she was underground, then they'd be comin' to stop ya diggin'. If nobody's comin' to attack us, that means yer guess is off," he said.

Fremy ground her teeth in frustration.

"Don't be feelin' down. At the very least, now we neow fer sure she ain't underground. That's results."

"But if she's not underground, then where is she hiding? Addy hasn't contacted us. So what should we do?" asked Rolonia.

"It's Goldof," said Mora. "He must hold a hieroform, after all. They're using its power to hide."

"Then Adlet should find them for us," Fremy countered her.

"We got to rethink it all from square one," said Hans. "Tgurneu must've been trickin' y'all, after all. Forget everythin' it said and take another look at the facts!"

"There's no point," said Fremy. "No matter what Tgurneu's game is, Nashetania still has to be within one kilometer."

"Then it has to be a fiend's power that's hiding her, after all," said Rolonia. "It would make sense if there's a species Fremy and Addy don't know about, and it's hiding her. There's nothing else it could be…" The three of them shouted at one another as the debate simply went around in circles.

Chamo spurted blood again. Watching her, Hans asked, "Hey, Mora, ya really can't meowve Chamo?"

"No," replied Mora. "Moving her even a hundred meters would be too much for her to bear."

"…Then I'll help look for Nashetania. We ain't gettin' nowhere at this rate."

"It looks like that's our only option," said Fremy.

Though they'd killed all the fiends in the area, more could still come later. If Hans was away at that moment, Mora alone might not be able to protect Chamo. Even so, Mora nodded. "Go. I'll protect Chamo, even if it means my life."

"Mew better. Chamo's more strategically important than you."

"…Rather blunt, aren't you? But so be it. You're right."

The moment Mora was done speaking, a voice called to them from outside the pit.

"This will not do." The voice was sexless, not clearly identifiable as male or female. A little creature stepped out from between the cracks of a smashed rock and slowly approached the group. It appeared quite odd, similar to a dog but also to a squirrel. It didn't look at all like a fiend, but there was clearly a horn on its forehead. "Please wait a little longer before you go hunting for Nashetania."

"Are you familiar with that fiend, Fremy?" asked Mora. The moment she saw it, she felt just the way she had when she'd faced Tgurneu, or when she'd fought Hans. Her senses told her it was a powerful foe. For what reasons, she didn't know, but it was wounded all over, large gashes marring its face and stomach. But she still had a gut feeling that defeating it would be no easy task, despite its injuries.

"I've seen it once before," said Fremy. "Here, in the lava zone. Tgurneu said it was Dozzu."

"Quite right. My name is Dozzu. It seems I owe you a considerable debt for your treatment of my comrade within the Phantasmal Barrier," said Dozzu, and sparks flared out around its horn. This was the traitor to fiends, and if they were to believe Tgurneu's information, also the mastermind between their battle within the Phantasmal Barrier. Tension shot through Mora's body.

"Incidentally," said Dozzu, "it seems you've encountered Tgurneu. What did you discuss? I would very much like to be informed."

"Not tellin'," said Hans, and he gave a hand signal to Fremy and Rolonia. It meant, *Go*.

"Can you handle it alone, Hans?" asked Fremy.

"Don't worry 'bout me. Worry ameowt Chamo." Hans smiled.

Fremy and Rolonia retreated behind him, then disappeared past a shattered rock hill. Dozzu ignored them.

"*Meow-hee?* Yer lettin' 'em go? Ain't ya come to slow us down?"

"It's surely enough to stall you, Hans. Nashetania has told me that you're more powerful than either Adlet or Chamo."

"*Mya-meow.* The princess has got good judgment," Hans said as cold sweat beaded on his forehead.

"Might I help, Hans?" asked Mora.

"*Hrmeow*, naw. You just keep protectin' Chamo." Hans raised his swords.

Then Dozzu said, "I think it may be better for us to move a little ways away. I doubt you want to involve the little lady in our battle."

Hans glanced over at his comrade. "All right, let's meowve, then. Pretty considerate for a fiend."

"Not at all."

"*Meow,* anyway, are ya okay with those wounds?"

"Thank you very much for your concern, but you need not worry on my behalf."

Mora silently watched Hans and Dozzu walk away together. Finally, Hans dropped into a fighting crouch, and sparks shot from Dozzu's forehead. "Now, then, Hans. Let's battle to the death."

The fight commenced.

"…What does this mean?" Adlet muttered as he sat on a broken rock.

He was already done searching the whole area of the gem's effective range. The only place he'd found traces of a hieroform's activation was that one tiny spot in that pit. What's more, it had been triggered some time ago. There was no hieroform currently in use within the gem's area of effect. Was that really how Nashetania was hiding? Something she'd used once a while back that continuously kept her hidden? If Adlet believed what Mora had said, then that shouldn't be possible.

Adlet examined the region again. Fremy's bombing had improved the view. The only thing around was some lowered mountains sparsely dotting the area. But no matter where he looked, he couldn't find Nashetania or Goldof.

Had Tgurneu fooled them? If so, then how, and what was the trick? Adlet thought back on what Tgurneu had said, but he just couldn't figure it out. The fiend had mostly just talked about Dozzu. It had barely said a thing about where Nashetania might be.

Was Nashetania camouflaging herself not with a hieroform but with a fiend? So then what the heck was the hieroform that went off before?

Adlet could feel his legs trembling a little. He'd never imagined that he'd come this far and still fail to get to the truth or even find any clues at all. But he had a gut feeling. He was overlooking something; there was something he couldn't see. He just needed something to get the ball rolling, and he could solve all these mysteries.

That was when Fremy and Rolonia ran over from Chamo's pit toward him.

"Fremy! Rolonia! You find her?" he yelled. But the question was pointless. If they'd found Nashetania, they would have already let him know.

"Bad news!" cried Rolonia. "Dozzu's come! It's fighting with Hans right now!"

"What?!"

Fremy and Rolonia explained the situation to him, and Adlet realized things had gone from bad to worse. But he couldn't go help Hans. He had no choice but to leave Dozzu to his ally.

"What should we do, Addy? About how much time do we have left?" Rolonia was on edge.

"...Goldof," Adlet replied. "He has the key. I can't think of anything else."

But just as they couldn't figure out where Nashetania was, they hadn't seen her retainer, either. As Adlet worried, Rolonia told him, "We did see him once."

Adlet looked at her. Fremy explained in Rolonia's stead. "Sorry we didn't tell you earlier. We saw him about thirty minutes ago. He was north-northwest of here, at the edge of the area of effect. We tried to kill him, but he got away."

"Which way did he run?"

"Out of the circle. The terrain was complex, and we couldn't find him."

Adlet didn't know what to say. He had thought Goldof was fighting to protect Nashetania. So why would he run? He wasn't going to fight Fremy or Rolonia? He wasn't going to join Dozzu to kill Chamo?

Suddenly, there was an explosion about fifteen meters off to Adlet's side. Reflexively, he lowered his center of gravity, but it was just hot steam shooting from the ground. Fremy breaking up the earth had destabilized the underground magma and water vein. A second spurt came up right beside Adlet. "Damn it, that scared me," he said.

"Let's go. Hurry," Fremy urged him, and he set off running.

As he forged ahead, he thought about Goldof.

What was his role in this fight? He'd drawn the party to this place, and then he'd shown up again to stop them from killing Nashetania. And if Goldof was the one with the hieroform, then he'd used it once for some yet unknown reason.

But that was all he'd done. If his goal was to kill the Six Braves, he could have accomplished that several other ways. He could have hindered their search or gone straight for Chamo. Adlet didn't get the man. Who was he?

They had multiple enemies converging here in the lava zone: Tgurneu, Dozzu, Nashetania, Goldof... What was going on behind the scenes?

"...Damn it!" Adlet barked, in spite of himself. There wasn't the time to be wondering about the truth behind it all. For now, searching for Goldof came first. That was all Adlet could do. They had forty-five minutes left. If they couldn't find Goldof, then this might be the end.

Mora swallowed as she watched the battle raging just fifty meters away. Hans and Dozzu's fight was a desperate mortal struggle.

"*Hrmeow!*" Hans spun wildly every which way to evade Dozzu's lightning strikes. Dozzu, on the other hand, was constantly moving out of Hans's range as its thunderbolts fell. Not a single strike hit Hans, though the attacks seemed to be completely unavoidable. It wasn't reflexes that enabled him to do this—it was his unique skill of foresight. If Hans misread a single move and messed up the timing of a dodge, Dozzu would burn him to a crisp.

Meanwhile, Dozzu was also frantic. If Hans got too close, Dozzu would be instantly sliced in two. As they fought, it darted all over the place to keep Hans at a distance.

Mora realized that it had been the right choice to let Hans handle this alone. She wouldn't have been able to keep up. One wrong move from her, and she would have surely made things more difficult for Hans.

"..."

Mora hugged Chamo hard. She wanted to get her out of there as soon as possible. She wanted to go with Adlet to search for Nashetania. But all she could do was send Chamo a small amount of energy that, at this point, was more a gesture than anything.

"Catboy's...fighting hard...huh?" The dying girl spoke for the first time in a long while.

"Don't speak. You'll only tire yourself," said Mora.

But Chamo didn't listen. "Listen...Auntie. This may be weird...for Chamo to say...but...this is kinda...nice."

"?"

She smiled. "You know...'cause of who Chamo is...no one's ever... worried."

"...Oh..."

"Who'da thought...everyone would...fight so hard...for Chamo. Especially Fremy... And catboy didn't say...*You're such a drag...I don't need you*...and just kill Chamo...after all."

"Really? You thought that?" Hans was still fighting Dozzu with everything he had.

"...Catboy's...a good guy, isn't he?" Chamo said, and closed her eyes. Mora could tell she was very near her limits.

"Move yer ass, ya stupid mutt!" Hans yelled as he slashed at Dozzu.

"I'm *not* a dog. How rude." Dozzu shot out a bolt of lightning, but Hans leaped sideways to dodge it. There was no end in sight to their battle.

Rock mounds still covered the space outside the gem's area of effect. All Goldof had to do to give his pursuers a hard time was stay low. Adlet, Rolonia, and Fremy split up and spread out to search for him. Fremy and Adlet stayed near the area of effect, while Rolonia headed farther out.

They must have been running for about fifteen minutes when Adlet found something unusual. The ground was glowing faintly. Someone had used a hieroform here, and it couldn't have been Nashetània. It was Goldof.

"...What the hell?" Adlet murmured. Now he was even more confused about the true nature of Goldof's enchanted object. Did it really have nothing to do with keeping Nashetania hidden, after all? If so, how on earth was she staying hidden?

Then suddenly, something small exploded in the distant sky. They had agreed that if any one of them found Goldof, that person would immediately throw a signal flare into the air to call the others. Adlet ran off as fast as he could. On the way to the explosion, he found Rolonia, and they continued together. They were headed back into the gem's area of effect.

"Why would he be there?" Adlet muttered. Once they had reached the circle, they immediately found Fremy running toward Goldof, who was about three hundred meters away.

Then Adlet noticed the knight's helmet. It was glowing faintly. *That* was the hieroform. The power behind the dim light couldn't be too strong, either. If Adlet could just figure out what that helmet really was, he could solve the mystery.

"…He's not gonna run?" Adlet muttered to himself, observing Goldof closely as they all closed in on him.

Fremy held him at gunpoint when she reached him, but he didn't fight back or even raise his spear.

"Be careful, Fremy!" Adlet yelled as he approached, and that's when he realized Goldof was standing where the three Braves had been just fifteen minutes earlier.

"You came…Adlet," said Goldof quietly, once Adlet was standing in front of Fremy with his sword drawn.

He wasn't looking at them. His head was turned to the side as he stared intently at the shattered fragments of a boulder. But he revealed no weaknesses to them. Attacking him would not be easy.

"What're you looking at?" Adlet asked him. Goldof didn't reply. He just watched the rock in silence.

His eyes were tranquil, his expression calm. Adlet knew it was the bearing of a man expecting to fight with everything in his life on the line.

"What's over there?" he asked again, but he received no reply.

Then finally, Goldof turned his gaze toward the three of them for just a few seconds and spoke. "Have you...found Her Highness?"

"Yeah, we're close," said Adlet. "You've been giving us a rough time, but...that ends now."

"...Have you figured out what's really going on?" Goldof's eyes were still locked on the rock.

"Who do you think you're talking to? I'm the strongest man in the world." It looked like Goldof was almost smiling. "Tell me about your helmet. What's that hieroform, really?"

"...Hieroform?" Goldof muttered.

"I'm going to kill you now," Fremy said, her finger sliding onto the trigger of her gun. "But before that, let me ask you this: Is it your hieroform that's keeping Nashetania hidden?"

"That question...is pointless. For you...and for me." Goldof shifted his spear from a one-handed to a two-handed grip.

Adlet swallowed. He had a grasp of Goldof's skill. Three-on-one, they wouldn't lose, even if they made a few mistakes. But now Goldof had something to overcome the difference in numbers.

"I'm disappointed...Adlet." Goldof looked at him calmly. "I thought... maybe...you'd figure it out."

"Figure what out?"

"Once it's...all over...I'll talk." Goldof lifted his spear, and the other three readied their weapons as well. Rolonia began whispering her invective under her breath.

"I will...protect Her Highness," said Goldof. And then, what he said next shocked Adlet. Rolonia stopped mumbling to herself, and Fremy's eyes went wide.

"And...I'll save Chamo...too."

He launched himself at Adlet.

Chapter 4

Goldof
Auora's
Anguish

Goldof Auora.

He was known all over the world as a gifted young knight, extolled as the pride of the Kingdom of Piena. But in truth, few knew of his background. His origins were unfamiliar not only to foreigners, but also to the people of Piena. Even some among the knights and nobles were unaware.

Goldof was born into the lowest class of Piena, in a tiny port town on the western fringes of the kingdom. His father was a rag-picker-cum-petty-thief who targeted the wallets and accessories of passers-by. Goldof had been told that his mother was a prostitute, but he didn't know her name or what she looked like.

He grew up in the slums, the territory of thugs and the abode of those who made a living stealing from honest people. Young Goldof's job was to search among the piles of refuse for anything that might still be useful and then sell it. To him, the upper classes and the royal family were so far beyond his sphere of interaction, he was barely even aware they existed.

Goldof was a very taciturn boy. He would rarely reply when spoken to, and when he did open his mouth, he'd mutter a word or two at most. He just expressionlessly followed the instructions of his father and the other adults in his life. The people of the slums all thought he was simply stupid.

But there was one thing about Goldof that distinguished him from the other boys: He was born exceptionally strong. He grew at double the speed of the other children, and his strength increased at twice that rate. Goldof had everything: reflexes, athletic talent, and the unique sharp instinct of a first-rate warrior. Why was he so strong? No particular reason at all. He'd never had a teacher, never labored for it, and had never once had any ounce of desire for it. He was just strong for no reason.

This was not necessarily a good thing. Goldof knew this firsthand.

The first time he killed a living being was when he was four years old. A stray dog had tried to bite him, so he swung it around by the tail, and it died.

The first time he'd broken a person's bones was when he was seven. He'd picked up a little ring by the side of the road and was on his way to take it to his father when a boy around his age came in to snatch it away. When Goldof grabbed the boy's arm as hard as he could, he heard a horrible sound in his grip. The boy crumpled, wailing. Goldof merely looked down at the squalling boy.

The first time he'd gotten into a fight had also been at seven.

The boys of the slums were all in gangs. They banded together to protect themselves from unfair violence and also to coordinate for a chance to pilfer from adults. They plotted their revenge against Goldof, and late one night they all took up their preferred weapons and boxed him in.

They punched him and kicked him, but Goldof didn't say anything. He didn't apologize to them or cry. When they hit him in the head with an iron bar, he remembered none of what happened next. A few minutes later, Goldof's fists were drenched in blood, and all of his attackers prone on the ground. Of the nine boys, two were wounded so badly they would never recover.

Goldof killed someone for the first time when he was eight. His father, the petty thief, had stolen a wallet from someone he perhaps shouldn't have. Some oafish men were kicking him around on the street. Goldof grabbed one of the men from behind by the hair, threw him to the ground, and snapped his neck. Instantly, the man lay still.

Two small girls came running out of the crowd that had gathered around the scene. They flung themselves on the man's body and cried, jeering and hissing at Goldof. The dead man was the girls' older brother. When one of them came at him with a knife, he kicked her as hard as he could in the stomach.

Goldof first hit his father at the same age.

In their back-alley hut, Goldof's father had grabbed him by the collar, ranting and yelling at him. *You're so violent, everyone resents me, too. I can't live in this town anymore! How could you?! This is your fault!* his father howled, crying.

Goldof head-butted his father in the face and kept on kicking it beyond all recognition. His father apologized and then begged for his life. When Goldof stopped, the man scuttled away in panic. The boy never saw him again.

He had hit people more times than he could count. Sometimes it was to protect himself. Other times it was for utterly trivial reasons. Ever since he was young, his heart had burned with hot coals. Those coals easily ignited whenever something rubbed him the wrong way. It didn't matter if the cause was something small or even if it was Goldof's fault. When the black flames flared up, Goldof plunged everything around him into a sea of blood—be it a little girl or even his own father, his only family. And once those flames were burning, Goldof could not snuff them out.

Everyone hated him. When good people saw him, they looked away. The boys his age hid or ran from him. Even the worst and the roughest wouldn't accept him. When they fought, it was ultimately about survival. Their way of life was incompatible with Goldof's. He only hit to break and to harm. They talked about him behind his back, always searching for a chance to kill him.

It wasn't that hitting people was fun for Goldof. Winning didn't make him happy, and he wasn't proud of being strong, either. He just wanted a normal life, to take pleasure in the small things like playing with friends and having a relationship with his father. But each time the black flames flared up, someone near him was injured. Goldof couldn't do anything about it.

Goldof spent his boyhood as a target of hatred and fear. Eventually, he discovered a single truth: The world didn't want him. There wasn't a single person in the world who wanted him to be alive—himself included, most likely.

And then, when he was ten years old, the boy loathed by everyone met a girl.

Goldof noticed that for the past few days, there had been a lot of noise in town. The soldiers of the noble ruling the city had been lurking about the streets. And these soldiers had never been much for maintaining the peace—they did nothing but extort the citizenry. They came to the slums, too. The neighborhood thugs were staying quiet and in hiding so as not to be blamed for anything.

At the time, Goldof was keeping himself fed by rag-picking. Whenever he showed up, the people of the neighborhood always looked away. Women and children quickly made themselves scarce. Even the merchant who bought the items of value that Goldof scrounged from the trash didn't talk with him more than was necessary. That was Goldof's day-to-day at the time.

The soldiers seemed to be searching for something in the back streets. They proceeded along the road, going into houses, scouring furniture and closets. As Goldof picked through trash, he eavesdropped on the soldiers' conversation. It sounded like they were searching for a girl. Goldof didn't know who she was or why they were searching for her. But from the bits of conversation, he understood that if the soldiers found her, they'd be paid very handsomely. The reactions of the residents varied; some were trying to find the girl to get rich quick, while others worried that this might bring trouble. Goldof was not going to get involved with any of it, however.

"Hey, kid. Have you seen—" one soldier called out to him.

But before the soldier could even finish speaking, Goldof glared at him and said, "Move." That one word made the soldier flinch. Wordlessly, Goldof passed the man by. He avoided interaction as much as possible. Avoiding people meant he could go without hurting anyone, or himself. Goldof had acquired this worldly wisdom at the age of ten.

"It's best if you don't talk to him, sir. He's crazy." Goldof faintly overheard a man behind him speaking to the soldier. Fortunately, the black coals did not flare to life. If they had, he probably would have beat to death both the man who'd said that and the soldier.

Goldof exchanged the once discarded items for money, bought his bread for the day, and headed home. He lived in a little hut in the filthiest district of the slums.

He was about to open his half-broken door when he noticed that someone was inside.

"..."

Was it a petty thief who didn't know about Goldof and had the poor luck to be searching his house? Or was someone with a grudge against him trying to set his place on fire? The black flames began burning inside him. *Guess I'll kill him*, Goldof thought, opening the door.

But then suddenly, it was as if Goldof was frozen; he couldn't move at all. "...Who are you?" he asked.

Inside his home was a girl. She lay curled up on the ground, her eyes closed. Her clothes were rags that even the children of the slums wouldn't wear. Her face was rather dirty, and her cheeks were sunken. Her long, golden hair shone softly.

The moment Goldof saw her face, the fire burning inside him was immediately snuffed out. It was the first time in his life this had happened. The black flames had flared up, but he'd gone without hitting anyone.

The girl was beautiful. She had to be in her early teens. Goldof approached her and gently reached out for her cheek. Just before his fingers touched her, his hand stopped one centimeter from her face. For some reason, he felt like he wasn't allowed to touch her—that if he did, she'd break.

"...Oh." The girl on the floor opened her eyes and looked straight at Goldof. That alone was enough to stun him, like he'd gone and done something he shouldn't have.

The girl looked at him, frozen with his hand outstretched, and tilted her head. "Is Meenia all right?" she asked, and rose.

Not understanding what she meant, Goldof was unable to reply.

"Oh, are you not one of Barbitt's men, mister?" Barbitt was the name of the noble who ruled the town. That was when Goldof realized this was the girl the soldiers were looking for. "I'm not going to run. Relax, please. Also, I think capturing me unwounded will net you the biggest reward."

Sitting on the floor, the girl wrapped her arms around herself. Goldof could tell she was afraid. He didn't know what to do, so he simply kept silent.

"Um…are you not going to capture me? Are you…the person who lives here?"

Goldof nodded, and the girl bowed her head to him.

"Oh. I'm sorry. I just barged into your home. I was so tired, I just wanted to rest. I can't do anything for you now, but I will make it up to you."

He tried to reply, *It's no problem*, but the words wouldn't come out. The girl's face kept him spellbound. He couldn't see anything else. It was like he'd forgotten everything in the world besides himself and her.

Then suddenly, a noise came from outside the hut. "Have you searched this house?!"

"Not yet!"

Soldiers burst into the hut without knocking. When they saw the girl, their eyes widened, approaching her with greed. "We've finally found you! You're not getting away again."

The girl stood up without a word. Her face drained of all color, stiffening in fear. Her legs trembled.

"Come with us. You can't tell us no."

"…I…under…stand," she said. The soldiers ignored Goldof's presence entirely. They grabbed the girl by the arm and dragged her out of the hut.

Instantly, the black flames flared again in Goldof's heart. They roared hot, more powerfully than they ever had before. He didn't know who that girl was or why the soldiers were chasing her, either. But he felt like he had to kill all of those soldiers immediately. He clenched his fists and took a step forward.

But then the girl yelled, "The gentleman over there!" Her sudden cry surprised the soldiers. Goldof froze before he could punch them. "He... was not a part of this."

The soldiers looked at Goldof and shrugged.

Then the girl smiled at him and said, "Mister, I'll be okay. Please, don't worry about anything."

The moment she spoke, the flames that had been burning in Goldof's chest were again instantly extinguished. *If she says there's no need to fight, then I don't need to fight*, he thought.

Surrounded by soldiers, the girl left the hut. Goldof watched her go in silence. She looked back one last time, bowing her head to him. "Mister, thank you very much, truly. I will not forget this debt." The soldiers were confused as to what she meant. But Goldof just stood there. He didn't know what he should do or why the girl had thanked him.

"...Oh...I get it." Then, after a while, he figured it out. The girl had realized he'd been about to attack the soldiers. She had thought the soldiers would kill him if he did, so she had stopped him. Then she had thanked him for trying to save her.

The girl had defended him. She might have been able to get away during the fight, but she had prioritized Goldof's life instead.

The moment he understood that, he dashed out of the hut.

Later, Goldof would find out that the girl's name was Nashetania Rouie Piena. A year after she and Goldof first met, the name Augustra would be added to that, as the title of the successor to the throne.

At that time, there was great political unrest in the Kingdom of Piena. The king, Nalphtoma, had suddenly gone mad. He'd started ranting about a heretical sect running rampant throughout the nation, and how these heretics who worshipped the Evil God planned the destruction of the world and plotted to kill him. Nalphtoma caused a bloodbath, slaughtering innocent citizens and aristocrats in the name of "saving the world." Finally, he accused even his own daughter, Nashetania, of heresy.

No matter how much the high chancellor and the knights investigated, they could find no such profane cult in Piena. But that didn't cure Nalphtoma of his delusions. Eventually, he ordered that Nashetania be disinherited and executed, and then he selected a distantly related prince from a different nation to be his successor instead. He rewarded those who killed the most heretics and bestowed important posts to them.

And so a civil war began. Many accused innocent nobles of crimes in an attempt to gain wealth or status for themselves. The king would either divest these nobles of their status or execute them.

Nashetania's life had been in danger, and so she was left with no choice but to disguise herself as a commoner and flee the capital. Three years later, she would become the Saint of Blades, but at this time in her life, she was still just a powerless girl.

The day Nashetania had met Goldof, she and her retainers were supposed to have gone to the noble who governed the town. But that noble had betrayed Nashetania instead, apprehending her knight guards and the maids who attended her. Without her guards, Nashetania had fled until eventually she had become separated from her one remaining maid, Meenia.

Finally, Nashetania had arrived at a tiny hut on the edge of the slums, where she had met Goldof.

Goldof ran outside his hut, the black flame searing in his chest. Eyes bloodshot, he panted like an animal. There was nothing in his head but the urge to fight.

He searched for the girl and the soldiers, but they had already withdrawn from the slums. He grabbed people on the street and half tortured them to find out where the girl had gone. Most of them knew nothing, but he did find one person who'd been eavesdropping on the soldiers' conversation. They said that the girl was going to be taken to the noble's estate and killed there. Goldof asked around for more detail about the girl's location. One person had witnessed her being loaded into a four-horse carriage and escorted out of the city.

"…The noble's…estate…" Goldof muttered. Then he seized a nearby carpenter's biggest hammer and headed out of town.

He sprinted along the main road. The noble's estate was about a half day's walk away. No matter how fast he ran, he was not going to be able to catch up to a carriage. The sun set, wreathing his surroundings in darkness. A wolf howled as Goldof kept his pace down the road.

When he arrived at the noble's estate and neared the front door, two gatekeepers brandished their spears at him. The black flame burned in his chest hotter than it ever had before. But this time the heat was not unpleasant. Howling like a beast, Goldof attacked the gatekeepers.

He didn't remember very well what happened after that. Weapon in hand, he struck down everything within reach. When the hammer broke, he stole a spear from a soldier and swung it around recklessly. But as strong as Goldof was, he was still barely ten years old, and this was also the first time in his life he'd ever used a weapon like this. There was no way he could match armed and formally trained soldiers. They stabbed him in the side, hit his head with a spear shaft, and pierced his foot with an arrow. But still Goldof's knees would not lower to the ground.

His consciousness dim, his vision hazy, Goldof noticed that there were others fighting with him. Ten knights had broken into the estate and were fighting the soldiers.

"The princess is safe!" someone yelled, and the moment Goldof heard that, he passed out.

When Goldof opened his eyes, he found himself swathed in bandages and lying on a soft, unfamiliar bed. He asked the young knight by his bedside where he was. The man replied that it was one of the Black Horns knights' barracks. He also explained that this was a special sickroom for nobles only, but Goldof was getting special treatment.

Goldof's next question was, "Is that girl safe?"

The knight laughed and replied, "Yes, Princess Nashetania is safe."

That was when Goldof first learned the girl's name. The knight was surprised to learn he hadn't known who Nashetania was. "You're saying you fought that hard for a girl whose name you didn't even know?"

Goldof nodded, and the knight shook his head as if to say, *I can't believe it.* But Goldof let that drop. What he really wanted to know about was Nashetania.

According to the young man, the Black Horns knights, one of the twelve knight orders of the Kingdom of Piena, had rescued Nashetania. By the time Goldof met Nashetania, the captain of the knights, Gazama, had already known that she was in danger. Gazama had spearheaded an attack on Barbitt's estate to rescue her. That had been merely half an hour after Goldof barged his way into the estate. The Black Horns knights had killed Barbitt, and Nashetania was now under their protection. Three knight orders had declared they would stay by Nashetania's side, so there was no longer any danger to her life. What's more, Barbitt's plan had apparently been to take the princess to the capital and kill her there. At the time Goldof attacked the estate, her life had not yet been in danger.

In other words, even if Goldof hadn't come to fight for her, the Black Horns knights would have saved Nashetania anyway. Basically, his fierce struggle had been entirely pointless. But the young knight said, "Your courage in facing the enemy all alone to save the princess was greater than that of any. Every knight should learn from your example." That confused Goldof—this was the first time in his life anyone had ever praised him for anything.

A knock sounded on the sickroom door. The knight snapped to attention and ushered in the guest. Wearing a simple white dress, Nashetania approached his bedside with graceful steps. Goldof felt hot, and his heart pounded so hard that blood oozed out from his unhealed wounds.

"So you're all right. First, let me ask your name." Nashetania spoke gracefully. She seemed completely different from when they had first spoken.

Blushing, he introduced himself.

"Goldof...That's a nice name."

He couldn't even hear what she was saying. He was so entranced, he couldn't think.

"Sir, a thanks is in order..." the knight beside them said.

But Nashetania indicated with a gesture that it was unnecessary. "Sir Bov, please step outside. I wish to speak with him privately."

"Very well, Your Highness."

As the knight left the sickroom, Goldof remained fixated on Nashetania. Once they were alone, her poise evaporated, and she gave him a carefree grin. "So your name is Goldof, mister? The truth is, I'm actually Nashetania. *Tee-hee*, does that surprise you?"

Goldof nodded. Nashetania reached out to him. He hesitated, but then accepted her handshake. It was the first time he'd ever touched a girl without violence.

"You don't talk much, do you?" she said. "I got that impression, when we first met."

"...Yeah."

"How old are you? Where did you learn to use a spear?"

"That was...my first time. I'm...ten."

"Really, te— Wait, you're younger than me?!" Nashetania's eyes widened in shock and she looked Goldof up and down. "Huh? What?! You don't look...Oh, well, I guess you've kinda got a baby face..." Embarrassed by her ogling, Goldof turned away. Nashetania's head tilted back and forth in bewilderment, but she seemed to be convinced, nevertheless.

After that, she asked about his wounds, touching him to make sure he was recuperating. His wounds were serious, but knowing they would all heal with time made her smile contentedly.

Talking with Nashetania evoked strange feelings from inside him. It made his heart turn clear, warm, and serene. Later, Goldof would come to understand that this feeling was called "peace."

"Well, mister—I mean, Goldof. I forgot to ask you something important. Why did you come to save me?"

Goldof hadn't even known what he was doing when he came after her. Unable to explain his reasons, he reflected. As he did, for some reason, he began crying. Goldof kept wiping the tears away, but they wouldn't stop.

"What's wrong?" she asked. "Are you hurt?" Goldof tried to say something, but it just wouldn't come into words.

Nashetania smiled and said, "You don't have to force yourself to talk. I'll wait until you're done."

Goldof continued sobbing for a long time after that. He'd first woken in the afternoon, but even after the sun set, the tears wouldn't stop coming. Nashetania waited patiently, never showing slightest sign of annoyance.

Goldof had always longed for praise. He wanted to be needed. He yearned for someone to tell him it was all right for him to live. For the first time, he'd found meaning in life. They were tears of joy. After Nashetania had left his hut, Goldof had thought to himself, *I want to protect her. I want her to need me. And I want to see her again.* And now she was safe, and she was right there in front of him. He wept with happiness.

Eventually, he stopped. After listening to his long confession, Nashetania said, "Goldof, I'm glad that you were born in this country. Thank you, truly, so much for saving me. Please, let me show you my thanks."

"There's...nothing...I want."

Nashetania shook her head. "You've done so much for me, even though you'd never met me before and you didn't know me. I have to repay you somehow."

But there was nothing that Goldof wanted now. He'd already gotten his wish—to see Nashetania one more time. For her to thank him. What more could he need? Goldof racked his brain, and finally he said, "I have...just...one request."

"What is it?"

"If...you're ever...in danger...again..." He hesitated to say it out loud. He was anxious, not sure if it was allowed. "Can I...come save you... again?"

When Nashetania heard that, she put a hand over her mouth. A hint of wetness welled in her eyes. "Of course, please, come save me. Come save me again and again."

Goldof was so relieved, the tears he thought had dried spilled out once again.

That was how Goldof became a knight in Nashetania's service. The civil war ended, and Nashetania returned to the capital. King Nalphtoma was stripped of all authority and reduced to a mere figurehead on the throne. Nashetania designated a high chancellor who would take on the responsibilities of governing the nation.

By Nashetania's decree, a lower-ranking knight named Kenzo Auora adopted Goldof, and so the boy's surname was changed, as well. Goldof learned how to read and write, how to wield a spear, manners and etiquette, as well as the tenets of chivalry.

Life for him at the royal palace couldn't be called comfortable. His humble origins made him feel obligated, and many of the other knights were jealous of his incredible strength. But none of that mattered compared to the joy he obtained by being with Nashetania. He could suppress the black flames in his heart if it meant being with Nashetania. He was able to forget his past violence. Goldof had been reborn.

But as Nashetania turned out to be an outrageous tomboy, Goldof was confounded by how often she caused trouble for everyone.

When Goldof was fourteen years old, he became the youngest-ever victor of the Tournament Before the Divine. As his reward, he was promoted captain of the Black Horns knights. But in practice, the previous captain, Gazama, was really in command. Goldof's title was in name only.

He also received one more reward: a hieroform that had been passed down through generations in Piena's royal family. Four hundred years ago, the King of Piena had ordered its construction in the utmost secrecy. Even the elder of All Heavens Temple didn't know it had been created. Goldof was not allowed to tell anyone of its existence or its power.

The hieroform was called the Helm of Allegiance, and it was charged with the power of the Saint of Words. When the wearer's liege was captured, the helmet would activate automatically. First, it would make a sound like a bell to alert the wearer to the danger. No one else could hear the sound. Then the wearer and their liege would be able to communicate at will. No matter how far apart they were, they could hear even the gentlest whisper from each other. The Helm had one drawback, however: It only activated when the wearer's liege was captured. If the liege was in danger, but not specifically captured, then the helmet would not react at all.

Goldof wore the helmet at all times, never letting it leave his person. He'd even worn it at socially inappropriate times, making him the butt of some jokes.

Goldof was in love with Nashetania; he wouldn't deny that. But more importantly, he had sworn a solemn oath of loyalty to her. Love did fade, but loyalty was endless, and Goldof believed that a bond of fealty was far deeper than one of passion.

Nashetania was a good master.

Her willfulness did often cause trouble. Sometimes she would sneak out of the castle on her own to talk to dubious characters. Sometimes, she would overwhelm her retainers with impossible requests. Her behavior was rarely befitting of a princess. The greatest stir she'd ever caused had been her tantrum because she wanted to be a Saint. But still, everything she did was, in her own way, with her people and the country in mind.

I will not be a princess who is simply there to be protected. I'll defend the people, she had said, puffing up with pride. That was Nashetania: the girl who made him worry, the girl who was dear to him, the girl who made him proud.

Nashetania was Goldof's *raison d'être.*

This must be a bad dream, Goldof told himself. If he closed his eyes and opened them again, he'd surely wake up. *Nashetania won't be the seventh; she'll still be the liege I swore to protect,* he thought, squeezing his eyes shut.

"…"

After a few blind moments, he opened them again. Nightmarish reality lay unchanged before him. He was in the Howling Vilelands. With him were the other five Braves and one impostor; his beloved Nashetania was not among them. *If this is a nightmare, let me wake up now,* he mentally implored as he opened his eyes, but the reality was the same.

It was the afternoon of the seventeenth day after the Evil God's awakening. The Braves of the Six Flowers had made it through the Cut-Finger Forest and now stood before the massive ravine dividing the Howling Vilelands.

"Meooow! That's huge! I've never seen nothin' so big!" Hans was prancing about in front of the ravine. It had to be more than a hundred meters deep. Its vastness stunned the others—Fremy alone maintained her composure. Goldof gazed vacantly at the gorge from a little ways away.

"I can't believe it. Fiends carved out this whole thing?" Rolonia marveled.

"The fiends have been preparing for their battle with the Braves of the Six Flowers for three hundred years. Digging a ravine like this is nothing to them," said Fremy.

"How will we cross it?" Mora asked. "Tgurneu will eventually notice our departure from the forest. The fiends will surge in, and we'll be surrounded." Their expressions were grave as they discussed the situation. Goldof didn't join in. He just stood in silence.

It had been four days since Nashetania had told them all that she was the seventh and then disappeared. For Goldof, those days had been an unending nightmare. Everything in front of him seemed so terribly far away. His thoughts wouldn't settle down, and he felt hollow, as if he'd abandoned his emotions somewhere. Was he sad? Was he angry? He couldn't even figure out that much.

All of his memories felt vague to him: Rolonia's appearance, their excursion into the Howling Vilelands, their fight with Tgurneu, Adlet figuring out Tgurneu's plot to trick Mora, their talk at the Bud of Eternity, and how they'd all worked together to get through the Cut-Finger

Forest. Goldof couldn't remember much of anything. Fremy and Mora had said that they were suspicious of him, and Adlet had tried many times to encourage him. But not even that mattered to him.

"Isn't there a bridge, Fremy?" asked Adlet.

"There is. One at the northern end, and another at the southern end. But I don't think either one is an option. Cargikk's minions are waiting for us there, and the bridges are set up to immediately self-destruct if we ever get close to crossing."

"Hey, Fremy," Chamo interjected. "Aren't there any secret paths? Like some way to get across safely without the bridges?"

"There'd be no need, would there? Since the fiends always use the bridges."

The group tossed around some ideas for how to cross the ravine. Goldof couldn't join in. Even if he did try, his thoughts wouldn't come together. If he attempted to talk, he wouldn't know what to say. Four days ago, Goldof had lost the ability to speak fluently. It had been a very long time since Goldof had been that taciturn boy. Over the past six years, he'd learned the speech and conduct appropriate for a knight. But now, he couldn't remember how he had talked before.

He looked out over the ravine. He wasn't trying to devise a way to cross it. He was looking for Nashetania. In the four days he'd been in the Howling Vilelands, his search for her had not stopped.

"..."

He recalled the events of four days ago, after Nashetania had confessed to her crime and fled into the forest.

Three of the Braves ran through the dark forest: Hans, Chamo, and Mora. They were in pursuit of Nashetania, who had just escaped them. Adlet was passed out on the ground while Fremy treated his wounds. It was well into the night, and dawn was close.

In the dark forest, Goldof stood alone, in front of the temple.

"Has Nashetania come this way, Goldof?" Mora asked him from within the forest.

He shook his head.

"We have no leads, either. It seems we've lost sight of her entirely. I'd rather kill her tonight, if possible, though," said Mora.

Mora had said that though the Phantasmal Barrier had been nullified, its effects would continue for a while until the mist had cleared entirely. Nashetania would not be able to escape the barrier yet, not for the whole night. Hans and Mora had said that if they failed to kill her within that time, she'd only cause more trouble down the line.

"She seems to be using some strange technique. She has vanished before my eyes many times, and Hans has witnessed the same. You be cautious, too."

Goldof didn't even nod. Mora sighed and left.

Sometime after Mora's departure, a voice came from within the temple. "It sounds like you have them fooled, Goldof." Nashetania emerged from the large hole in the temple floor. Her armor was cracked and her sword broken, and she was pressing one hand to a gash on her arm. Her face revealed her deep exhaustion. "If you hadn't been here, I would've died...Hans really is a terrifying man," she said, smiling.

The Braves had her cornered. She didn't stand a chance against Hans or Chamo, and the assassin had already figured out her mysterious disappearing technique. When she'd run to Goldof, he'd covered for her without hesitation.

"The barrier's effects will wear off soon. Maybe I can get away now... *ngh*." She grimaced. The wounds Hans had given her must have been painful.

"...Why...?" Goldof questioned.

"That's a rather vague inquiry. What are you trying to ask me?" Nashetania spread both arms with a wry smile. That was the Nashetania he knew: willful, mischievous, honest, and without artifice. Always brimming with confidence, she treated people of every station equally. Though she caused the citizenry trouble, she was also beloved. The girl he knew was still right there.

"Why...why...have you...?" Confused, he couldn't put it into words.

Seeing his condition, Nashetania gave him a smile that said, *Oh, you're hopeless.* "You may not believe this, Goldof, but I *am* the seventh. I came here with the intention of killing the Braves of the Six Flowers."

No matter how many times she said it, he couldn't believe it. He didn't want to.

"No one is controlling me. I'm not doing this because I have no other choice. I fought of my own free will, and I lost. But I won't give up. I must keep fighting, as long as I live."

"...What...for? What was the reason...you betrayed us?"

"For the sake of my ambition," said Nashetania, and for the first time, the look on her face became something unfamiliar to him. Her eyes were filled with serene strength of will and unwavering determination. "I have an ambition and I fear no hardship in accomplishing my goal. No matter what sacrifices I must make, even if it destroys my reputation, so be it. I'll stake my life on it."

"...Ambition..." Goldof muttered. That word didn't sound like her at all.

"Yes. I can't describe my feelings as a 'dream' or an 'ideal' or any other pretty-sounding words. Dreams can be abandoned, and ideals can be discarded, but when you have an ambition, you can't be stopped until you're dead." She leaned in toward him. Her face scared him. He'd never seen this expression on his liege, whom he'd sworn to spend his life defending. But this was who she really was.

"You wouldn't understand. Someone who's never had ambition could never understand how I feel." Nashetania watched Goldof fall silent and giggled.

Thinking about it now, his relationship with Nashetania went back a long way. But perhaps they'd never spoken candidly to each other before, not even once. Goldof wanted to protect her, but he'd never gotten to know her that deeply.

"What will you...do now?" he asked.

"I'll escape, and then go meet my comrade to think about what happens next."

"Your...comrade?"

"That's right. I have a colleague named Dozzu who has been with me since before I met you. We share the same passionate ambition, and we fight together. I would never betray Dozzu, and Dozzu would never betray me, either."

"Who...is he?"

"The traitor to fiends. The other fiends are trying to kill him. I'm a traitor to humans, and he's a traitor to fiends. *Tee-hee.* A beautiful friendship, don't you think?" Nashetania joked. "I must be going. The barrier has just about expired. It will be quite a rough battle, but I should be able to manage an escape, at least."

"...Your Highness..."

"If you survive, I'm sure we'll meet again. Will we be enemies then, or allies? I would rather you be my ally."

Goldof wanted to beseech her, *Please, come to your senses!* But he couldn't. She was serious about waging war on the Six Braves. The only way he could stop her was to kill her.

Nashetania was about to walk out of the temple when Goldof called after her. "Your Highness...what should I...do?"

"We're enemies now. You don't have to address me by my title anymore." Nashetania started walking away. "Do what you think is right. That's all I can say."

"What...does that...?"

"You need to find that out for yourself. I won't resent you or be disappointed in you. Even if you kill Dozzu or me. Not if you believe you made the right choice."

"...Your Highness...what's...your ambition?"

She put one hand on her chest and said with pride, "Didn't I tell you before? It's to create a world of peace. To see all the people of the world smile. To build a nation where we can make humans and fiends alike happy. That's all."

"Even if...you have to sacrifice...five hundred thousand people?"

"I'd rather have as few human deaths as possible. But my ambitions cannot be fulfilled without some loss of life," Nashetania stated, and she left the temple.

Was it all a lie? Goldof wondered as he stood alone in the temple. *The kind things she said to me when we first met, wanting to protect her, all of it. Was I just another person for her to deceive?*

Then he heard Nashetania outside. "I'm sorry I lied to you all this time. It wasn't want I wanted. But it had to be this way."

"…Your Highness…"

"But just let me say this. Six years ago, when you told me your wish, it made me so happy I wanted to cry. Someone cared for me from the bottom of his heart. Someone would protect me, even if it cost him his life. I couldn't believe it." Nashetania's voice cracked, just a little. "I've lied to you many times, but *this*—this is true."

And then he could hear her no more. After a while, he heard Hans's and Mora's voices, then the sounds of battle being joined. Goldof stood frozen the whole time.

Goldof didn't tell anyone that he had hidden Nashetania from them or that he had spoken with her. In a way, he'd already betrayed the group. As they made their way through the Howling Vilelands, he wondered non-stop. What was this objective of Nashetania's?

If what she wanted was to see everyone in the land smile, then she could just rule as a good queen. She would have been able to do that. Was her ambition to have the whole world under her control? If so, that should have been within her reach, too. With the power of the nation of Piena, Goldof, and herself in battle, along with Nashetania's fame, it would have been doable. Why did she need to betray humanity, join forces with a fiend, and fight the Braves of the Six Flowers?

And who was Dozzu? Fremy had said that Dozzu was the traitor to fiends, that it fought against Tgurneu and Cargikk. When and why had Nashetania met the traitor fiend?

And who was Nashetania herself? Was the woman he'd loved nothing more than a fabrication? No matter how much he pored over these questions, he found no answers.

Goldof continued to agonize. What should he do now? Nashetania was bound to come after the Braves of the Six Flowers again. Would he fight her then, too? Would he be able to? He couldn't. She was everything to him. He couldn't exist without her.

Then would he fight the other Braves to protect Nashetania? No, he couldn't do that, either. What would happen to the world if all the Braves of the Six Flowers fell? There was no way that Nashetania could actually create a world in which humanity and fiendkind lived together. Goldof couldn't even consider destroying his race with his own hands.

He was suffering. Who was Goldof? Was he a knight who defended Nashetania, or a Brave who safeguarded the world? If he were forced to choose between the two, then which should he pick? He had to protect the world—but the world he wanted to fight for was one that had Nashetania in it. Without her, it was worthless to him. Nashetania had told him to do what he thought was right, but Goldof didn't know what that meant anymore.

As Goldof brooded over this, the others were moving on with their discussion. It sounded like they still couldn't find a way to cross Cargikk's Canyon.

"Anyway, standing around talking won't get us anywhere," Adlet was saying. "We'll split into three groups to look for a way across. Find us something we can work with, no matter how trivial. Hans and Mora, you go north. Me, Rolonia, and Goldof will go south. Chamo and Fremy, you stay here and guard our backs."

"This is shaping up to be a more troublesome obstacle than I expected," said Mora.

Goldof couldn't tell the others about his troubles. They wouldn't understand, anyway—no one besides him could.

Tormenting himself over this was exhausting. The mental back-and-forth had whittled away at him. He'd never been a bastion of emotional fortitude.

Right now he wanted only one thing: to see Nashetania one more time. He longed to see her and talk with her. That was the only answer he'd gleaned from this directionless agonizing. But now Goldof couldn't even make that tiny little wish come true.

"Let's go, Goldof," said Adlet. Apparently, the three of them were going to look for a means to cross the ravine.

Gazing out over the ravine, Goldof wondered, *Will she be there, on the other side of that gorge? Will I get the chance to see her safely one more time?*

Not long before, the traitor herself had been in the volcanic zone to the southeast, sitting on a boulder and watching the distant sky. Dozzu was on her lap, and Nashetania was holding him, her arm loose around its neck. There were more than fifty fiends around her—a lizard-fiend with rock skin, a long and lithe monkey-fiend, a silver-pelted wolf-fiend. They silently awaited her orders.

"I wonder what Goldof is thinking right now," Dozzu muttered softly, for Nashetania's ears only.

"Oh, I'm sure he's worrying over things—whether to join us or stick with the Six Braves. And most of all right now, he wants to see me. That's probably all."

"I'm sure you're right."

"This is Goldof we're talking about. Of course I know what he's thinking," she said with a smile.

"You've grown up to be so cruel. I actually feel sorry for the boy, being used like this."

"What are you talking about? This is precisely what he's always craved, I'm sure—for me to use him." Nashetania fiddled with Dozzu's ear, grinning wickedly. "And besides, you're the one who made me this way, aren't you?"

"Quite right. You've grown to be so wonderfully ruthless." On her lap, Dozzu smiled, too.

"It won't be long until our preparations are complete. Let's trust in Goldof. I'm positive he'll do a fine job for us."

*   *   *

Searing-hot steam hissed up from the bottom of the ravine. Goldof leaned forward, feeling the scalding vapor on his cheeks as he peered down. No matter how carefully he examined the area, he couldn't find anywhere that looked viable. In a similar fashion, Adlet and Rolonia were surveying the area. When Goldof happened to glance up at the sky, he caught sight of a moth-fiend flying southeast.

"...Hey, Addy," called Rolonia.

"Did you find something?"

Adlet and Rolonia were discussing something. They seemed to be concerned about the moth-fiend, but Goldof wasn't bothered. He vacantly returned his gaze to the depths of the chasm.

Then it happened. Suddenly, without warning, it began.

The ring of a bell reached his ears. He lifted his head and looked around. There was nothing nearby that would make that sound. Adlet and Rolonia didn't seem to have heard anything. Deep in conversation, they were focused on the sky. No one else could hear the ringing.

That was when Goldof realized it was coming from the Helm of Allegiance. This was the first time it had activated since he'd first received it two years ago. This would happen only when the wearer's master had been captured. Someone had taken Nashetania.

The noise inside the helmet was piercing, like someone flailing a bell around in a panic. Goldof recalled what Nashetania had told him—it rang like this when the wearer's master was in grave danger.

"Your Highness? Your Highness? What happened?" His hands jumped to his helmet, and he called out to her.

"...dof...if you're still...my..." He could hear Nashetania's voice coming from the helmet. It sounded broken, like she was struggling to breathe.

The moment Goldof heard her voice, a jolt of dread shot through him. It felt like something was coiling around his heart and squeezing. "Your Highness? Who's captured you? Where are you?" he called out to her quietly. He'd completely forgotten that she was his enemy.

"Tgurneu's captured me…south of the Cut-Finger Forest…the lava zone…in a fiend's stoma—"

Then came a noise like something collapsing under pressure, and after that, pained rasping and a retching sound. Instantly, he realized that her throat had been crushed.

Goldof's rational mind was telling him, *You don't have to go save her. She's the Braves' enemy; she's a traitor; she's abandoned you; she's sided against the human race.* But his emotions descended upon him with a vengeance, urging him to rescue her. Someone was killing her. He'd lived to protect her. Abandoning her would mean the death of his soul.

His heart was wreathed in black flames. It felt just like when he'd charged into that noble's mansion alone, six years ago, to save Nashetania. When this fire was burning, reason, fear, presence of mind—everything turned to ash, and Goldof could think of nothing but battle. He stood and began marching south. He had to.

"What's wrong, Goldof?" Rolonia called as he set out.

But he didn't stop. Starting slow and gradually accelerating, he headed southeast.

"Hey, don't just run off. We're not doing anything over that way right now." Adlet grabbed his shoulder.

Don't get in my way, thought Goldof. Everyone who hindered him should drown into a sea of blood. He grabbed Adlet's wrist reflexively and hurled him to the ground.

"Addy!" Rolonia cried out. But Goldof couldn't hear her anymore.

"What the hell are you doing, Goldof?" Adlet stood in his path.

Don't get in my way. That one thought occupied his whole mind. "…Her Highness…is in danger…" His fists nearly knocked Adlet down of their own accord. He held himself back with what little reason he had left.

"What happened?" asked Adlet. "Did something happen to the princess? Did something happen to Nashetania?"

Goldof wasn't thinking about the Braves of the Six Flowers, the Evil God, or even about himself. The only thing that occupied his mind was saving the princess.

"Wait, Goldof. Explain to me! What's going on with Nashetania?"

"Her Highness is in danger...I'm going...to save her..."

"What are you thinking? Nashetania is the enemy!"

The moment Adlet said that, Goldof reached a conclusion. *So he's my enemy, then.* Instantly, his sense of reasoning vanished. He drove his fist into Adlet's stomach, and the winded boy dropped to his knees. Rolonia screamed and ran up to them.

"Adlet...Rolonia...I'm...going...to save...her."

"W-why now, all of a sudden?!" Rolonia implored.

Goldof explained himself plainly. "Listen...up. Just...listen. Don't... get in my way. I'm going to...save...her." He had no misgivings in his decision to go save Nashetania alone. Adlet and the others were her enemies. If he stayed with them, they'd be sure to try to stop him. *Just leave me alone,* he thought. *They have their fight, and I have mine.* "I'm...going... alone. Don't...follow me." He turned from the two of them and began striding away.

"Wait, please, Goldof!" Rolonia called after him. "What happened?!"

"The situation...has changed. If you get in my way...I can't let you live."

"C-can't let us...live?" Her face stiffened in fear.

Goldof was serious. The flames raging in his heart were now beyond anyone's control. In his current state, he would probably kill anyone who hurt Nashetania. But he didn't want to fight his allies, and so he wished for them to let him be. He left Adlet and Rolonia and their confusion behind him, breaking into a run. That was when he realized he was crying. "... Your Highness...I'm going...to save you now..."

Some vestige of discretion remained in his head. His reason was whispering to him, *This could be a trap.* Nashetania could be trying to trick him and kill him, or maybe she wanted to use him to eliminate the others. But even knowing that, Goldof had to do this.

I'm sorry, he silently apologized as his feet thudded against the earth.

Goldof maintained his rapid pace out of the valley and into the plains. Three fiends appeared from beyond a hill to rush toward him. Immediately, he knew what to do with his spear to kill them all. He attacked, handling his weapon as his instincts commanded. Mere seconds later, the fiends had all been impaled, spewing blood from their mouths as they fell.

His senses felt sharper. His eyes and ears were keener than any moment in memory, and he understood everything around himself so clearly. In that moment, he was probably stronger than he'd ever been.

Suddenly, he remembered what Nashetania had said. *In a fiend's stomach,* she'd told him. Goldof dissected each fiend's belly in a single incision with the point of his spear. No one was inside. He ran off again.

"Can you speak, Your Highness? Where are you? What kind of enemies are around you?" Goldof put a hand to his helmet and called out to Nashetania. He could just faintly hear suffocated rasping, but no words. Her throat must have been destroyed, after all. She wouldn't be able to communicate through the Helm of Allegiance if she couldn't talk. Nashetania had said that it was Tgurneu who had captured her. Dozzu had betrayed the fiends, so the Six Braves would not be the only ones after their lives.

Thirty minutes later, Goldof was past the plains and heading into the forest. Every fiend in his way fell to his spear in less than ten seconds before he sliced its stomach open in search of Nashetania.

When he reached the lava zone, Tgurneu would be there. Three days ago, the Braves had failed to take down the fiend commander, even four-on-one. But Goldof wasn't afraid at all. When he was fighting for Nashetania, any traces of trepidation vanished from his mind. The Helm of Allegiance clamored incessantly in his head. Nashetania was still alive, and she was still in danger.

As he raced on, he began having doubts—why had Tgurneu captured Nashetania? Now that it had her, what did it plan to do with her? But there was no point in considering those things now.

Another creature appeared before Goldof, and the sight of it left him stunned. He understood immediately that it was a fiend—the horn on its forehead was proof. It was small enough to be cradled in his arms, with an odd form like something between a dog and a squirrel. But it also looked familiar to him. Aside from that horn, it was the spitting image of a pet of Nashetania's. She had been particularly fond of that strange dog called Porta. "...It couldn't be..." Goldof pointed his spear at the fiend. It was wounded with cuts, burns, and bruises all over its body.

"It's been a long time since I've last had the pleasure of seeing you, Goldof." The fiend folded its hind legs and sat to bow politely to him.

"It can't be. You're..."

"Yes, indeed." Anticipating what Goldof was about to say, the fiend continued. "I am Dozzu, one of the three commanders of the fiends, and Nashetania's comrade. For a time I was also her pet." Goldof recalled that this fiend had been with Nashetania even before he had met her. She had told him that she'd happened to see him in the forest, and she'd adopted him because of his funny appearance.

"So you...lured her...to your side?" Goldof said.

"No." Dozzu shook its head. "Nashetania endorses my ideas. She became my ally, and she fights together with me for the sake of our ambitions. I did not in the least *lure* her."

It's the same thing, thought Goldof. *If this fiend had never showed up, then she'd...* He clenched his spear. He aimed the spear at its heart, ready to end its life in one stab.

"Goldof, though it shames me, I must ask something of you. Please, save my partner Nashetania."

"?!" Goldof's spear stopped.

"Tgurneu has captured her. She should still be alive, but she could be killed at any moment. I cannot hope to face Tgurneu's entire force alone. Please, Goldof." Dozzu groveled, pressing its cute face to the ground.

Goldof watched the fiend, lowering his spearpoint. Then he approached Dozzu. "Later...we'll talk," he said, snatching Dozzu by the scruff of the neck. Lifting the tiny creature, he ran off with the fiend dangling from his grip.

"Wh-what are you—" Dozzu was bewildered.

But Goldof paid him no heed. Nashetania had said that Dozzu was her one and only comrade, that she would not betray it, and neither would it betray her. It would be hard to rescue Nashetania by himself. He'd need an ally. "I will…save…her. You don't…have to…tell me."

"Goldof…are you serious?"

"If I weren't…I wouldn't have come alone."

Dozzu's eyes widened. "You came here by yourself? Unbelievable. I worried over how I should request this of you. I didn't imagine you would simply come yourself."

"Where…is she?" Goldof asked.

"We were in the lava region when she was captured. It's around an hour's run from here. I believe she'll be around there."

That meant Goldof had been heading in the right direction. He glared at the suspended fiend and said, "You're going to…talk. About what was… going on with you two."

"Yes, I understand. Fortunately, it seems we have enough time for a chat," Dozzu agreed, and the fiend quietly divulged its story. "I have an objective: to end the conflict between humankind and fiendkind. To build a world where both can live together. Two hundred years ago, with this ambition in my heart, I left the Howling Vilelands and ensconced myself in the human realms."

"It…just sounds like…a fantasy to me."

"Anyone would think so, the first time they heard it. But I'm certain it's an achievable goal, and so is Nashetania."

"…Her, too…huh…"

"I cannot tell you as of yet how we will realize this goal. This is a strict secret from those who aren't our comrades. Please understand."

"…Keep talking."

Dozzu continued. "I needed allies in order to realize my goal. There were very few fiends that would fight with me, and I was the only one with real combat abilities. I had to make a human my comrade—and not just any human, but a gifted warrior who would be chosen as a Brave of the Six Flowers. In order to find such a partner, I established a secret society and nurtured its growth slowly over the course of two hundred years."

What had the fiend done to create that society, and by what means had it cultivated it? Dozzu didn't say. There were other questions that Goldof would rather ask, anyway.

"My society's influence extended almost to the core of the Kingdom of Piena. Nashetania's late mother, Latortania, and her elder brother, Chrizetoma, who passed away young, were my allies. They brought Nashetania to me, and she became our accomplice as well."

"…"

"I had comrades among nobles, merchants, neighboring nations, and even your Black Horns knights."

Goldof recalled the King of Piena, Nalphtoma, who was currently semi-confined. Six years ago, his claims about a world-destroying cult running rampant through the land had sparked a civil war. So that had been no delusion at all.

"I'd believed Nalphtoma to be a simple fool, but his instincts were sharper than I'd expected. That civil war he caused six years ago was a disaster for us."

This was enough to make Goldof shudder. The homeland to which he had sworn loyalty was already long under the control of a fiend. "…Why are you…fighting us? If world peace is your goal…then you should just do that."

"I'll explain that as well. No matter what, we had to kill three of your group in order to force Tgurneu and Cargikk to bow to us."

"What do you mean?" Goldof asked without thinking. That didn't seem connected to Dozzu's argument.

"Before I left the Howling Vilelands, Cargikk, Tgurneu, and I made a contract through the Saint of Words. Whichever of us killed three of the Braves of the Six Flowers first would become the sole commander to rule all fiends, and the other two would submit to their new leader. Any who broke the contract would die. That was the agreement."

"…"

"If I had killed three of your group, then Tgurneu and Cargikk would have been forced to submit to me. Then there would no longer be any obstacles to our goal. We bet it all on that fight four days ago in the Phantasmal Barrier."

"But…"

"You know what came of that. With Adlet's ingenuity and resourcefulness and Hans's insight, Nashetania was defeated, and she fled. Were it not for those two, the world would have had a different fate!" Dozzu ground its teeth.

"I don't understand," said Goldof. "Why would…Tgurneu and Cargikk…agree to that contract?"

"That goes without saying. Because I tricked them," Dozzu said readily.

Five fiends appeared before them. Dozzu still dangling from his grasp, Goldof slaughtered them with his spear, then cut open their stomachs to check inside.

"This is a waste of time, Mister Goldof. Nashetania is not going to be there," said Dozzu.

Goldof knew that. But he couldn't help but search for her. After he had killed the fiends, he hastened onward. It wasn't much farther to the volcanic area. "…I get your situation," he said. "But what I care about…is Her Highness. What's happening with her?"

"Yes, allow me to explain. After Nashetania's defeat, she spent a day swimming through the sea to join up with me. Then Tgurneu's forces appeared. All we could do was flee."

"…And then?"

"We gathered our remaining comrades in the lava zone, lured Tgurneu in, and began our final showdown. I thought that if we took him down, the way would open for us. But he has gotten much stronger over the past two hundred years, so strong I can't match him. My comrades were annihilated, and he captured Nashetania," Dozzu finished.

"There's a few things…I want to ask," said Goldof.

"Please do."

"Who's the seventh?"

"…I have an idea, but I don't know for sure."

"What?"

"The seventh among you is not one of ours. I'm quite certain that

Tgurneu was the one who arranged that one. Sending in an impostor to kill the Braves of the Six Flowers from the inside…This may be hard for you to believe, but Tgurneu and I had prepared the very same ploy."

"I can't…believe that."

"Neither can I. When my ally who was investigating your group told me that there was yet another Brave, Nashetania and I were both dumbstruck."

"…I still have more questions. How did you get…that fake crest she has?"

"That I cannot answer," Dozzu replied flatly.

"Then one last thing. Do you…do you two…still plan to fulfill your ambition?" The way Dozzu described their plight, it and Nashetania seemed near despair.

But Dozzu thought for a moment and replied, "One with ambition cannot stop until they are dead. Even if our chances of this goal being realized are near zero, as long as we're alive, we have to keep fighting." That was exactly what Nashetania had said back in the Phantasmal Barrier.

"You and I are enemies," Goldof said in no uncertain terms. "I want to…protect Her Highness. I want her…to live. I have to stop her from keeping on with this reckless fight…no matter what it takes."

"Unfortunately, that's quite impossible. Nashetania will persevere in the fight for her aspirations as long as she lives. If what you want is to protect her, then you must fight together with her to realize her goal."

Goldof fell silent. He couldn't give Dozzu that answer yet. "…I…"

"I won't ask you for a response right now. Choose the path you believe is right. That's what Nashetania said."

Goldof had made up his mind to protect Nashetania. But who should he fight in order to do that? If he killed Dozzu, would she stop? Or was there no way to protect her other than to eliminate the Braves of the Six Flowers?

Goldof put off the decision. Thinking about what would happen next was pointless. Right now, he would save Nashetania from Tgurneu. That was everything.

"Tgurneu will have a hard time killing her, though," said Dozzu.

"What do you mean?"

"One year ago, a comrade from the Howling Vilelands came to me in the royal palace to inform me that Tgurneu wanted to see me. I found this peculiar, but I responded to the summons. I changed shape and headed to the location specified as our rendezvous point. Oh, I didn't explain this before, but I'm able to transform myself. My current form was not the one I was born in."

"And?"

"Tgurneu was there with the Saint of Words, Marmanna. He then made a request of me—that I not kill Fremy Speeddraw."

That's strange, mused Goldof. Fremy had told them that Tgurneu had planned all along to get rid of her. If that was true, it would be odd for Tgurneu to arrange a contract like that. Or was Dozzu lying?

"I agreed and made my own request in return: that Tgurneu would not kill a certain individual whom I would later give proof of comradeship. Tgurneu agreed quite willingly, and we sealed our contract through Miss Marmanna. The one to whom I handed that proof was, of course, Nashetania."

Goldof mulled over it. Was what Dozzu said true, or not? But without a contract like that, Tgurneu would have no reason to let Nashetania live. Why was she still alive, and why hadn't Tgurneu killed Nashetania after capturing her? Goldof couldn't come up with any other explanation. "What will…happen to her…now?" he asked.

"I expect that Tgurneu intends to hand Nashetania to Cargikk. I didn't make a contract with Cargikk, so Tgurneu must be planning to have him kill her."

"…Is Fremy…the seventh?" Goldof asked.

"I have no definitive proof, but I think that's the most likely."

A Brave of the Six Flowers carried the fate of the world on their shoulders. He should have immediately gone to Adlet and the others to tell them about this and then interrogated Fremy to evaluate Dozzu's claims. But Goldof's feet kept on course to the lava zone.

He would save Nashetania. That was the only thing driving him. "Never mind...about Fremy right now. I'll save Her Highness...and that's all." He couldn't trust Dozzu entirely. It was a fiend and an enemy of the Braves. But he had to cooperate with it in order to help the princess. At the very least, it was true that Nashetania had been captured and was in trouble, because the Helm of Allegiance activated only when the wearer's master was in such a situation.

"..."

Then Goldof remembered—Nashetania had also been the one who'd given him this helmet. It could be part of her plot, too. But his feet continued forward anyway. Nashetania might truly be in peril. So Goldof was forced to keep going, even if it was a trap.

As he ran, he happened to look back. What were Adlet and the party doing now? He wanted them to ignore him and cross the ravine. He didn't want anyone else walking into this trap.

At some point, the trees around him had grown sparse, the ground gray and rocky, and the undergrowth thinner. Goldof was entering the lava zone.

As Dozzu dangled from Goldof's hands, the fiend thought to itself that the boy most likely did not entirely believe what it had said. This was still good enough, though. Dozzu had never expected to be able to deceive him completely. Goldof was heading into the volcanic region, just as Dozzu and Nashetania had anticipated, so they had achieved their goal. The problem was what came next.

Would he ever figure out the truth? If he did, then when? Would Nashetania and Dozzu's plan succeed?

All of it was riding on Goldof.

Chapter 5

A String
of Battles

Goldof and Dozzu pushed on through the lava zone. Their line of sight was obstructed in every direction, so if they wanted to avoid getting taken by surprise, they'd have to proceed cautiously. But the pair raced forward without the slightest hesitation. Here, too, they fought several fiends, and each time, Goldof sliced their stomachs open in search of Nashetania.

"Listen, Goldof, Nashetania won't be in there," said Dozzu.

Goldof agreed with Dozzu. If Nashetania was in a fiend's stomach, it probably wouldn't be one of the rank and file. But he still couldn't help himself from checking.

"More importantly," Dozzu added, "has she not contacted you at all?"

"No. I think…she can't…talk…right now," Goldof replied, putting a hand on his helmet. He could hear the bell warning him she was in danger, but nothing else.

Goldof had told Dozzu all the information he'd learned from the Helm of Allegiance. When he had told Dozzu that Nashetania was inside a fiend's stomach, it had grimaced. It would be difficult to find out which fiend held her. Without more information from Nashetania, it would be nearly impossible to pinpoint her location.

The two of them ventured deeper into the land over the magma chamber. After they climbed a stone hill, a large trapezoidal mound came into view. Dozzu saw it and said, "Over there—that's where Nashetania was taken." Goldof clambered up the slope to the top. In the hill's center was a large pit filled with piles of bodies. They all seemed to be still. It appeared Tgurneu and Nashetania had already left.

"Are these...your...comrades?" Goldof asked Dozzu beside him as they descended the slope.

"They were all so brave. I'll roll in my grave if we fail to see their passion rewarded," said Dozzu. The fiend lowered its nose as it ran down the slope, snuffling along the earth. "Please wait just a moment. I'm trying to pick up which way Nashetania went."

Goldof nodded and then scanned the area for anything of concern. But he had no idea what he was looking for, so clearly he wasn't going to find anything. He called out to Nashetania through his helmet over and over, but still received no answer. Curbing his impatience, he waited for Dozzu to find something.

"I've figured it out," it said. "I can't find Nashetania's scent, but I know now where Tgurneu and his followers are headed. Most of the surviving fiends headed southward. Tgurneu, and most likely Nashetania as well, are among them."

"All right. Then let's go," said Goldof. He dashed off, Dozzu following after him. "What is Tgurneu...heading south...for?"

"He must plan to get rid of her, after all. Tgurneu can't kill Nashetania himself, so he'll hand her over to Cargikk's fiends to have them do it instead."

"Any other...possibilities?"

"Alternatively, he may be planning to use Nashetania as a hostage to threaten you. That would be the only worthwhile use he could get out of it."

"...I see." As Goldolf used his hands to scale a steep slope, he wondered—was Dozzu really telling the truth? Maybe it wasn't Tgurneu who was trying to lure him in to kill him, but Dozzu. Was Nashetania actually in danger?

But still, Goldof couldn't stop. The princess could die. As long as that possibility existed, he had to go save her. If this was a trap, then he'd just have to break out of it on his own.

Goldof and Dozzu traversed over the waste for another fifteen minutes. Then, apparently puzzled, Dozzu stopped sniffing the ground.

"What is it?" asked Goldof.

"This is odd. The fiends are moving too slowly. If their plan is to hand Nashetania off to Cargikk's followers, they should be moving faster."

"So what's…going on?"

"I don't know what Tgurneu is trying to do. But regardless, at this rate, we should catch up to them soon." Still looking perplexed, Dozzu started running again.

When they crested the next rock hill, they arrived at a somewhat open expanse. The moment they got to the top, Goldof was stunned. There had to be fifty fiends waiting for them, clearly anticipating their arrival. But it wasn't the enemies that shocked him. What left him breathless was Nashetania, right there in the center of the crowd. She was sitting on the back of a giant rock-skinned lizard, fiddling with the slim sword in her hands. The armor she wore was different than he remembered, but it was clearly her.

"Your Highness!" Goldof called out to her.

Without a word, Nashetania pointed her sword at him, and the fiends charged en masse.

At first he was suspicious, thinking it was a trap after all. But when he looked at Dozzu beside him, he noticed the fiend's eyes were wide with shock.

"Nashetania! You were safe?!" Dozzu cried, running up to Nashetania.

The charging fiends attacked it. Dozzu rolled to one side to avoid the assault, but then a score of blades sprouted from the ground, drawing blood where they grazed its tiny body.

Goldof couldn't understand it. If this was a trap and the goal was to kill him, then why attack Dozzu, too? Nashetania had told him that the fiend commander would never betray her and she'd never betray it, either.

The fiends descended on him, and Goldof raised his spear to repel the onslaught crashing toward him. These he couldn't kill in one stab. They were clearly superior creatures, very different from the cannon fodder he'd been fighting before.

"Your Highness! What's going on?!" Goldof cried out to her, but she didn't reply. She continued her merciless barrage of blades at Dozzu. Wordlessly, she smiled and kept up the fight.

His next suspicion was that perhaps this Nashetania was a fake. Adlet had told him that some fiends could transform. But even a shape-shifter wouldn't be able to mimic her power over blades. That meant this Nashetania was real. And the Helm of Allegiance's ringing hadn't stopped. She was still captive and in peril. Goldof didn't understand what was going on. He couldn't manage to muster anything but bewilderment.

"What are you doing, Nashetania?! We came to save you! Don't you recognize us?!" Dozzu yelled, dodging attacks from the fiends closing in around it. Horn sparking, it roared and called down lightning in every direction. Two enemies fell in a single blow. "Nashetania! Why?!" Dozzu tried to run to her, but she retaliated with a blade that impaled it from stomach to back, suspending it in midair. Dozzu twisted itself off the spike and backed away from Nashetania.

"*Ngh!*" Distracted by Nashetania and Dozzu, Goldof had left himself open to an attack from behind. Another three fiends approached him from the front. He raised his spear high, feinting a downward swing onto the one before him but then jamming the butt into the ground instead. He leaned on the spear, vaulting himself up with a wide leap, flying high and somersaulting in the air to land past the fiends. Then he charged toward Nashetania. Of course, he wasn't going to kill her. He was planning to slay that stone lizard-fiend and then hit her in the jaw or stomach to knock her out.

"...Hee-hee." Nashetania giggled, and blades sprouted up from the ground at Goldof. Most of them pinged off his armor, and the rest he deflected with his spear, but one managed to bite into his foot.

"*Gah!*" Goldof collapsed, and immediately, fiends rushed in around him to attack together. But still, he reached out toward Nashetania.

A blade stabbed up through the ground and skewered his outstretched hand. Blood streaked down the metal, dripping onto the ground. *Why?* he thought, rising and rolling to the side to dodge a fiend attack. He couldn't get any closer. All he could do was keep on the defensive and run. "Your Highness!"

Nashetania ignored him and slapped the head of the stone lizard-fiend under her. The creature began a sluggish lope away from Goldof.

"Mister Goldof! Follow her, please!" Dozzu cried.

But the others were blocking Goldof's way, and he couldn't follow her. A few followed her in her retreat northward.

"Where are you going?! Nashetania! Nashetania!"

Dozzu shouted, but she didn't even look back. She simply continued over a rock hill and out of sight.

The foes surrounding them were all powerful. It took nearly half an hour to finish off the whole group. Whenever Goldof tried to pursue Nashetania, they hounded him, trapping him in the area. Once they'd finally defeated them all, Goldof regarded Dozzu with a look of utter loathing.

"...What's going on, Dozzu?" he demanded. The Helm of Allegiance was still telling him Nashetania was in danger. But it was clear that she was not anyone's prisoner.

"Mister Goldof, is the Helm of Allegiance still ringing?" asked Dozzu.

"Yeah."

"Then...Nashetania is still captive."

"...Explain," Goldof said, pulling a needle and thread from beneath his armor as he spoke. Still standing, he swiftly stitched up his wounds and pasted medicine on them to stanch the bleeding.

"Tgurneu commands fiends known as specialists. They're tools that lack the ability to fight, but in exchange, each of them has a unique power that other fiends cannot imitate. One of these may be able to control humans. Controlling a human is very difficult, but it may be possible for them."

"You're saying...she's being controlled? Do you have proof?"

"No. The powers of these specialists are a mystery. But I can't think of anything else."

Goldof tried to follow Nashetania northward, but the pain from the stab wounds she'd given him prevented that. He pulled a small metal bottle out from beneath his armor and swallowed a gulp. This medicine was another of the treasured hieroforms that had been passed down through Piena's royal family. It didn't heal wounds—it cleared pain and exhaustion so you could force yourself to fight. It was half medicine, half poison.

"I believe this fiend is probably like a parasite," said Dozzu. "If we can remove it from her body, that should solve the problem."

"Anyway…this means we have no option but to catch her." Goldof hadn't seen this coming. He couldn't have imagined that he'd have to fight Nashetania in order to save her. But still, it wouldn't be impossible. One-on-one, he was stronger than her.

The two of them began running northward. That was when Dozzu said, "Can you hear that, Goldof? Just a moment ago, a fight started north of here. I think it's near the pit where Nashetania was captured."

"What? Who is it?" Goldof listened closely. The noise coming from the Helm of Allegiance interfered, making it difficult to hear, but he could still just barely pick out the crack of gunshots. "I told them…not to come…" The others had followed him. He silently cursed Adlet. They should have just ignored Goldof and focused on crossing the ravine.

"The Six Braves must be fighting with Nashetania. We have to stop them. At this rate they'll kill her," said Dozzu.

As they ran, Goldof agonized. Adlet and the rest of the Braves were certain to kill Nashetania. He'd have to fight them to free her. They would never forgive him for that, and Goldof knew it. Even if Tgurneu's fiend was controlling Nashetania, she was still their enemy. Goldof had feared this inevitable situation ever since they had set foot in the Howling Vilelands. Finally, the time to make a decision had come. His feet came to a halt. He couldn't keep going when he still hadn't reached any answers.

"What will you do, Goldof?" Dozzu stopped as well. The fiend seemed to understand Goldof's dilemma. "I'm of the same opinion as Nashetania. If you say you can't fight an ally, then there's nothing for it."

"Shut up," said Goldof. Clutching his chest, he recalled the sound of Nashetania's voice as she had cried for help through the Helm of Allegiance.

A fiery blaze seared his heart, screaming at him to kill all who would harm her. It was burning in him, urging him to go to Nashetania's aid just like it had on that day six years ago. He'd always known he would have to destroy everything that would hurt her. "Let's go, Dozzu. We'll save her."

"Thank you, truly. And I'm very sorry," said Dozzu, approaching his feet. "Goldof, how many times have you fought her now?"

The sudden question confused Goldof. "The first time was during the tournament. That last fight…was the second."

"Has she ever escaped from you?"

"…Why ask me that?"

"…Pardon me. This isn't the time for idle chat. Let's go," Dozzu said, scampering off. Unease colored the fiend's expression—even desperation.

"What're you…talking about?"

"Nothing, nothing at all."

They had been running for about five minutes when suddenly Goldof realized that the distant sounds of battle had stopped. The Helm of Allegiance was still ringing. Nashetania was not dead.

Then Mora's voice echoed toward them from far away. **"GOLDOF! GOLDOF! CAN YOU HEAR ME? NASHETANIA HAS NEARLY KILLED CHAMO!"** Reflexively, the young knight stopped. **"NASHETANIA HAS PUT A HIEROFORM INTO HER STOMACH! WE MUST DEFEAT HER, OR CHAMO WILL DIE! NASHETANIA HAS FLED FROM US! CHASE HER DOWN AND KILL HER!"**

Goldof looked down at Dozzu. The fiend was bristling, its expression sour. "It seems the situation…has worsened even further."

Goldof stood two kilometers from Chamo's pit. Mora had explained what had happened with her mountain echo. Chamo was dying because of a blade gem that Nashetania had put inside her. The only way to save her was to kill Nashetania, and the princess had to be within one kilometer of the pit. They had three hours until the girl was dead.

Now that Goldof understood the situation, he clenched his spear, pointing it at Dozzu. "So...this is what's going on, Dozzu?"

"Wait, please, Goldof!" Dozzu backed away.

"...You weren't after me...you were after Chamo...weren't you? You used me to lure the Braves here...Then you activated that blade gem thing...Is that it?"

"No! We didn't put that blade gem in her. You must already know that Nashetania can't create hieroforms."

"..." Goldof thought back. Once, two years ago, Nashetania had suddenly stolen his spear, telling him she was going to modify it to make him stronger. Being without his weapon of choice had inconvenienced him for a time. One month later, she had announced she had failed and returned the spear to him. Nashetania couldn't make hieroforms. But could he be truly certain that wasn't an act?

"This is another of Tgurneu's tricks," said Dozzu. "He's trying to kill Chamo and making it seem as if it's Nashetania's doing."

"You think...I'll believe that?" Slowly, Goldof edged forward.

Dozzu continued. "Tgurneu must have had one of the old Saints of Blades create a hieroform and then put it in Miss Chamo's stomach. It's only activated now."

"..."

"Tgurneu is using Nashetania as a decoy, making the Braves believe she's the one responsible in order to keep them from figuring out the truth."

"That couldn't..."

"He will make Adlet kill Nashetania, and while that's going on, kill Chamo with the blade gem. That's Tgurneu's goal," Dozzu rapidly explained. "Please, calm down and think about it, Goldof. If Nashetania had the power to create a blade gem, she would have used it earlier. If she'd triggered it while you were all running around inside the Phantasmal Barrier, she could have killed one of you, at the very least. She could have gotten Chamo out of the way ahead of time, before all of you were assembled."

"…But…"

"But she didn't. That proves it, more than anything, doesn't it?"

Still clenching his spear, Goldof faltered. Was Dozzu his enemy or his ally? He didn't know who his adversaries were. He had no idea who he should fight to protect Nashetania.

"The one most likely to have implanted the gem was Fremy. She fought Chamo once and lost. I couldn't say how she did it, but she must have done it then."

That did make sense. But Goldof couldn't trust Dozzu anymore. The Helm of Allegiance was still ringing, warning him of impending danger. But was Nashetania really at risk? He wasn't sure anymore.

"It's far too late to be asking you to trust me," said Dozzu. "That would be unreasonable. But this much is true: At this rate, they'll kill Nashetania!"

"Shit!" Goldof yelled, running off again. He just couldn't discern what was real. But Nashetania was in trouble, and he had to help her.

At this point in time, Goldof did not yet feel that he had betrayed the Braves of the Six Flowers. He had no intention of killing his allies. While he was trying to save Nashetania, he was also looking for a way to help Chamo. But he didn't reply to Mora's summons, instead choosing to work together with Dozzu, his enemy. Objectively speaking, he was already a traitor.

As Goldof ran over the heated earth, he heard the sound of explosions far away. Those were Fremy's bombs. The pair turned westward.

"I'll assume…for now…you're telling…the truth," said Goldof as they ran. "First…I'll catch Her Highness. You…remove the fiend…that's controlling her. Can you do that?"

Dozzu nodded. "There are methods to deal with them. Though this can only be done if Nashetania is unconscious and there are no enemies around."

"Then…I'll do that. Once you've dealt with it…you take her…and leave the gem's area of effect."

"Understood."

"Then the others'll…realize that she's not the enemy. Then I'll…find the one who's really using the gem…and save Chamo."

"It seems…this will be a difficult battle," Dozzu muttered. It surely would be.

But Goldof wasn't afraid. He'd win, no matter who his enemy was—or so he told himself.

He might have to fight Nashetania herself to protect her. So there was something he had to make sure of first.

"Dozzu…that stealth power…she has… If you focus on looking… and hurt yourself…you can see through it…right?" he asked.

Dozzu's expression changed. The fiend pensively regarded Goldof. "That's exactly right. You do know. That's good; it saves me the trouble of explaining."

Was it something to be glad about? Goldof couldn't figure out what Dozzu was thinking. "If she…doesn't leave…the area of effect…I'll know you were lying. Then…I'll kill you. I swear I will."

"Understood."

They crested another rock hill, and now the blade gem's area of effect was just ahead. Nashetania was running with her group of fiends. Goldof picked out Adlet, Fremy, and then Rolonia following her. It didn't appear any of the other Braves were after her.

The fiends were attacking Adlet in an attempt to slow him down, but Rolonia's whip and the redhead's sword sent them scrambling. Goldof saw Fremy's bullet skim past Nashetania's head. Ice-cold chills ran down his spine.

They were attacking her. She was about to be killed. The sight instantly ignited the flames in Goldof's heart. All his mental faculties were extinguished, and all he wanted to do was slaughter Adlet and the rest. Clutching his chest, he desperately attempted to calm the impulse. "I'll… stop the Braves. I can stop three…or at least two. You restrain Her Highness," Goldof said, dashing ahead.

Dozzu called after him, "Goldof, watch out for her power."

"Of course," Goldof replied.

"Please, come on! Can't you run any faster?!" Nashetania yelled. It seemed like she might meet a bloody end any moment now. Goldof judged that it would be impossible to resolve this through discussion. He wasn't good with words like Adlet was. Besides, the others were suspicious of him. They probably wouldn't listen, anyway.

Goldof removed the chain connecting the spear to his wrist and lobbed it as hard as he could. Meanwhile, Dozzu ran to intercept Nashetania.

Adlet and Rolonia turned to Goldof, while Fremy pursued Nashetania. Goldof had to stop Fremy. He started after her. A bomb formed in Fremy's palm, and she hurled it at him. He dodged to the side, weathering the subsequent blast. The wounds from his fight with Nashetania throbbed.

"Oh no, you don't!" Adlet cried, and Goldof just barely avoided his poison needle. But as he darted away, Fremy's second bomb hit him in the chest. The thickest part of his armor blocked it, but it still sent him soaring backward.

Goldof had to stop all three of them. If he didn't give this fight everything he had, he was going to lose his life. He had to be prepared to hurt them.

"Fremy! Rolonia!" Adlet yelled. "You follow Nashetania! Let me handle Goldof!"

"…I can't let you go," said Goldof.

Fremy and Rolonia were gaining on the fleeing Nashetania. Goldof desperately tried to catch up, but Adlet was approaching from behind to attack him. Goldof managed to block Adlet's smoke bomb, but Rolonia's whip and Fremy's bullets formed a merciless fusillade. He somehow managed to take Adlet and Rolonia down unarmed, but while he was busy with them, Fremy raced off far beyond his reach.

"Fremy! Don't worry about us! You can't lose sight of Nashetania!" yelled Adlet.

Goldof was about to run behind them to stop her, but before he could,

Adlet and Rolonia blocked his path. He was forced to give up the chase. "You...handle Fremy!" he shouted to Dozzu, who'd gone after Nashetania. Goldof had no choice but to leave Fremy to the fiend. He would stop Adlet and Rolonia. "...You're in the way," he declared and spread his arms before the two of them.

Adlet yanked the spear Goldof had thrown out of the ground, pointed it at its owner, and said, "Why, Goldof? You get what's going on, don't you? Chamo is about to die. We have no choice but to kill Nashetania to save her. Didn't you hear Mora's mountain echo?" Of course Goldof had heard Mora. That's why he was doing this.

"Please stop, Goldof! We have to defeat Nashetania. We have no choice if we want to save Chamo." Rolonia, too, urged Goldof to stop.

Goldof believed they were both kind people. Even this late in the game, they hesitated to kill him. He felt a little guilty about fighting them.

"Goldof, talk to us. Who tricked you? And how?"

"It's the same as what happened with Mora, right? You've been coerced to fight us somehow, right? Haven't you?"

Adlet, then Rolonia, attempted to start a conversation.

Maybe they were right. Maybe Goldof was just being deceived. But still, he couldn't stop this fight. If he let them go now, they were sure to kill Nashetania. Even if she was the enemy, even if she was a traitor to the human race, Goldof wanted her to live.

Enough hesitation. You can't beat them if you don't make up your mind, he told himself. "I can't let you...go beyond this point."

"Goldof..." Adlet trailed off.

"If you want to get past me...you have to...kill me first." Once those words left Goldof's mouth, the look in Adlet's eyes changed. The kindness and naïveté vanished. Goldof hardened his resolve. *He intends to kill me.*

He had to stop both of them right there until Dozzu could excise the fiend controlling Nashetania. That was his only task now. He was at a steep disadvantage here, two-on-one, and Adlet had Goldof's spear, too. But still, he was not afraid.

The fight began.

*   *   *

Rolonia's screech rang out across the heated earth:

"Diediedietraitoryougottadieorthesunwon'trisetomorrow!"

Goldof blocked her whip strikes with his armor. If the lash hit his exposed flesh, he wouldn't survive this. As he defended himself, he reached out toward Adlet for his weapon. Adlet stabbed and kicked at him, trying to keep Goldof from taking it back. A smoke bomb burned Goldof's eyes, and the blows from Rolonia's whip stung his wounds. But even then, he kept on struggling.

As the battle raged, Goldof thought to himself—somewhere in their hearts, Adlet and Rolonia were probably still hesitant. They still weren't sure whether or not they should kill him. As he grappled with them, his eyes darted in the direction Nashetania had gone. Had Dozzu pulled it off? Had it managed to stop Fremy and extract the fiend controlling Nashetania? Dozzu had a difficult task to tackle, too. All Goldof could do now was pray for Dozzu's success.

"Adlet...don't kill...Her Highness," Goldof said during their fight. He knew full well that Adlet was not going to listen.

"Whywhywhywon'tyoudieyouwon'tdiedon'ttouchAddydon'ttouch-Fremydon'ttouchChamoDIEEE!" Rolonia shrieked as she cracked her whip at him. He dodged, and when he found an opening in her whip's trajectory, he darted through to steal back his spear.

Adlet took one hand off the spear to pull a tool from his waist. Goldof immediately grabbed Adlet's hand to snatch the needle away. He threw it at Rolonia's face as he recovered his own weapon, and as he drove Adlet back, he remembered what Dozzu had said—that Fremy was the seventh and that she was the one who put the blade gem in Chamo.

Finally, Goldof figured he'd share the information with Adlet and Rolonia, too.

"Listen...the enemy...isn't Her Highness... It's Fremy," Goldof said, and then he thrust the butt of his spear into Adlet's stomach. He wouldn't be able to move for a while, not after that body blow.

That'll be enough to slow them down, Goldof thought, and he stopped his assault. They shouldn't have tried to prevent him from saving Nashetania, but that was no reason to kill them.

More importantly, he had to go to help Dozzu. He couldn't even guess as to how things were going on that front. He ran after Nashetania, crossing over a rock hill to find Fremy fighting a crowd of fiends. These were the same ones that had accompanied Nashetania only moments ago. His liege herself was nowhere to be seen, and neither was Dozzu.

"Better than…I'd hoped," Goldof muttered. This was doubly advantageous for him. Fremy would be pinned on the spot for a while, and now the fiends around Nashetania would not be bothering Goldof and Dozzu. Goldof ran past Fremy, continuing in a clockwise arc.

Now he just had to catch up to Nashetania. He'd knock her out and remove the human-controlling fiend that Dozzu had claimed was inside her, and then he'd carry her out of the gem's area of effect. After that, Adlet's party would stop trying to kill her for the time being. If Dozzu was lying, and Nashetania was the one who'd put the blade gem into Chamo, then Goldof would kill Dozzu, seize Nashetania, and forcibly move her away from the gem. That would save both Nashetania and Chamo.

"I won't…let them die. Not Her Highness…and not Chamo," Goldof muttered. The Helm of Allegiance had never stopped ringing all this time. Nashetania was still in danger.

Goldof went on about a half-circle counterclockwise, and there he found Dozzu. Ahead of the fiend, he could see Nashetania racing away. "Dozzu!" yelled Goldof.

"I'm over here!" Dozzu called back.

Ten more minutes of running and Goldof caught up to Dozzu. They'd reach Nashetania soon. "I've…slowed them down. Not for long… though," Goldof said as they chased Nashetania together.

"I knew you'd be able to manage it." Dozzu smiled.

Nashetania was ascending the steep slope of one of the slightly higher hills, and Goldof and Dozzu were right behind. Goldof used his hands to scale the hill. *I'll catch up to her at the peak*, he thought.

"Goldof, I'll stop her with a lightning strike," said Dozzu. "Please push her down and constrict her throat to knock her out."

"Got it."

They hit the top of the hill, and at the summit was a big pit. Nashetania stood in the middle of it, her sword raised and ready to fight back. Focusing everything he had, Goldof leaped off the rock, about to charge at her when—

It happened in an instant. Sensing a threat, Goldof launched himself sideways instead. A bolt of electricity hit the spot where he had just been standing. The strike was so powerful, if it had hit its mark, he wouldn't have stood a chance. Dozzu had been waiting to stab him in the back after all.

"It missed?"

Nashetania swiped at him with her sword. Goldof rolled farther to the side to avoid a blade piercing from the ground, then dodged again to evade Dozzu's second attack. The blitz was relentless—lightning from behind, knife edges from below.

Goldof was not shocked. Hardly. *I knew it.*

It had all been a lie. Nashetania and Dozzu had tricked him. All along, the plan had been to use him and then murder him.

Tgurneu had never captured Nashetania. She had been the one to put the blade gem in Chamo's stomach, and that story about a fiend of Tgurneu's controlling her was also false. Her goal had been to lure the Braves of the Six Flowers here, kill Chamo with the blade gem, make Goldof careless, and then kill him when his guard was down. That was the truth. He'd expected as much.

"Dozzu! Don't let Goldof escape!" Nashetania yelled.

Dozzu's horn charged with fat sparks, and then the fiend unleashed its most powerful thunderbolt yet. Figuring he couldn't dodge it, Goldof threw his spear instead.

There was a roar as the lightning hit the weapon, stopping short of Goldof. But the heat still scorched him. This was the first time in his life he'd ever experienced the pain of a lightning strike. He fell, rolling down the slope as Nashetania's blades stabbed at him. He just barely wrenched his vital organs away from the spikes.

"Aaggh!" He screamed in pain as he tumbled down the hill.

Oddly enough, he wasn't angry. He didn't feel like he could be outraged at the deception. He and Nashetania had been enemies all along. It was his fault for falling for it.

The instant before the final lightning strike descended on the boy rolling down the slope, he grabbed one of the blades thrusting from the ground. Fingers bleeding, he snapped it off and flung it at Dozzu. The keen edge skimmed Dozzu's face, the lightning missed, and Goldof barely kept his life.

He tried to go for Nashetania, but razors stabbed up from below, blocking his way and piercing his side. Blood dribbled from his mouth. Another electric bolt seared through him, and his entire body went numb. He couldn't move anymore. But still Goldof kept on fighting. Even now he wasn't considering killing Nashetania. The only thing in his mind was protecting her.

Dozzu and Nashetania stopped attacking. They were both out of breath.

"I can hardly believe you're human," Nashetania said, panting heavily. "We surrounded you with fiends, made you fight with Braves, and ambushed you, and you still won't go down. What a monster." Pleased by the compliment, Goldof smiled, just a bit.

"I have something to request of you, Goldof. Would you please die without a fuss?" Nashetania gave him a wicked smile. "If we can kill you and also manage to keep running around until Chamo dies, it'll be just one more step to victory for us. If we can eliminate one last Brave, Tgurneu and Cargikk will submit to us."

"...Your Highness..."

"Die to save us, Goldof."

Goldof closed his eyes for a while. Then he checked the ground at his feet and replied, "Yes. Very well, Your Highness."

"Huh?"

"Goldof?".

Shock made itself plain on Nashetania and Dozzu's faces. Goldof seized the moment to make his move, kicking a nearby rock as hard as he could. The rock smashed into Nashetania's face and shattered into pieces.

"Sometimes...I..."

Everything happened in an instant. In the blink of an eye, Goldof was advancing on Nashetania, rolling forward to dodge the blades from below. He swept her feet out from under her, and when she lost her balance, he grabbed her face, slamming it against the ground, hard.

"I...lie...too."

"Gah-hah!" The impact drove the breath from her lungs, and then she was still. He hadn't killed her. She just wouldn't be able to move for a while.

Goldof stood and glared at Dozzu. Now all he had to do was kill the fiend. He felt the black embers in his heart blazing brighter than ever. This one he couldn't let live.

Dozzu's horn sparked right as Goldof tore off his iron plate, throwing it at the fiend in an attempt to avoid the lightning. But only one piece of armor wasn't enough to block the whole strike. Goldof jumped backward, but the sparks still singed him all over. "Aagh!"

As Dozzu mustered power in its body, particularly fat sparks scattered from the horn on its forehead, and an instant later the fiend unleashed the most massive bolt of lightning yet. The moment Goldof saw the flickering, he rolled to the side. But even after avoiding a direct hit, the heat still penetrated his armor, searing his skin.

Even now that it was one-on-one, this was no easy fight. Once Goldof saw a strike was coming, it was already too late to dodge it. If he wanted to avoid getting hit, he had to move out of range. But if he did, he'd have no way to attack. The only commonsense choice would be to run. But Goldof tore straight ahead.

"...Foolish," said Dozzu. Right as the deadly charge descended, Goldof kicked a rock at his feet. The missile shot toward Dozzu, but the fiend easily avoided it. "I've already seen that move," it said. And then, without a pause, the next strike found its mark, shooting through Goldof's body. Slowly, he sank toward the earth.

"This is the end," said Dozzu.

Mid-crumple, the moment before Goldof's face would connect with the ground, his hands shot out.

His right hand grabbed a rock, and his left hand and both feet propelled him forward in a leap.

"!"

Goldof had figured it out. He'd analyzed Dozzu's technique. If Dozzu used all its strength, it would probably be able to hit him with a bolt powerful enough to be instantly lethal. But Dozzu's attacks were only ever just strong enough to slow Goldof down. Goldof figured that a full-power lightning strike would leave Dozzu wide-open afterward. Its plan was to hit him with one bolt to stun him and then charge up a second, fatal strike. Goldof was going to take advantage of the brief moment between the first and second strike. He let the first attack land, making a gamble that his body and his willpower would hold out.

"What?!" Dozzu cried as the shards of a rock Goldof had crushed in his hand stabbed into its eyes. When Dozzu tried to back away, Goldof reached out, grabbed the tiny fiend, lifted it into the air, and hurled it into the ground with all his strength.

"Ah...gah!"

Goldof raised his leg and smashed it to the ground. The limb bounced back up and descended again. He could feel the unpleasant sensation of bones breaking.

"Argh...ughhhh..." As Dozzu moaned, crawling on the ground, Goldof went to retrieve his spear from where it had fallen on the slope. He lifted it and approached Dozzu, raising the weapon to finish the fiend off. But then what Nashetania had said flitted through his mind.

My comrade, Dozzu.

He remembered how proud she'd looked when she'd said Dozzu's name.

"We share the same passionate ambition, and we fight together. I would never betray Dozzu, and Dozzu would never betray me, either."

"..." Goldof lowered his spear. She would surely mourn if he finished off Dozzu. And the fiend couldn't move anymore. Goldof figured he should just leave it be. "Her Highness...is more important."

Nashetania's eyes had rolled back in her head entirely. She didn't appear to be feigning unconsciousness.

He approached her. If he carried her unconscious form in his arms, he could run out of the gem's area of effect within five minutes. That would save Chamo, too. Then this fight would be over.

What should he do after that? Return to the other Braves, or take Nashetania and run?

But he didn't have the time to be thinking of the future. *Right now I just have to get her out of the area of effect*, he thought, but the moment he reached out to her—

"...Goldof." He heard her voice from the Helm of Allegiance.

"Huh?" For the briefest moment, he was stunned. How could he hear Nashetania's voice from the helmet when she was unconscious? The moment Goldof figured it out, he shot backward.

A moment later, a cluster of blades stabbed up from the earth where Goldof had been. If he'd been just a moment later jumping away, he would have been skewered to death. More and more pierced up below him. Goldof ran, keeping them away with his spear.

How could Nashetania be using the power of blades when she was unconscious? How had he heard her voice from his helmet? The answer was clear: This Nashetania was a fake.

The blade attacks stopped. Lying on the ground, the girl changed shape before Goldof's eyes into a fiend that looked like a thin monkey: a shape-shifting fiend. Strangely, even now that the monkey's true form was revealed, its left arm was still human.

"I must repeat the previous question—are you *actually* a monster? How did you dodge that attack? To say nothing less of how you avoided Dozzu's sneak attack."

The voice was coming from underground. A fiend resembling a thin snake emerged from the earth. The scales growing from its skin were silvery metal.

The snake-fiend continued. "Oh, I see. The real Nashetania interfered, didn't she? That woman never knows when to quit, either." Its tone sounded familiar to him—though he'd only heard it briefly, in the Ravine of Spitten Blood.

"...Tgurneu...huh?"

"Alas, you've found me out. Oh, well. Hello, Goldof." The snake-fiend—Tgurneu—flicked out its tongue and smiled. "What do you think? The fake was rather convincing, don't you think? It didn't only fool you—it fooled all the other Braves, too."

Goldof couldn't even hear what Tgurneu was saying. The reality that Nashetania was a fake was like ice freezing his spine. The Helm of Allegiance was still ringing its bell, warning him that she was in danger. Goldof understood that the real Nashetania was still captive somewhere. "Where is she?" Goldof pointed his spear at Tgurneu.

"Where is she? Now, where do you think she is, Goldof?" The gaze of the metallic snake felt like a tongue sliding all over his face.

"Where is she, Tgurneu?!" Goldof yelled, stabbing out with the spear.

Wearing a nasty smile, Tgurneu easily evaded the attack. "Now, why would I tell you that? You may be a fool, but you understand that much, don't you?" said Tgurneu.

Goldof reflected on the events so far. With the voice from the Helm of Allegiance as his guide, he'd headed out to save Nashetania. He'd run into Dozzu and come to the lava region. Then he'd heard that Chamo was dying because of a blade gem. Then Dozzu and a fake Nashetania had attacked him.

He couldn't comprehend what was going on. He didn't understand anything—not who was deceiving him, who his allies were, or who his enemies were. His mind was all mixed up. He felt ready to scream.

"...Keh-heh-heh, heh-heh-heh, AHA-HA-HA-HA!" Tgurneu threw back its head and burst into laughter. "You really are stupid! I've known as much for quite some time, but I never imagined you were quite *this* stupid!" Tgurneu's tongue flicked out as it leaned in toward Goldof, tickling his cheek as if petting a cute little animal. "You're incompetent. Hopelessly incompetent. I utterly fail to understand how Nashetania could have trusted you."

"...You vile..."

"Tricking you has been so much fun. It's been so easy, it actually made me suspect you were plotting something!" Inches from Goldof's face, Tgurneu's eyes narrowed. "I almost want to tell you the truth. If I were to simply kill Chamo and Nashetania right now, it wouldn't be the least bit interesting to me."

"The truth?"

"You should be grateful. What I'm about to tell you now is the pure and unaltered facts. You know, it's quite rare that anyone can get something out of me that doesn't include lies. It only happens once every few years."

Chapter 6

All for His Liege

While Goldof squared off with Tgurneu, Mora was still in the pit of corpses. Blood poured nonstop from Chamo's mouth as Mora's hand rested on her back, sending energy into her body. Hans was scrambling all around the pit, killing every enemy that came in after Chamo.

"Auntie…it hurts. Still…?" Chamo gasped, dribbling blood.

"Don't worry. Adlet and the others will catch Nashetania soon. Those three will have no trouble subduing someone like her."

"Ah-ha…yeah. I…hope so," Chamo replied with a laugh.

Mora didn't know anything. She had no idea of Adlet's predicament or the threat Goldof faced.

Meanwhile, Adlet was a kilometer and a half away, battling fiends with Fremy and Rolonia. They hadn't resolved their questions, either. They hadn't discerned any of the new information—not that the Nashetania they'd been chasing was a fake or who the real mastermind behind this fight was.

And at the same time, Nashetania was trapped inside a fiend's stomach. She was constricted, suffocating, sweltering. The heat pitilessly choked sweat from her body, while slimy, hot mucus clung all over her. Her wounds were severe. Her left arm had been torn off at the shoulder, and the wound was tied off casually with a rope to stop the bleeding. A tentacle wrapped around her throat had crushed her windpipe and her vocal cords. Her back was gouged open, and a great maggot-fiend had buried its face in the wound.

She tried to scream. But all that came out was a wheeze.

Inside the fiend's stomach, Nashetania desperately waited for Goldof to come save her, to figure out Tgurneu's plot, and to find her. If Goldof didn't make it in time, then her chances of survival were zero.

"The truth is quite simple," Tgurneu began calmly. "Dozzu and I are fighting each other. Nashetania is Dozzu's pawn, while the other seventh is mine. Until your battle in the Phantasmal Barrier, I didn't know about Dozzu's plan, and neither did Dozzu know about my seventh. This is all true. It's also factual that we forged a contract two hundred years ago."

Tgurneu continued its story. After losing in the Phantasmal Barrier fight, Nashetania dove into the sea and swam for a whole day to go meet up with Dozzu on the shore of the Cut-Finger Forest. Meanwhile, Dozzu had been in negotiations with Cargikk. It had offered a ceasefire to Cargikk—this was in case Nashetania failed to kill three of the Braves of the Six Flowers. But Cargikk rejected the proposal and sent its elite fiends out to kill Dozzu instead.

"Dozzu, Nashetania, and their fiends were running around in the Cut-Finger Forest. Their subordinates were killed, Nashetania was injured, and Dozzu had nowhere to run. He was backed into a corner. So then this morning, they came asking for my help."

That morning, Dozzu had come to tell Tgurneu that they had put a blade gem into Chamo's stomach. They offered to use its power to kill Chamo and give Tgurneu the point for it, too. In exchange, Dozzu wanted Tgurneu's protection. Tgurneu had accepted their proposal. It was still struggling with Chamo, so if a point was offered on the table, too, there was no reason to refuse.

So Tgurneu had killed all of Cargikk's followers. The bodies in Chamo's pit were from the fight between Cargikk and Tgurneu. Once Tgurneu had dealt with that little bit of interference, it had swiftly come up with a plan to kill Chamo and begun preparations.

"However…" Dozzu interrupted, pushing itself up from the ground and dragging its legs over to interject. "Tgurneu never intended to protect us. His plan was to finish us off once he was done with us and Chamo was dead." Tgurneu didn't deny it. It just smirked.

If Dozzu knew that, then why didn't it run? Goldof was skeptical. That was when, finally, he figured it out. He despaired, realizing what a fool he'd been. Nashetania had been taken hostage, forcing Dozzu to do whatever Tgurneu wanted. Dozzu's ploy and attempt to kill him had all been on Tgurneu's orders. What a complicated, bizarre situation. Fiends deceiving, killing, and using each other.

Tgurneu continued explaining. First, it had restrained Nashetania and threatened Dozzu to make the other fiend submit. It had sealed away Nashetania's special abilities with one of its specialists, number thirty-one, the Saint-sealing maggot.

Next, it created a fake Nashetania to trick the Braves, using a team of two fiends. The first was a transforming type disguised as the princess. The other was a snake with the power to control blades. The snake had been underground, hurling up blades to fake the Saint's power. Pretending to be the Saint of Blades, however, was not possible for a lesser power. So Tgurneu had made the snake-fiend eat its fig body in order to strengthen its abilities. The shape-shifter had been hiding in the royal palace in Piena until just days ago, which was how it knew Nashetania's habits and manner of speech. The fiend knew her so well, it could deceive Adlet and even Goldof.

The real issue had been Rolonia. She'd be able to pick out a fake just by licking its blood. To handle that problem, Tgurneu extracted some of Nashetania's blood and tore off her left arm. He then attached the arm to the transforming fiend, poured her blood into it, and ensured that Rolonia would taste the real Nashetania's blood from it. That was why even Rolonia hadn't realized that it was an impostor.

"Her arm… You…you sick…" Goldof trembled with rage.

Tgurneu paid him no mind and continued. Luring in the Six Braves had been simple enough. It had just used the Helm of Allegiance to alert Goldof to Nashetania's predicament, and the young knight had come running just as planned. The other Braves had followed him into the region.

Then the mastermind had instructed Dozzu to trick Goldof into separating from the group, persuade him to fight the other Braves, and then finally, to have him killed. Tgurneu had put a fiend into Dozzu's body that sent information back to it, so it knew about everything Dozzu had told Goldof. With Nashetania as hostage, her comrade had no choice but to follow orders.

"How was that? Even a fool like you can understand when I break it down so thoroughly, I'm sure?"

"Where…is she? Tgurneu…tell me!"

The fiend scoffed at him. "The real Nashetania is somewhere here in the lava zone. One of my pawns is particularly adept at keeping things hidden." It leaned in toward Goldof. "'Where is she? What sort of power does this fiend have?' Why would I tell you any of that? I intend to keep her hidden until Chamo dies—which, I estimate, is two hours from now at most."

"Give her…back."

"No. I've told Nashetania that if she tries to run, I'll kill her, and if she cancels the blade gem without permission, I'll kill her then, too. If Dozzu tries to help her escape, I'll kill her. If he attacks me, I'll kill her. Just one easy little signal from me, and she'll be dead."

"You…shouldn't be able…to kill her."

"That was a lie. Of *course* that was a lie. What are you talking about?"

"Give…her…back."

"No, I said. And while I'm at it, I'll tell you something else: Once Chamo is dead, I'm going to kill Nashetania on the spot. You don't mind, do you? Since she's the enemy of the Braves, anyway." Smiling broadly, Tgurneu watched Goldof shudder with fury. "The truth is, I thought you would be the greatest obstacle to this plot. I imagined the information she sent you through the Helm of Allegiance combined with Adlet and Hans's brains might lead you to find her. That was why I separated you from the other Braves and arranged it so that you wouldn't be able to share information with them. Well, you ended up breaking off from the group on your own, so it turned out I didn't need to bother."

Goldof ground his teeth.

"You were such a good fool. I was listening in on your conversation with Dozzu. Frankly, I had a hard time restraining my laughter. I was the one who ordered Dozzu to incite you to fight the other Braves, but I didn't think you would actually take it so seriously for me!"

Tgurneu drew back, and then a blade sprouted from its body and impaled the other commander.

"I know what you and Nashetania were after, Dozzu. You planned to have Goldof save Nashetania for you, didn't you?"

Goldof was taken aback. Dozzu gave a small nod.

"Of course you would," said Tgurneu. "That was clearly the option that could have kept both of you alive. But it's just as you see: Goldof, you are incompetent. There's no way you can save Nashetania. Chamo will die. The rest of you will also die here. And then it will be over."

Dozzu glared at Tgurneu, but it was not bothered at all. "Hey, do you know why I'm babbling on and telling you everything?" This time, the fiend faced Goldof.

"What?" said Goldof.

"It's because your knowing won't hinder my plans at all. If you pass on what I've told you to the other Braves, I'll kill Nashetania."

"!?"

"It's true that would mean I couldn't kill Chamo. But I know you'd never abandon Nashetania. And besides, I had a different plan for killing Chamo, anyway. If this stratagem fails, it won't bother me one bit. If you tell the others, the seventh will let me know—and just so you know, I'm not bluffing. If you talk, I will end her life."

"...The princess... You'd...you'd kill..."

"You want to save her? Then I think you should hurry up. The other Braves as searching for her. They may be able to find her, too."

"If…Adlet…finds her…" Goldof trailed off.

"Heh-heh-heh. I'm sure they'd kill her, of course." Smiling, Tgurneu got close to him. "Hey, Goldof. Give me a good look at your face."

"…What?"

"I like looking at humans' faces," Tgurneu said, examining Goldof's. "They reveal many things to me: anger, panic, sadness, despair, and the last threads of faintest hope. I like seeing all of those feelings."

"…"

"I love human emotion. By greeting someone, you create a connection. Through speaking, you can understand one another. You look at someone's face, and you can pick up on what they're thinking. I relish drinking in the feelings of humans I've defeated. That is what I fight for, and what I live for." Tgurneu flicked its tongue out and licked Goldof's cheek again. "I could kill you right now, but that wouldn't be fun at all. I want to see your anguish, your confusion, and your regret. I want to give you the hope of possibly saving Nashetania so I can savor your despair when you fail."

Goldof was looking for his chance to kill Tgurneu, but it didn't seem to be the least wary of him.

"That's a nice look on you. You—no, all of the Braves of the Six Flowers—are truly a wonderful spectacle."

Dozzu said, "You can't kill Tgurneu, Goldof. He would execute Nashetania at the same time."

Hearing that, Goldof was unable to do anything but keep silent and bear it.

"Hey, Goldof," said Tgurneu. "Do you think you can save Nashetania? You can't unravel any of my plots, and you're a mess after fighting Dozzu, to boot. I doubt you can fight anymore."

"…You monster…"

"And what's more, you're fighting solo. You attacked the other Braves. If they see you, they're sure to immediately come after you with deadly purpose. You've been terribly foolish."

"…Goldof…" Dozzu said sadly.

"Yes, a good look on you. You're truly incompetent. I love seeing your powerlessness."

Tgurneu pulled away from Goldof, and then a fiend with the head of a crow and the body of a yeti approached it. The yeti-fiend stuck its hand down Tgurneu's throat, withdrawing a fig from deep within and biting into it.

The yeti was now Tgurneu. It crushed the head of the snake-fiend it had been using as its body. Apparently, it was done with that one.

"Now, then, I suppose we'll get going," it said. "You should run, too, Goldof. Adlet and his friends will be coming soon."

Goldof glanced beyond the hill. Tgurneu was right. Adlet would be after him and Dozzu, and if he stayed here, it would only be a matter of time before they found him.

"Dozzu," Tgurneu continued, "you fry everything around here with your lightning bolts, and once you're finished, rest for a while to heal. I know you can recover quickly. You should be able to fight again within an hour, I'm sure. After that, go kill the three in the crater. You can't refuse."

"Understood… Not that I have a choice," said Dozzu.

"Indeed. See you, Goldof," Tgurneu said, departing.

Left behind, Goldof remained in a daze. He had come here to save Nashetania. He'd meant to crush whoever it took in order to do that. But what was the reality? All along he'd been dancing in the palm of Tgurneu's hand. The word *incompetent* echoed in his head. He couldn't deny it.

"Goldof." That was when Dozzu spoke to him.

"Dozzu…is what…Tgurneu said…true?" Goldof asked.

"It was all true—aside from just one thing."

"Just…one thing?"

Dozzu looked Goldof straight in the eye and said emphatically, "You are not incompetent. You're the most capable knight in the whole world. It's not impossible for you to save Nashetania."

"But…"

"Right now I cannot save her. You're the only one who can."

"I…"

"I swear to you: If you save her, we'll immediately release Chamo. I swear this is no lie."

"...Really...?"

"Now, please run. At this rate, Adlet and his companions will kill you. You're our only hope. You're her only chance," said Dozzu.

Goldof trudged away, heading out of the gem's area of effect. He hurt all over. Even moving was hard. The spear dangling from his grasp felt like dead weight.

Save...her.

Those were the only words racing through his head.

Running was impossible for Goldof now. The fake Nashetania's blades had pierced his arms and legs. He'd endured Rolonia's whip and Fremy's bullets and burns from Dozzu's lightning strikes. And the exhaustion seeped into his bones.

He forced himself onward through the barren land. About three kilometers from where he knew Chamo was, he stopped. The burns had left his throat parched. The pain and thirst alone made him feel like he would die.

"...The princess..."

He found a geyser and approached it. He figured for now he'd quench his thirst. But the moment he put his lips to the water to take a sip, agony shot through his tongue and nose. Moaning, he spat out the boiling water.

His knees hit the ground. He couldn't move anymore.

He had to drink something. At this rate, he wouldn't even manage to live through the next few moments. Plus, he had to treat the wounds from his fight with Dozzu. He wasn't carrying much in the way of medicine, but still, something was better than nothing.

Goldof looked back. He had to return to the lava zone right away to rescue Nashetania—before Chamo died and before the others found him. He had a mountain of things to do. But he still couldn't move.

He sensed a presence behind him. Ten fiends were licking their chops, watching him.

"Givén up yet, Goldof?"

"I'll protect...her." Goldof raised his spear and stood up. His body heavy like lead, he fended them off. With every breath, his throat stung. With every movement, his body ached. The pain, thirst, and exhaustion leeched his willpower. His hope of delivering Nashetania was draining away.

"We've caught hím!" A giant earthworm wrapped itself around him. Goldof hacked its head off with his spear, but the fiend continued squeezing him tight, even in death.

A dog-fiend lunged for his neck to bite him, but Goldof dodged and smacked it away with a fist. "I will...protect...her..." he muttered to encourage himself. But despair was gradually creeping up, starting at his feet. Could he really find Nashetania? Tgurneu had said a certain fiend's power kept her hidden. It had sounded quite confident that Goldof would never find her.

Could he figure out Tgurneu's scheme? He wasn't smart like Adlet and Hans. He didn't have Fremy's knowledge of fiends, either. What could someone like him do?

"Díe!"

Goldof shook off the worm-fiend, but the dog bit into his leg next. He stabbed it in the torso with his spear, but its jaws stayed clamped on his armor.

The other fiends seized the opportunity to rush him. Goldof fled, dragging the corpse of the fiend biting him. He tried to rip it off as he ran, but his fingers felt weak. "Damn it!"

The other Braves saw him as their enemy. If he encountered them, they'd immediately try to kill him. He couldn't expect them to go easy on him like they had before. Now he didn't even have the strength to survive another fight against them. If he got close to the gem's area of effect, he'd meet a quick end. Forget finding Nashetania—he couldn't even get near her.

"He's rünning!"

"After him! We can finish him off now!"

He couldn't count on Dozzu's help, and neither could he hear Nashetania's voice. He had no clues as to how he could keep her alive.

Goldof fled the fiends. When one nearly caught him, he killed it and then kept running. Another loomed close, and he slaughtered that one too without stopping. He repeated the same thing over and over—there was nothing else he could do.

How much time had passed? Goldof could only think of one way out of the situation.

And that was to abandon Nashetania.

Tgurneu had informed Goldof that if he shared the truth with the other Braves, it would immediately kill her. His liege's death meant that Chamo would live. What Goldof should do was kill these fiends, head back to Adlet, tell them the truth, and beg forgiveness. Adlet wouldn't kill him without hearing him out. Goldof would fight Tgurneu and its minions, destroy the Evil God, and then just disappear somewhere. He should forget all the time he had spent with Nashetania, like how a dream evaporates upon waking. That would solve everything.

Goldof killed the last of the gang of enemies, a leopard-fiend. Then he looked to the south, where he knew Adlet and the others were.

"…Princess…" Emotion swelled in his chest. The shock of their first meeting. His elation when he'd headed out to save her with nothing but a hammer in hand. How moved he'd been when she had listened to his request afterward. His confusion upon finding out what an outrageous tomboy she was. Anger at being the target of her mischief. Attraction, as day by day she became a woman. Bewilderment when she'd first declared she would become a Saint. Worry when he'd found out she was throwing herself into severe training with no care for her own life. Joy at watching her grow into her power as the Saint of Blades. Then regret for how he'd gone easy on her in the Tournament Before the Divine, when he'd handed victory to her.

Unease when she had been chosen as a Brave of the Six Flowers, and then determination to fight when he made up his mind to see her back safely from the Howling Vilelands. His slight jealousy of Adlet. And finally, the relief of knowing she was alive in his heart.

"If I could...forget it...like a dream..." A single tear welled in his eye. "It would be...so much easier." Goldof took the corpse of the leopard-fiend lying at his feet, lifted it up, and bit into its neck. He noisily sucked down what remained of the fiend's blood. The moment had to be a first for humanity—a man eating a fiend. The blood quenched his thirst.

Removing his armor, Goldof daubed what medicine he had left on his wounds and then quaffed the secret tonic passed down through Piena's royal family. This medicine was so powerful it was practically poison. Agony rippled down his throat and into his stomach. He hunched over, resisting the urge to vomit.

"..."

Then he rose to his feet. He clenched his fists and gave his spear a few swings. He could move. *I can still fight*, he thought, and he calmly began striding away. He'd made a decision—no matter what difficulties stood in his way, he would protect Nashetania.

About eighteen hours earlier, Nashetania and Dozzu had been in the Cut-Finger Forest. Hiding in the undergrowth, they leaned in close as they convened.

Their comrades weren't with them. Every single one had died after their fight with Cargikk's fiends. Dozzu was bleeding all over, and Nashetania's wounds were even more severe. A fiend's horn had impaled her, and the puncture wound reached all the way to her back. There was a deep cut in her leg, too, and the tendon was severed. Nashetania was fused with a fiend, so her capacity for recovery was far greater than a normal human's, but these injuries were grave, even for her.

Cargikk's forces had surrounded them with wave upon wave of fiends. How many more hours would they be able to keep running around? It was uncertain if they would even live to see the sun rise.

"Nashetania," said Dozzu. "I'll cut a path for you. Flee, please."

"Dozzu..."

"If you die, it's all over. As long as you're alive, we'll still have hope. Please, you must survive this."

"I can't! I can't do anything by myself. Both of us must survive this, or our ambitions will fall apart."

Dozzu was about to say, *We have no other choice.*

But then Nashetania suggested something unbelievable. "Let's ask Tgurneu for help."

"...Are you out of your mind?!"

"I'm not crazy. It's our only option. We'll use the blade gem in Chamo's stomach as leverage to negotiate. We'll have Tgurneu defeat Cargikk's fiends for us, and we'll kill Chamo in exchange," said Nashetania, looking toward the western side of the forest. She estimated Tgurneu's position based on the movements of the fiends. "I think Tgurneu will agree, since he's been having trouble with Chamo, too. We'll be protected until we kill her."

It could work, possibly. But Dozzu just couldn't agree to it. It knew better than anyone just how formidable Tgurneu was. There was no way it would actually end up helping their situation.

"If we can make it through this," said Nashetania, "then things will get better. We have to survive, no matter what it takes. We don't have any other options now."

Dozzu knew that, but it still couldn't agree. "Nashetania, after we kill Miss Chamo, Tgurneu will be done with us. I can't imagine he'd let us live."

"We'll only be working with him temporarily. Once he's eliminated Cargikk's minions, we'll escape—before we kill Chamo."

"You're underestimating Tgurneu. He would never allow it," Dozzu said.

Nashetania replied, "If Tgurneu captures me, then Goldof's Helm of Allegiance will activate. He'll come to rescue me."

"...But he..."

"The Helm of Allegiance only activates if I'm held captive, so I can't call for him right now. But it Tgurneu catches me, it's another story. The helmet will let him know I'm in danger."

"You're saying he'll come save you? Really?"

"I trust that he'll come."

Dozzu closed its eyes and thought about Goldof. During its time pretending to be Nashetania's pet, it had observed the knight. It knew quite well that Goldof's loyalty to her was absolute. In Dozzu's whole life—which had by no means been a short one—it had never seen such a loyal boy. He was so faithful, Dozzu found it tragic.

That loyalty had been the reason they had decided not to bring him into the fold. Goldof would not fight to achieve his ambitions—he would only fight to protect Nashetania. Dozzu's goal was bound to endanger her life many times over. Goldof might have tried to interfere for the sake of her safety.

"You betrayed him," said Dozzu. "I don't doubt his devotion, but your evaluation of him is plainly naive."

"You don't understand him, Dozzu. He can't live without me."

"…Nashetania…"

"He's been like that ever since we first met, and he's still the same." There was a rustling sound behind Dozzu. Cargikk's fiends were already close. "Goldof will come," she insisted. "He *will* come to save me. Please, Dozzu. Believe, as I do."

"Could he do it? Could he save you if Tgurneu captured you?"

"He could," Nashetania said, smiling. "The strongest person in the world is not Chamo—and it's certainly not a dunderhead like Adlet. I believe that when Goldof is defending me, he's the strongest man in the world."

Dozzu closed its eyes and nodded.

On the outskirts of the lava zone, Dozzu heard Goldof roar. Its hearing was far more sensitive than that of a human. When Dozzu heard the cry, it knew Goldof had not yet given up on Nashetania.

Everything was unfolding just as she had known it would. Tgurneu had readily agreed to their proposal and killed all of Cargikk's forces for them, and then it had taken Nashetania captive to force Dozzu to do its bidding.

It was clear that Tgurneu did not care to let them live. Dozzu knew that once Tgurneu was done with them, it would kill Nashetania. She had predicted everything beforehand. Dozzu and Nashetania had lured the Braves of the Six Flowers into their trap, and also just as Nashetania had anticipated, Goldof came to the lava zone to save her.

The problem was what happened next. If Chamo died, Tgurneu would kill Nashetania. It would be about another hour and a half until then. Nashetania couldn't escape on her own, and Dozzu couldn't rescue her, either. The only way for her to survive was for Goldof to save her. What's more, if Adlet discovered Nashetania first, he would be sure to dispose of her. Her chances of survival were incredibly low. Would Goldof be able to fulfill his role?

Dozzu knew how Tgurneu kept Nashetania hidden, but it couldn't tell Goldof. If it did, Tgurneu would immediately end her life.

Tgurneu had cultivated a specialist with formidable abilities. Dozzu doubted the boy would be able to figure out its powers—though, granted, his chances weren't zero. Still, Dozzu had no choice but to trust him. All it could do was pray that Goldof would save Nashetania.

Would Tgurneu's scheme succeed or would Nashetania's? Everything depended on Goldof.

The knight returned to the outer fringes of the gem's area of effect. Hunkering down in the shadow of a rock hill, he quietly poked out his head to check on the situation.

Clouds of dust billowed over the lava zone. From far away, he could hear the sound of explosions and see stone hills falling one after another. He didn't know what was going on, so he ventured toward the explosions.

Within the haze of debris, Rolonia and Fremy were examining the ground, hunting for something. They appeared to be searching underground. Goldof figured they had to be looking for Nashetania. They must not have realized that the one they had been chasing was a fake. To them, she'd suddenly disappeared. They thought she was underground.

"Where...did it hide her?" Goldof muttered, concealing himself in the shadow of a rock hill. She was within a kilometer of Chamo's location—Mora had told him as much with her mountain echo. Goldof was positive that was true. And Nashetania herself had told him she was inside a fiend's stomach.

Then where was it? The area had a radius of just one kilometer. There was no way it could stay hidden without using some special ability.

So what was that ability? That was where Goldof's train of thought ran into a brick wall. He couldn't even guess as to what kind of powers it was using to hide her. He wasn't educated about fiends like Adlet and Fremy were, and he didn't even know where his target was, either. He was stuck.

Don't give up, he told himself. But self-encouragement would not compensate for his lack of knowledge. As Goldof listened to Fremy blast the earth, he kept pondering.

"Hmm. Shallow thinking, Fremy."

Meanwhile, Tgurneu was flying far above. This time it occupied the body of what was now just a crow-fiend head. After the Braves had attacked it and driven it away, the commander had been observing the situation in the lava zone from the air. With the crow-fiend's sight, it could discern quite clearly what Adlet and the others were up to.

Fremy and Rolonia were blowing up the terrain to search underground. The very idea made Tgurneu laugh in derision. It would never hide Nashetania via such simplistic methods. Adlet was barking up the wrong tree, too. Tgurneu had tricked him into believing in a hieroform that didn't exist.

I've won this one. How long would it take for them to realize their mistake? By then it would be too late. "...Hmm." Then Tgurneu found Goldof outside the gem's area of effect. He was hunched low, searching for something. *So he still hasn't given up*, it noted with surprise.

Goldof's presence was convenient indeed. The boy had lured the Braves into the trap, and his foolish behavior had confused the others, too, distracting them from what was really going on. Even now Goldof was trying to save Nashetania all by himself, withholding his valuable information from Adlet. There was no way in hell Goldof would manage to save her. The other Braves would soon kill him.

Just in case, Tgurneu had instructed its pawns to finish him off, but that would probably not even be necessary. Reassured, it continued surveying the scene below, eagerly anticipating the look on Goldof's face when all his hopes were dashed.

Still hidden behind the rock hill, Goldof kept thinking. There was only one fiend power for hiding he knew about, and that was Nashetania's stealth power. But Fremy had said that even that ability could only be used to hide a person for ten seconds at most. There was no way a fiend could hide for hours on end.

Or maybe Fremy was the seventh, and some stealth-fiends actually could hide for long periods of time. But Goldof was forced to reject that possibility, too. Adlet had said it was impossible to maintain that hypnosis for hours on end. If Fremy was the seventh, that meant Adlet was a real Brave, so if both of them said something was true, Goldof had to believe it was.

So then, what other way could there be?

Maybe there was a fiend that could put Nashetania in its stomach and then shrink itself. If so, then it would make sense that Adlet and Fremy couldn't find Nashetania no matter how much they searched for her. Or maybe some fiend could expand the blade gem's area of effect, meaning she was even further away. Various ideas popped up in his mind, but without any clues to go on, he couldn't sort any of his ideas out. He realized that he was just wasting his time with wild speculations. He had no evidence, and no clues to guide him.

"..."

Once more, Goldof looked over toward Fremy and Rolonia as they kept blasting every section of earth. Maybe they were right and Nashetania was hiding underground. A burrowing fiend—that was a simple sort of ability, and certainly plausible. Some of Chamo's slave-fiends had similar skills. He could just keep waiting for Fremy and Rolonia to find Nashetania. The moment they did, he'd attack them and take her to safety. That was the only idea he could come up with.

But would that be enough? Was the fiend that had swallowed Nashetania actually underground?

"…"

No. Goldof was sure that if it were, Tgurneu would have done something to stop Fremy. Since it would want to avoid Nashetania's discovery, it would have been forced to act.

So she wasn't be buried anywhere. At the very least, they weren't going to find her using Fremy's methods. There was some other kind of power keeping her hidden, and he had to find out what it was.

The wheels in his mind kept turning.

In the lava zone was a fiend. Looking up at the sky, gazing at the sun, it wondered, *How much longer now until Chamo Rosso is dead?* No matter how long this dragged on, at this point Chamo couldn't last longer than an hour and a half. If the fiend could stay hidden until then, its mission would be complete. It would have helped to kill Chamo, the strongest of the Braves of the Six Flowers. It was eagerly awaiting that glorious moment. The death of a Brave was a fiend's greatest joy.

The creature was a large lizard-fiend with stone skin. It stood stock-still, about eight hundred meters from Chamo's location. It had been there for two hours with Nashetania inside its stomach. Its tongue was wrapped around her throat to keep her still, and Tgurneu had instructed it to immediately strangle her and crush her windpipe if she tried to say anything. Right now it seemed she was unconscious.

The fiend had no name. If it had to give one, it might say "specialist number twenty-six." It was one of the fiends with unique abilities that Tgurneu had cultivated. About a century ago, its superior officer had ordered it to refine its talent for concealment, and it had spent the past century remaking its own body. This had made it fragile and markedly decreased its capacity for combat, but its stealth abilities had been honed until they were peerless.

About four hours earlier, the fiend had tucked Nashetania into its stomach. Then, when Nashetania had called out to Goldof for help, it had crushed her throat so she couldn't talk anymore.

About two hours earlier, the Braves of the Six Flowers had arrived in the lava zone. As ordered by Tgurneu's fake Nashetania, the lizard-fiend had fought with the Six Braves. Anticipating when Chamo would attack, it had then sent a signal to Nashetania, inside its stomach, to activate the blade gem. If she had refused to obey, the plan was to kill her immediately.

After the girl complied, the lizard-fiend fled the Braves and came to its current hiding place. Checking that there were no enemies around, it had activated its ability to conceal itself. After that, it had remained in place the whole time.

The Braves of the Six Flowers had passed right by its nose. The fiend had caught sight of Goldof, too. It had even stood beside him, only a few meters away. But not one of them had picked up on its presence. No one, be they human or fiend, would ever be able to find it unless they understood its powers.

Half an hour ago, a messenger had come from Tgurneu with new instructions: to do whatever it took to prevent Goldof from saving Nashetania. And if it couldn't, it was allowed to kill her.

But the fiend wasn't concerned about a thing. Nobody would be able to find it.

Figuring he should go somewhere else—he had to look for clues—Goldof began creeping away so as not to be noticed by Fremy and Rolonia. But when he stood up, he sensed danger and flattened himself again. A bullet zipped right above his head.

"He *was* there!" he heard Rolonia yell. Unawares, Goldof had been noticed. He stood up and sprinted away.

This time was different from the last time he'd fought them. Their attacks were merciless attempts to kill him instantly. If he fought them now, he'd have no chance.

Fremy was aiming for the gaps in his armor. If he ran in a straight line, he'd be shot. Goldof darted in a zigzag pattern, using the complex terrain to shield himself from the bullets.

"We can catch him, Rolonia!"

"Yeah!"

He could hear the pair's voices behind him. Rolonia's footsteps were coming closer. His body aching, Goldof kept up the pace.

Fremy launched a bomb at him. The blast struck him in the back, making him stagger. An instant later, Rolonia was in range, screeching. "FuckingdietraitorIwon'twon'twon'tletyoukillChamoshowmeyourguts!"

His armor couldn't block it all. He slapped aside Rolonia's whip strikes with his spear. Her weapon was whirling in from all directions, and he was blocking on instinct alone. But he couldn't afford to stop and exchange blows, either. Fremy was right behind her and getting closer. If she scored a hit with her bombs or bullets, it was over.

Blocking the whip with his spear, Goldof charged straight at Rolonia, taking advantage of a split-second opening to kick her in the chest. His powerful leg struck out hard enough to knock her back ten meters, armor and all.

"Rolonia!" Fremy fired a shot at his face. His helmet stopped the bullet from entering his forehead, but it flung him back violently, and for a moment he was close to blacking out.

Goldof turned away from the two of them and sprinted off again. Rolonia's whip was thirty meters long. He absolutely could not let her within range. Desperately, he dodged.

"ReleaseChamoifyoudon'tI'llkillyouI'llkillyouI'llkillyouI'llkillyou-Goldof!" He could hear her screaming.

I only wish I could, thought Goldof. But Tgurneu had Nashetania captive and was forcing her to kill Chamo. If she refused, Tgurneu would simply murder her. As Goldof escaped, he thought, maybe it would be better to tell someone the truth, everything he had learned. There was no way he could find Nashetania all on his own. Tgurneu had said that if Goldof talked, the seventh would let it know. So maybe Goldof could tell someone trust-worthy, in secret, so the seventh wouldn't find out.

"...Ngh." Running, Goldof glanced back. He couldn't tell the two behind him the truth. There was no guarantee either of them weren't the seventh. The others who were most likely real Braves were Mora and Chamo. But Hans was with them, and Goldof couldn't say for sure that he was trustworthy. *Then what about Adlet?* Goldof considered.

"Hurry up, Rolonia!"

"Rottenbrutejustwon'tgiveupI'llsuckoutyourbloodandspititout!"

But that was a no-go, too. Goldof still couldn't say for sure that Adlet was a real Brave. He just couldn't be certain Adlet wasn't the seventh. The others trusted him because Nashetania had nearly killed him. But Goldof knew that the other seventh wasn't on the same side as Nashetania, so Adlet still could be the seventh.

When it came down to it, he couldn't tell anyone the truth. He was on his own, and there was no avoiding that.

"Rolonia! Don't chase him too far!" Fremy yelled after some minutes of running. Rolonia stopped, and Goldof escaped. "Adlet is all on his own! Tgurneu or Nashetania might go after him!"

"Y-you're right! Let's head back now!"

I'm saved, Goldof thought, leaning back on a boulder as he panted. He had to look for clues to save Nashetania, but he couldn't even get near her.

As he gazed up at the sky, his mind turned to Adlet. Back in the Phan-tasmal Barrier, he had been all on his own, too, and he'd solved all the mysteries and won. But Goldof couldn't fight like him. Adlet had smarts, along with the mysterious ability to win people's trust. Goldof had neither of those. Now that he was in the same situation Adlet had been in, he understood just how amazing the other boy was.

I can't compare to Adlet—but that doesn't mean I can give up, he thought, but his mind just kept spinning around in circles.

Meanwhile, Nashetania was inside the fiend's stomach, waiting for salva-tion. The remains of her left arm hurt. It was so suffocating inside her prison, she couldn't think straight. She felt on the verge of passing out. But she bit her lip and clung to consciousness.

She had fused with multiple fiends in order to make their powers her own. Now she desperately tried to use those fiends' powers to heal her crushed throat. She had to tell Goldof where she was. But with her throat in such a condition, she'd only be able to say a few words to him.

"...*Your Highness...are you safe? Where...are you?*"

Occasionally, she could hear him speak in her head. He was still searching, still trying to save her. Hope was not yet dead.

What she knew was that she was inside a fiend's stomach, and it was holding her somewhere within the gem's radius. She knew it was staying perfectly still and not moving at all. That was it. Nashetania didn't know how it was staying hidden.

In the darkness, she heard sounds. Fiends' footsteps as they thudded along in a pack. Adlet, Fremy, and the rest fighting the fiends. She heard bomb after bomb detonating all around her. From these noises, Nashetania could guess that she was aboveground, not underground, and that Braves had passed right by her multiple times. As for why none of them could find the fiend that had swallowed her—it was so baffling she could hardly take it.

"..."

Nashetania tried to keep every muscle still, pretending she was unconscious so as to make the fiend that had swallowed her lower its guard. She also listened intently for anything that could help her understand what was going on outside and where she was so that she could tell Goldof. She wondered what she could tell him that would be helpful. What would lead him to her?

She remembered what Goldof had said to her six years before. He had told her his wish was to save her one more time. She had yet to grant that request.

Hiding outside the circle, Goldof continued pondering. He contemplated everything that had happened since he'd first heard Nashetania's cry for help—what she had said, what Dozzu had said, what Tgurneu had said, and what Adlet and Mora had said—wondering if maybe a clue lay somewhere in all of that.

But nothing came to mind. Mora had only told him the situation with Chamo. Adlet hadn't found any clues. Tgurneu had chosen its words carefully to ensure Goldof wouldn't find Nashetania. And Dozzu was under surveillance, so it couldn't tell him anything.

One more time, Goldof reviewed everything from the beginning. One by one he diligently scrutinized each thing he had seen and heard in all the fights so far. Nashetania had told him that she was south of the forest, inside a fiend's stomach, in the lava zone. As asked, he'd come.

That was when a question floated up in Goldof's mind. One of the most fundamental elements of this situation didn't make sense to him: Why the lava zone? If the goal was to lure out the Braves of the Six Flowers in order to activate Chamo's blade gem, it shouldn't matter if they were in the forest or anywhere else. But Tgurneu had clearly chosen the magma hotspot as their battlefield.

There had to be a reason—a reason the scheme had to be set here.

"!"

Staring into empty space atop the hill, deep in thought, Goldof had been distracted by his questions and ignored his surroundings. Adlet was two hundred meters away, and Goldof was within his field of view. Panicking, the knight slowly lowered himself down and out of sight.

"..."

If Adlet had spotted him, he would have called for Fremy and Rolonia, and they'd have come to surround Goldof and kill him. Should he move out from this spot and defeat Adlet before he called for help? But he couldn't manage that, either. *Don't notice me*, Goldof prayed, waiting for the redhead to pass him.

After some time, Goldof poked his head out. Adlet was moving farther away. Goldof immediately ducked down and left the vicinity.

It appeared Adlet was searching for something, and his eyes were emitting a strange light. He didn't seem to be wandering aimlessly. Had he found some kind of clue? What was he looking for? What had he noticed?

"I don't…have time," Goldof muttered, and he continued his analysis.

Inside the fiend's stomach, Nashetania had her ears open. She could hear explosions going off nonstop all around her. That was probably Fremy. Nashetania couldn't see anything, so she didn't know what was happening outside.

It wasn't just Goldof who was looking for her—the others would be on the hunt, too. If Fremy found Nashetania first, she would kill her. Stifling her terror, Nashetania focused on the sounds outside.

"…It's no use, Fremy. There's nothing."

"Looks like it."

The voices were very close. The first was Fremy. Nashetania didn't know the other, but it was safe to assume it was Rolonia.

"She's not underground? Then…where the…" said Fremy.

"Maybe she's gone even deeper down? There could be a fiend with powers like that."

"But still, that would leave traces. There's no way we'd tear up the whole surface and find nothing."

The two of them hadn't noticed the fiend carrying Nashetania in its stomach. But they were close by, so close that Nashetania could overhear them clearly. Nashetania's captor didn't move a muscle. Was it trying as hard as it could to disappear and avoid discovery? Or did it simply not believe it would ever be found?

"There are still places we haven't searched yet," said Fremy. "The pit where Chamo is…and the hills around there. Let's search over there."

"And what if she isn't there?"

Their voices departed, and eventually Nashetania couldn't hear them anymore. They must have left. They'd given her no ideas as to her location, and neither had she been able to gain any information worth telling Goldof. So she kept her ears open for any other clues.

*   *   *

"There has to be…something." Having escaped Adlet, Goldof was now examining ground zero of Fremy's blasts. He'd made sure that Adlet, Fremy, and Rolonia were nowhere near, but he couldn't yet set foot within the area of effect. He'd decided that if he did enter, it would be after he had found answers.

Why this region? Goldof was convinced that if he could answer that question, he would find Nashetania—though he had no basis for that belief.

There was something in the volcanic area that was absent elsewhere. Heat. The warmth permeated up from the ground—could it be used to hide? Goldof considered the idea carefully, but nothing came to mind. He picked up a rock at his feet. Did the stone hold some kind of secret? He stared at it hard enough to bore holes into it but found no answers. He had no ideas, but thinking was all he could do. There was a key in this zone; that was the only clue Goldof had uncovered.

As Goldof pondered, he heard lightning strikes far away. The sounds were coming from the pit where Chamo was. "…Dozzu, I guess." He recalled that Tgurneu had ordered Dozzu to keep Hans busy. Dozzu must have wanted to rescue Nashetania, but Goldof couldn't rely on its help if it couldn't oppose Tgurneu.

"…"

Again Goldof reflected on the whole fight from the beginning, Nashetania's information, and Dozzu's. *So Tgurneu's been watching Dozzu, and Dozzu's to do what Tgurneu says. But has Dozzu done nothing at all to help Her Highness?*

No, that couldn't be. Dozzu must have done something to ensure that Goldof could help Nashetania. It must have given him a clue indirectly to escape Tgurneu's notice. That was what Goldof would have done if he were in Dozzu's position.

Again Goldof examined each and every thing Dozzu had done, one by one. Out of every action it had taken, Goldof remembered just one thing it had said that seemed off. It had been right as the fake Nashetania was fighting the Braves, immediately before she activated the blade gem inside Chamo's stomach.

"Goldof, how many times have you fought her now?"

The sudden question had confused Goldof. When Goldof had replied that it was the second time, for some reason Dozzu had given him an uneasy look. Next it had asked if Nashetania had ever escaped him.

Why had Dozzu inquired about that? Nashetania was captive. The previous times he'd fought her shouldn't be important. And furthermore, what did her escaping him before have to do with it?

Goldof thought further. Had Dozzu done anything else unnatural? Goldof didn't only consider what Dozzu had said—he even called to mind its slight changes of expression and eye movements. He recalled that for some reason the look on Dozzu's face had changed a few times. That had been before Goldof fought Adlet to save the fake Nashetania.

"Dozzu...that stealth power...she has... If you focus on looking...and hurt yourself...you can see through it...right?"

When Goldof had said that, Dozzu's expression had changed. It had given Goldof a brief, pensive look and eventually replied, *"That's exactly right. You do know. That's good; it saves me the trouble of explaining."*

"...It couldn't be..."

What Dozzu had been trying to confirm was that Goldof knew about the stealth ability. Upon finding out that Goldof knew how to see through it, its expression had changed to one of relief. The fiend's attitude had been superficially curt, but it had clearly been glad.

That power of concealment. Was that how the captor was hiding?

When he realized that, it hit him. Fremy had said before that when a fiend used the stealth ability, a sweet scent would hang in the air around it. Goldof now understood why Tgurneu had chosen this hot spot as their battlefield. The smell of sulfur hung over the whole area. A few minutes there and your nose went numb. Tgurneu had elected to carry out his scheme here in order to disguise the smell of the stealth ability.

"...I've got it," muttered Goldof, seeing a faint light in the darkness. He had figured out the true nature of the enemy's powers.

*   *   *

Goldof sprinted around the outer circumference of the area of effect, keeping out of sight. He was in danger of being discovered by the other Braves, but he couldn't afford to worry about that anymore.

Fremy's bombs had drastically transformed the landscape. Even from outside the area of effect, Goldof could get a glimpse of the situation within.

"...Hmm..." Goldof found Adlet about five hundred meters away, squatting down, head lowered in thought. It was unlikely that he'd notice Goldof, but it would still be dangerous to get too close. Goldof stopped and backtracked.

He was certain now that there was a fiend with a stealth talent somewhere within the gem's area of effect, and inside its stomach was Nashetania. Adlet had said that the ability was a kind of hypnosis. Fremy also explained that a fiend would scatter a special chemical while emitting a sound that human ears couldn't detect. And Goldof knew the way to see through it. He could weaken the effect of the hypnosis by causing severe pain to himself. Then, if he concentrated his mind and focused his eyes, he'd be able to see the fiend.

How was the fiend staying hidden when this power generally only lasted for just over ten seconds? Goldof didn't have an answer. But if Nashetania's captor was using the same technique, he should be able to defeat it the same way.

"*Ngh!*" Running, Goldof stuck a finger under one of his nails and pried it hard until it split. The pain should weaken the hypnosis's hold over him. He braved the discomfort and focused his eyes. But in the expanse of the lava field, nothing became visible. *Not here, then?* Goldof thought. He tried another location and tore off the broken nail. He peered hard once again, but still, he didn't find anything. "...Damn it!"

The sounds of Fremy's bombs had already halted. She'd probably given up searching underground and was on the lookout for some other clue.

He had to find Nashetania before the others did. But even after he combed through the entire circle and broke every nail on his hands, he couldn't find anything. Had his deductions been wrong? Was pain not enough to see through the stealth ability? Maybe there something else he needed in order to find Nashetania? He had less than thirty minutes left. Panic was clouding his thoughts, and irritation weakened his concentration.

Visibility in the rocky area was much better now. And there, specialist number twenty-six continued its observation of the Braves of the Six Flowers. Inside its stomach was Nashetania.

About twenty meters away, Adlet, Fremy, and Rolonia were having a discussion. The fiend was certain they wouldn't figure out its true nature. There was also no indication that Hans and Mora would come out of that pit, so no problems on that front, either. The only issue was Goldof. He was running the circumference of the area of effect in search of something. He might have deduced the fiend's ability to cloak itself.

Two hundred years ago, Tgurneu had told the fiend that its ability was weak. It could vanish for just over ten seconds. It was intensely exhausting, and once it had used the skill, it would be unable to do so again for a while. What's more, it couldn't even vanish perfectly, and once its opponents found out how to overcome the hypnosis, it was useless.

At most, it would only serve catch the Braves of the Six Flowers by surprise. And Tgurneu had said that even if it startled them, it probably wouldn't be able to defeat a warrior strong enough to be chosen as a Brave.

But Tgurneu had also said that this power had potential. Even simple concealment might lead to the death of all the Six Braves, depending on how it was used. The fiend joined the group known as the specialists, and the number given to it was twenty-six.

It could only make the stealth effects last for a few scant moments. No matter how much it evolved, it couldn't change that. So then it had an idea. If the effect held for only a dozen-odd seconds, it should just trigger it multiple times in succession—just use it continuously tens, hundreds, thousands of times. But after triggering its illusion, there was a cooldown of a few minutes, and no matter how much it developed the talent, it couldn't improve this, either.

So then it thought it should just make more of itself. It should split itself into thousands, tens of thousands of bodies. It remade its form and mutated itself to create a new organ inside itself: an ovary. By splitting its core, it acquired the ability to spawn eggs. The children it bore were about one centimeter long and one millimeter in diameter. They had no organs for eating, and neither could they drink water. Once the children were born, they would die in about a day.

Like their parent, the offspring could use the same drug and sound wave. The offspring would hypnotize nearby humans, hiding themselves and their parent by altering their perception. The fiend had dispersed about fifty thousand children across approximately three kilometers throughout the rocky plain. When one offspring's hypnosis wore off, another would immediately pick up the slack. When the second round ended, another offspring would instantly trigger its ability, and it was by repeating that over and over that the fiend remained hidden. Fremy's bombs had killed many of the offspring. The fiend itself had also been wounded by the blasts. But still, enough remained to maintain the illusion.

Goldof must have already realized that the fiend was using this stealth ability. But its hypnosis was far from weak. He would not be able to reveal his foe easily, even if he injured himself to do it. He'd never be able to break through the hallucination unless he focused on one spot and stared continuously at it. It wasn't possible to find the fiend in a mobile search, like he was doing now.

Thirty minutes left. The fiend's powers would hold until then.

"…Goldof. He has the key. I can't think of anything else," said Adlet.

Adlet, Fremy, and Rolonia, who had been conversing nearby, seemed to have come to a conclusion. Foolish. They were trying to go look for clues, totally unaware that their target was right beside them.

But right as Adlet and the others ran off, suddenly two explosions occurred in succession. Boiling water burst from the earth. All Fremy's blasting had disturbed the magma and water vein underground. It was startling, but no serious cause for concern, or so the fiend thought.

Nashetania was biding her time inside her prison for an opportunity to communicate her position to Goldof, hoping for a hint as to her position. Pretending she was unconscious, she waited to hear something.

Her throat had already recovered somewhat, and speaking was entirely possible for her. But once she'd spoken, she would immediately be strangled again. She could only give Goldof a brief message.

"…Goldof. He has the key. I can't think of anything else."

She heard Adlet and the others talking. They were close by. She thought about telling Goldof that—but that wouldn't be enough. Was there no information that would help him pin down her location?

That was when Nashetania heard the double explosions. For a moment she didn't understand what they were. Then she realized the sound belonged to hot water spraying up from the ground. She made up her mind. If she was going to relay something to Goldof, this was it.

"Goldof. Just now, close by, two geysers went off," she said quietly, and the moment the words left her mouth, the tentacle around her neck constricted, sending her mind careening into instant darkness.

Goldof was still on the prowl for the stealth-fiend when he heard a voice. After many hours, Nashetania had fed him information again.

"Goldof. Just now, close by, two geysers went off." Her voice was so hoarse, he almost couldn't believe it was her.

He immediately dashed off. Fortunately, there was no sign of Adlet's trio within the gem's area of effect. It seemed they were looking for something beyond the boundary. Goldof would probably be discovered within ten minutes. He had no choice but to find Nashetania and save her before his time was up.

He hurtled across the ground. He found one geyser, but not another spray of steam nearby. He ran farther and found another. Not this one, either. Forgetting the pain of his fingers and his other injuries, Goldof ran and ran.

Specialist number twenty-six felt its blood freeze. Nashetania, whom it had thought unconscious, had told Goldof where she was.

The boy would come immediately. The fiend desperately began to move, but it was slow, no faster than a human's walking speed. It had expended all its strength on camouflage, and Fremy's bombs had wounded it. It couldn't move quickly.

Tgurneu had said that under no conditions should it allow itself to be found by Goldof, in particular, and that if he seemed close to rescuing Nashetania, to kill her. Goldof would reach the fiend eventually. So what should it do? The creature desperately racked its brains. It had to carry out Tgurneu's orders no matter what. To a fiend, failure to follow its master's orders was an agony more terrifying than death.

"...Oh? Has something happened?" Tgurneu muttered, far, far away. It was still aloft, observing the situation down below. Goldof had suddenly dashed into the gem's area of effect, while specialist number twenty-six began lumbering off. The child couldn't have figured out where Nashetania was, could he? From afar, Tgurneu couldn't tell what was going on.

"Hmm. What's to be done here? Well, this time, I suppose I'll trust in my pawn. Let's leave it to number twenty-six." Tgurneu understood that its subordinate was in danger, but it couldn't come up with any ideas as to how to assist. If Tgurneu charged in, it could be exposed to danger itself. Just a little while ago, it had had a close call, and it wasn't keen on experiencing that again.

"All right, number twenty-six. I've decided to cheer you on from up here. You can do it. You can do it. Don't give up," Tgurneu urged gleefully as it continued to observe the spectacle.

"Is that...it?" Goldof found two adjacent holes spurting steam. Already, five minutes had passed since he'd received that message from Nashetania.

Goldof bit his broken fingertip. The bone grated, shooting a spike of pain through his appendage. Amid the aching, he focused his eyes. It seemed a part of his field of vision shimmered just a bit. He concentrated on that spot and bit his finger harder. The mirage-like fluctuation grew, and when he continued to stare, a fiend came into view. It was turned away from him, trying to escape. The moment Goldof started after it, he heard a voice.

"Stöp, Goldof." When the fiend spoke, it appeared clearly—a lizard-fiend with rock skin. When it turned toward him, he stopped automatically.

"...Monster..."

The fiend's mouth was very slightly agape, and inside he could see Nashetania's face. The sharp teeth pierced her skin. That alone told him immediately what it was about to do. If Goldof took one step forward, it would kill her.

The fiend was about thirty meters away from him—too far for even Goldof to cross in an instant. He knew it wasn't bluffing. Tgurneu would want to avoid her rescue at all costs. It would surely rather kill her than let him save her, even if that meant the plan to deal with Chamo would fail.

"...Not a single step." The fiend spoke skillfully, even with its mouth blocked. It wasn't going to hand over the girl. It would never let him save her. A glance was enough for Goldof to apprehend its determination.

"I'm...almost there..." The Helm of Allegiance was still telling him that his master was in danger. How much longer until Chamo died? Depending on her strength, she could fade at any minute. If she died, Nashetania would immediately follow.

"I will...save her." Goldof took a slow step forward. The sharp teeth bit into Nashetania's face. Blood dripped from her forehead onto her cheeks. He could even hear her bones grating, or so he though. "Your Highness... Please...open...your eyes..." Goldof called out to her. But her limp body didn't so much as twitch. And even if she did wake, there was nothing she could do, anyway. Tgurneu had said that the power of one of these special- ists prevented her from controlling blades.

Goldof shifted forward very slightly, less than a full step. But the fiend didn't miss the movement. It clamped her face even harder. He couldn't get near it.

Can't I create an opening? he thought. But the fiend was eyeing his every action. He couldn't approach. *Then I should throw my spear,* he thought, but the fiend had already anticipated that. The instant he moved his arm to ready his spear, the fiend's mouth tensed.

What's more, Goldof realized that if he failed to kill the fiend in one strike, the next thing it would do was crush Nashetania's face. If he aimed for its head, he'd kill her, too. He couldn't aim for its heart because he didn't know where that was.

"…I'll never give her to you."

Sweat beaded on Goldof's face, left tracks down his jaw, and dripped on the ground. He kept perfectly still as he and the fiend stared each other down.

He racked his brain, trying to think of a way to kill the fiend in one strike, a way to guarantee it would die instantly, without time to bite Nashetania's head. And the more he thought about it, the clearer it became that such a method didn't exist. There was no way for him to succeed with his own power and weapons.

He couldn't back off for now to find a way to save her, either—he couldn't afford to. There was no time. If he left, the fiend would go into hiding again. Right here, right now, was his only opportunity to save her.

That moment, the fiend's eyes crinkled. Goldof could tell it was smiling.

"…"

The boy didn't take his eyes off the fiend—but he knew what was happening. He had sensed the presence of someone to the right, as well as a bloodthirsty aura sharp enough to pierce his flesh.

Fremy was thirty meters away, gun trained on. "Adlet and Rolonia will be here soon, Goldof," she said. She couldn't see what he was looking at. "Just so you know, if you release Chamo, we'll let you live. What will you do?"

Goldof didn't reply. His gaze never left the fiend. He could tell Fremy was a little irritated at being ignored. *What kind of nonsense are you talking about?* he thought. He wanted to free Chamo, too.

Fremy didn't fire. She wasn't looking to see if this was a trap. She was waiting for Adlet and Rolonia. Before long, the two of them arrived as well.

Goldof knew what the fiend was after. It was waiting for the other Braves to kill him. "You came...Adlet," he said.

"What're you looking at?" Adlet asked him. Goldof didn't reply. "What's over there?" Adlet asked again.

That was when Goldof understood—Adlet hadn't found a thing. He hadn't even figured out that there was a fiend with stealth powers here. Still, Goldof asked him anyway, "Have you...found Her Highness?"

"Yeah, we're close," said Adlet. "You've been giving us a rough time, but...that ends now."

"...Have you figured out...what's really going on?"

"Who do you think you're talking to? I'm the strongest man in the world."

Goldof could tell immediately that was a bluff. Adlet was a surprisingly bad liar.

"Tell me about your helmet. What's that hieroform, really?"

"...Hieroform?" How did he know about the Helm of Allegiance? And why was he asking about something so trivial right now? Goldof didn't know, and it didn't matter.

The fiend was watching Goldof, eyes narrowed. Now it just had to wait for the three of them to kill Goldof. That had to be what it was thinking. And the fiend's assessment of the situation was entirely accurate. Goldof doubted he could win the other Braves over this late in the game. Whatever Goldof said, they'd try to kill him, regardless. He could tell that clearly, from the vicious looks they directed at him. He didn't imagine he had a chance, not against the three of them. If he could hold on for even a minute, he'd accept that as a good fight.

Then, in that single minute, he'd win.

Goldof focused every nerve in his body, steadied his breathing, felt his blood pound in his veins, tensed every muscle. And then he trusted that he *would* be able to save Nashetania.

"I'm going to kill you now," said Fremy. "But before that, let me ask you this: Is it your hieroform that's keeping Nashetania hidden?"

"That question…is pointless. For you…and for me." *What a stupid question*, thought Goldof. They really didn't know anything. They hadn't even managed to puzzle out a sliver of the truth. Fremy and Rolonia aside, Goldof had thought that Adlet, at least, might be able to figure out something. Unconsciously, the gaze Goldof had leveled at them grew contemptuous. "I'm disappointed…Adlet."

"About what?"

"I thought…maybe…you'd figure it out." Goldof raised his spear, and while the others were raising their weapons, Goldof observed the red-haired Brave—and the variety of tools at his waist—closely. Adlet inched forward, while Rolonia began to whisper invective under her breath.

Finally, to show them his determination, as well as to shock them, Goldof announced, "I will…protect Her Highness." He crouched low and readied himself to charge. "And…I'll save Chamo…too."

That seemed to startle them. That instant, Goldof launched himself at Adlet. Their confrontation lasted only an instant, and the fight reached its conclusion in mere seconds.

"StinkingGoldofI'llscatteryourinnardseverywhereyoudemonI'llspillyourbloodandwringyououtandcrushyoutrashworm!" Rolonia's lash danced as she tried to intercept Goldof's charge toward Adlet. Fremy leveled her gun while Adlet, too fast for the eye to follow, whipped out a chain with a metal fitting on one end.

Goldof knew the longer this battle went on, the more disadvantageous it would be for him. So he used his strongest move first, spinning as he advanced, using the centrifugal force to fling his spear. He'd unchained it from his wrist beforehand. The heavy weapon spun toward Rolonia.

He was aiming for Adlet—or that was what they'd think. They'd assume Goldof wouldn't let go of his spear since he had to beat all three of them. That was why the shaft of the spear landed a hit on Rolonia's chest. Thanks to her armor, it probably didn't hurt her much. But it did jostle her whip away from Adlet's defense. Adlet seemed a bit worried, but he quickly prioritized killing Goldof. If he'd been distracted by Rolonia, even just a bit, it would have made things easier, though.

"Haa!" Adlet jumped to the side as he flung the cuff and chain. This was the same tool he'd once used to restrain Tgurneu. Goldof tried to avoid it, but he wasn't fast enough. The binding caught his now weaponless right arm.

Meanwhile, Fremy was firing at a gap between his armor plates around his stomach. She had probably chosen that rather than his head so it would be harder to avoid. Goldof didn't block her shot and let the bullet pierce his body. If it went right through without hitting bone, it wouldn't stop him. Feeling the hot slug pierce his stomach, he kept racing forward. Adlet strafed sideways, yanking the chain in perfect time with the moment when both Goldof's feet left the ground. Goldof's upper body jerked forward.

"!" If he landed on his stomach, Fremy would immediately shoot him in the face. If he caught his fall with his hands, he wouldn't be able to use them for what came next. So he deliberately drove his forehead toward the ground. As he descended, he used his left hand to rip off his right bracer. His face scraped the ground, but a moment later, his arm was free. Fremy shot at his head, but he blocked it with an armored shoulder. As his body rotated from the impact, he grabbed the chain he'd just removed and yanked with all his strength. The unsuspecting Adlet stumbled toward him.

Discarding the chain, Goldof reached out for the boy's throat. Adlet drew his sword and swept it horizontally in an attempt to slice the hand away. But the attack at his throat was just a feint. Goldof immediately snatched his hand back and crouched to grab Adlet around the waist.

That was when Rolonia recovered from the earlier blow and cracked her whip at Goldof. Fremy charged toward him, too, reloading in preparation for a near-contact shot. As Adlet toppled backward, he landed with practiced technique and tossed a poison needle at Goldof.

The very next moment decided the fight. Goldof dodged the needle, released Adlet, and rocketed backward. In his hand, he now held a twenty-centimeter-long spike.

"Yaaaagh!" he screamed as he threw the weapon he'd stolen from

Adlet at the stealth-fiend right beside them—which had been dispassionately observing them.

That missile was called the Saint's Spike—one of a set of four, the most powerful weapons Atreau Spiker had ever made, entrusted to Adlet.

Only one weapon could kill the stealth-fiend, which had its fangs sunk into Nashetania's head, with a single instant, infallible attack—and that was Adlet's Saint's Spike. Goldof had not been stuck frozen and passive. He had been waiting. Biding his time for Adlet, the one with the weapon that could save Nashetania.

"Guh...gurgle-ugh...gyahh...gahhh!" The Saint's Spike piercing its flesh, the fiend writhed and spasmed. As Rolonia's whip skimmed his body and Fremy's bullets thudded into his armor, Goldof sprinted toward the fiend with zero hesitation.

"!" His behavior confused Fremy and Rolonia. Then they turned in the direction of the screech. To them it must have looked like Goldof had suddenly flung the spike at nothing, and then that nothing screamed.

"What was that?!" said Fremy, firing at him. Goldof turned aside to avoid the bullet, but it grazed his cheek, taking a strip of flesh with it.

"WaityoutraitorrottenGoldofyou'renotwatchingmespillyourblood!" Rolonia's whip cut through the air.

"Your Highness!" Goldof yelled, and then he plunged his hand into the fiend's mouth to grab Nashetania's shoulder. Feeling her presence filled his heart with joy. He'd done it. Tasting the feeling of accomplishment, he dragged her out of the maw. "Your Highness!" he cried again, and then, with Nashetania in his arms, sprang sideways. Rolonia's whip, Fremy's bullet, and Adlet's poison needle all landed where Goldof had just been.

It was too early to relax. He had to stop the three of them and make them understand that the battle was over. "Your Highness! Release Chamo! Hurry!" he kept yelling at the unconscious Nashetania. She just barely opened her eyes, gazing into his face. Then she smiled.

Meanwhile, back in the pit, Hans and Dozzu's fight had reached its climax.

The residual sparks from the lightning had burned off Hans's clothes, leaving him naked from the waist up. He was red all over and flecked with burn marks. There was a deep gash in Dozzu's right foreleg and a large wound on its face. The situation was about even, as were the skills of both parties. However, Hans was at a disadvantage. He had to kill Dozzu as quickly as possible so he could head out to look for Nashetania—even if there wasn't much time left.

Mora watched over their fight with the feebly panting girl in her arms. She mustered all her strength to pour energy into Chamo. If there was even the slightest break in the stream of energy, Chamo would die.

"Cat...boy."

Chamo spoke, which startled Mora. She should have already been too drained to speak.

"Catboy..." She was smiling. The strength had returned to her eyes.

"Chamo? It couldn't be..."

"Chamo'll help you out!" The girl opened her mouth wide and shoved a finger down her throat. Up came buckets of blood, along with a black fluid, and before their eyes, the fluid took the form of her slave-fiends.

The moment the youngest Saint shouted, Dozzu turned away from Hans to dash away. Hans didn't follow it, running up to Chamo instead. "Chamo!" he said. "They saved ya?!"

"Catboy! You can't relax yet! We'll kill them all—Goldof, and that little animal, too!" From her attitude, one wouldn't think she'd been dying just moments ago. No, she must have still been in pain. But even after coming back from death's door, she was as belligerent as ever.

"CHAMO HAS BEEN SAVED! ADLET! CHAMO HAS BEEN SAVED!" Mora's enhanced voice thundered.

As Dozzu escaped, it glanced back at them. To Mora, it seemed to be smiling.

What had happened? Utterly confused, Adlet stood facing Goldof. A fiend had suddenly appeared, and then Goldof had immediately pulled Nashetania out of its mouth. Adlet didn't understand, so he decided to ignore all that and just attack. That was when Mora's mountain echo reached them. All three of them, right about to descend upon Goldof, froze at the same time.

"It's over? Why?" Rolonia murmured.

Fremy's eyes were wide. Did this mean Nashetania had surrendered? What was that creature that Goldof had killed with the Saint's Spike?

Adlet was half joyful and half confused. He couldn't understand what was going on here. He eyed the girl in Goldof's arms. She wore no armor, carried no sword, and her clothing was in tatters. She was wounded all over, and most noticeably, her left arm was missing from the shoulder. It looked painful for her to even breathe. Cradling her, Goldof glared at the trio as if to warn them that if they took so much as one step forward, they were dead.

"It sounds like...Chamo's been saved." Fremy lowered her gun. She must have been unable to judge whether or not she should fight Goldof and Nashetania.

"What a relief! We did it! We did it, didn't we?" Rolonia cheered, now back to normal and sounding elated.

Fremy asked her frostily, "Did what? What did we do?"

Rolonia couldn't give her an answer.

"Thank you...for stopping," said Goldof. "Don't...kill her. She can't...hurt you anymore. We don't...intend to...fight anymore."

Adlet considered his next course of action. Nashetania was their enemy—as was Goldof. Though he didn't have a full handle of the situation, that much was still true. Should they kill the pair here and now?

No, we shouldn't, he thought. "Fremy, Rolonia, put away your weapons. Leave them be."

"...Adlet...I..." Goldof began.

"I know," said Adlet. "You don't want to fight anymore, right? First, tell us what happened."

"I'll tell you...everything."

Fremy and Rolonia put their weapons away, but Goldof still didn't let go of the young woman in his arms. Nashetania, breathing weakly, looked to be faintly smiling in victory.

"You're okay with this, Adlet? We're not going to kill Nashetania?" asked Fremy.

"..." He couldn't reply to her. He had stopped the fight because he'd wanted to hear what Goldof had to say—and because he thought that if they tried to kill Nashetania, they'd have no guarantee of winning. Even now that Goldof was disarmed, wounded, and exhausted, Adlet didn't feel like they could beat him. Goldof would make it through any trial for the sake of protecting Nashetania, or so it seemed.

"I want to ask you one thing, Goldof. What was your goal?" Adlet asked.

Goldof replied, "...I wanted to see her."

"That was it?"

"Yes. Nothing more...than that. I couldn't think...about anything... else." His expression was different now. No longer the monstrous warrior who had barred their way so many times, he was now just a boy. Adlet noticed the distinct youthfulness of his face. Tears overflowed from Goldof's eyes.

"...Gol...dof..." Nashetania whispered in his arms. Her voice was hoarse because of her crushed throat. "...Now, I've...granted it. Your request...six years ago." She smiled.

Goldof bowed his head to the woman in his arms and said, "Your Highness...thank you...so much."

From what Adlet could see in this situation, Goldof had been the one to save her. So why was he thanking her? But the meaning behind that was surely meant for just the two of them, something he would never be privy to.

Epilogue

An Alliance Formed

Night fell, and the group returned to the Cut-Finger Forest from the hot, sulfuric area. If they lingered, Tgurneu's fiends might come to attack them next. In a corner of the woods, they sat together, keeping as quiet as possible.

After Adlet's trio had finished fighting Goldof, they'd headed over to meet up with the other Braves. They told Nashetania and Goldof they'd put the fight on hold for the time being so they could learn the truth about what was going on. Chamo didn't seem pleased, but since she had no choice, she did as Adlet said.

When Dozzu discovered they'd stopped fighting, it had returned from where it had fled to come meet up with them.

Chamo removed the blade gem from her slave-fiend's stomach and then meticulously inspected the rest of her pets. Dozzu, meanwhile, spat up the parasite in its mouth that had been feeding information to Tgurneu and immolated the Saint-sealing fiend on Nashetania's back.

In the faint glow of light gems, Adlet's party faced Dozzu. A short distance away from where the Braves huddled together sat Goldof, holding Nashetania firmly against his chest. Dozzu situated itself right next to the group of six, telling them the truth behind their fight. It explained the contract between Cargikk, Tgurneu, and Dozzu, about how Cargikk's fiends had chased Dozzu and Nashetania, how the pair had chosen capture by

Tgurneu over the alternative, and how they'd had Goldof save Nashetania. Dozzu did most of the talking. Nashetania's throat was destroyed, so she couldn't speak, and all Goldof's nerve had been consumed protecting her.

"I swear that all I've said has been completely true. Please, I do hope you will trust that," said Dozzu, tying up the long story.

The six looked at each other, silent. They had no guarantee that everything Dozzu said was genuine—but still, it didn't seem to be lying.

Adlet was shocked. Now he knew just how far from the truth he'd been, and the degree to which he had been manipulated. The hieroform he'd been chasing had just been a tool for Goldof to speak with Nashetania. The traces of the hieroform that he had mistaken for a clue had been from their communications. Tgurneu had tricked him and won.

"So in other words, it was mew guys, the Dozzu camp, who won this one?" said Hans, ignoring Adlet as he reflected upon this humiliation.

"Exactly. We achieved our goal, which was the survival of both myself and Nashetania. That was all," Dozzu replied, quite composed.

"So you used Tgurneu in order to escape from Cargikk," Fremy reflected, "and to escape Tgurneu, you used Goldof. Quite a pair you are."

"I will take that as a compliment. Thank you." Not even Fremy's sarcasm bothered Dozzu.

"Hey, so now that we're done talking, Chamo can kill it, right? Chamo just can't hold back anymore."

"…Miss Chamo." Dozzu lowered itself and pressed its face to the ground. "You have my deepest and most sincere apologies for everything that has happened. I realize that this is not a transgression that can be forgiven, but I beg of you, please, have mercy."

"…Um…are you apologizing?" Taken aback, the girl tilted her head in bafflement.

"Chamo, our original purpose was never to cause you harm. It was something we were forced to do to survive," said Dozzu, and behind the fiend, Nashetania bowed her head as well.

"Well, Chamo doesn't know what to do with an apology," she mused, scratching her head.

"We should kill them, no? They're our enemies," said Mora.

Dozzu lifted its head. Seeing that, Fremy took aim at the fiend. Goldof, still holding Nashetania, put his hand on his spear and rose slightly. Hans lifted his blades to dissuade Goldof.

"Wait, please. It's true, we are your enemies. But it's not our intention to fight right now," said Dozzu.

Adlet gestured for his allies to sit. He'd expected as much. If Dozzu had wanted a fight, it wouldn't have gone to all this trouble to tell them the truth.

"Please, Dozzu, could you explain what you mean?" said Rolonia. Adlet wondered why she was being so polite to a fiend.

"If we killed three of the Six Braves," Dozzu explained, "Tgurneu and Cargikk would surrender to us. That was ultimately the only reason we arranged that battle in the Phantasmal Barrier. Killing the Braves in and of itself is not our goal."

"...So?"

"With our current forces, we can't kill three of you. Perhaps it could be done if we sacrificed ourselves, but that wouldn't help us realize our ambition." Dozzu surveyed the entire group and said, "We would like to defeat Tgurneu and Cargikk. They are the greatest obstacles to the fulfillment of our objective. We would like to join forces with you in the name of that goal."

Face stiff, Mora objected. "That's far too great a demand. Your actions nearly brought about Chamo's death."

"And we do apologize most sincerely for that. However, that was not our original purpose," Dozzu countered. "We wanted to meet with you earlier to make this proposal, but we were unable to do so. By the time we arrived at the Bud of Eternity, you had already left. We immediately set off after you, but you were running hither and yon in the Cut-Finger Forest trying to avoid Tgurneu, and it was impossible to pin down your location."

"So if we'd stayed a little longer at the Bud of Eternity..." Adlet trailed off.

"That's right, Adlet. In that case, this battle never would have happened at all, since we would have had no reason to deceive you or fight with you."

This was an absurd tale indeed. That meant this whole day of fighting had been completely unnecessary.

"Please, I beg that you agree to this alliance. I believe this proposal will be of benefit to both parties," Dozzu said, and it bowed its head one more time.

All eyes gathered on Adlet—the final judgment was his responsibility.

Chamo, beside him, offered her opinion. "Chamo is way not convinced about this. Adlet, can you just tell us to kill 'em?"

"But, Addy," said Rolonia from his other side, "we'd have more allies. That's a good thing."

Adlet sat sandwiched between Chamo and Rolonia and their conflicting opinions.

"But would they truly be our allies, Rolonia?" said Mora.

Dozzu spoke. "I won't pretend that this is a noble act. Let me be frank: We're your enemies. We would be cooperating solely to defeat Tgurneu and Cargikk. After their fall, I'm sure we will end up fighting one another."

"S-so then…"

"Nevertheless, I would still hope you accept this offer of alliance," said Dozzu.

Adlet asked, "What's in it for us?"

"I am a considerable asset in combat, and Nashetania as well, once she's recovered. We can also offer your group much information about the Howling Vilelands, fiends, and the Evil God."

"Would that information be useful?" asked Adlet.

"I believe so. You haven't even managed to find a way to cross Cargikk's Canyon, and beyond the ravine, many more obstacles await you. Without our cooperation, you'll never arrive at the Weeping Hearth," said Dozzu.

Adlet couldn't counter any of that. It could've been all true.

"And we have still more intelligence to offer. While we don't know the identity of the seventh among you, we have a clue—information I can say with certainty will lead you to discover their identity. We can also tell you about the origin of the fake crest."

Adlet fell silent. Like him, the others all had their eyes on Dozzu. This wasn't even something that needed consideration—he wanted that knowledge so badly he could taste it. Adlet scanned his allies' faces. Judging from their expressions, none of them opposed this alliance. Even Chamo and the deeply doubtful Fremy didn't seem to object.

"Goldof," said Adlet.

Still holding Nashetania, Goldof shifted his eyes to Adlet.

Adlet had come to realize that the knight was probably a real Brave. Would it even be possible for him to work for Tgurneu without Nashetania and Dozzu noticing at all? The very idea that a master and retainer with such a strong connection could each be communicating with different enemies was just so improbable. And in the end, Goldof had saved Chamo and thwarted Tgurneu's scheme. Goldof opposed Tgurneu and therefore couldn't be the seventh.

"...What is it...Adlet?" asked Goldof.

"Are you in favor of this alliance?"

After a silence, Goldof spoke. "I want to protect Her Highness. If it will help me accomplish that...I'm in favor."

When Adlet heard that, he thought, *He's already left our side.* "Goldof, after we've killed Tgurneu and Cargikk, will you fight with us?"

"...I will...protect Her Highness. That's the most important thing. The Braves' victory...is second most." Goldof didn't explicitly say he would fight them, but he had essentially declared that he would be apart from the Braves of the Six Flowers. Something that should not be, something that they all had thought impossible, had just happened.

One of the Braves had betrayed them.

There were eight humans here. Nashetania sided with Dozzu, and the seventh worked for Tgurneu. Now Goldof had joined Dozzu's side, too. It was enough to make Adlet dizzy. Three of the eight humans here were enemies. How should they fight in a situation like this?

"So, Adlet. Will it be possible for you to accept this alliance?" Dozzu pressed him.

Adlet wanted to do everything he could to avoid fighting Tgurneu and Cargikk. Their goal was, ultimately, the overthrow of the Evil God. But he wanted the information that Dozzu had, by all possible means. He concluded that they would join forces for now, and then eventually cut them loose. In proposing this, Dozzu had most likely anticipated Adlet's choice.

"I'd like to accept, but first I want to ask something," said Adlet.

"Then I'll answer. Go ahead," Dozzu replied.

"You said before that you want to create a world where humans and fiends can live together. How do you plan to accomplish that?"

"I simply cannot answer that question. If I do, then our victory will slide even further from our grasp."

"Your ambition just sounds like a crazy delusion to me. I don't want to join forces with lunatics. Just tell me part of it, whatever you can."

Dozzu glanced at Nashetania, and she gave a tiny nod. "Understood. If we're going to cooperate, then it can't be helped." Adlet's whole group gave Dozzu their full attention. Goldof, too, leaned forward to listen.

"Our goal is to replace the Evil God."

"What?" Adlet didn't understand what Dozzu was saying. The Evil God was the Evil God. You couldn't just replace it like a king or a temple elder.

"We will destroy the current Evil God...that ugly, mad monster, and birth a new deity. It will have a righteous heart, love fiends, love humanity, and love peace. There wouldn't be any point in replacing the Evil God otherwise. Under the rule of a new god, all fiends will be reborn, transformed from creatures that loathe humans into creatures that can live together with them."

"No way," breathed Adlet. "That's just...unbelievable, though..."

Dozzu ignored him and continued. "And then, with our new god, we will storm the human realms, destroy the rotten kings, the nobles that drown themselves in decadence, and unify the world. That is our ultimate goal. And that's all we can tell you at present."

It was all so extravagant, Adlet's brain just couldn't parse it.

"What do you know, Dozzu? Answer me—what on earth is the Evil God?" Fremy pressed, her tone agitated.

Dozzu's expression was still calm as it looked at the group and said, "The Evil God, the fiends, the Saint of the Single Flower, the Crest of the Six Flowers, the conflict between Tgurneu, Cargikk, and me, and the two fake crests might all seem like independent elements, but in truth, it's all one single complex matter."

The group said nothing. They just waited for Dozzu to continue.

"I'll start from the beginning. Three hundred years ago, I encountered a Saint. Together we took on the mysteries of the world. Her name was Hayuha Pressio, Saint of Time."

All the Braves' eyes widened. Everyone who lived on the continent knew that name. Hayuha, the Saint of Time, had defeated the Evil God three hundred years ago. She had been one of the Braves of the Six Flowers.

"The first fake crest, the one that Nashetania has now, originally belonged to her, and she gave it to me three hundred years ago."

AFTERWORD

It's been a long time, everyone. This is Yamagata.

I finally submitted *Rokka: Braves of the Six Flowers* volume three without incident.

Did you enjoy the book?

I have five whole pages for my afterword this time, so I've been thinking I have to add more lines somehow.

This is an advertisement: The manga adaptation of *Rokka: Braves of the Six Flowers*, which is currently being serialized in *SD & GO!* (Super Dash Bunko's bimonthly manga magazine), has been published in volume format. The artist for this series is Mr. Kei Toru. His art is beautiful and powerful. He's drawn such wonderful work. Mr. Kei Toru, thank you very much, and I'm very happy you'll be working on this series.

I think his work has a certain appeal that's just a touch different from the novels, so I'll be glad if you pick it up.

Now, I suppose I'll report on my current state of affairs.

My poor quality of sleep has always been a source of anxiety for me. Just about every night, immediately after falling asleep, I'll have a nightmare and jump off my futon.

Typical nightmares include strange women strangling me, hands growing from the floor to drag me underground, something really heavy and creepy sitting on my stomach, or something holding my legs to keep me from moving when I really have to go to the bathroom. Less common dreams include a character from an eroge I played before bed cutting off my legs and taking them away, and a dream of a plump, fortysomething male I've never met before coming into my apartment to take a dump.

I get these kinds of nightmares at least once a night, and at worst, two or three times a night. Every time, they wake me up.

I've been dealing with these nightmares for more than ten years now, and I've tried many times to fix the problem—like by taking a long bath before bed, or listening to relaxing music before bed. The psychological approach has had some effect, but ultimately, wasn't enough to resolve the problem. I've tried various other schemes, like exhausting myself with exercise before bed, or just staying up so late that I couldn't keep my eyes open, but that just made it worse.

I've also tried more spiritual methods, such as leaving salt in my room for luck, or visiting the temple, or reading sutras before bed, or meditating before bed, but none of these worked, either. It seems my problem is not within the jurisdiction of the gods and buddhas.

If I drink to my heart's content, the nightmares stop, but that just causes other, health-related problems, so it's not something I can do often.

I was utterly at my wit's end. What should I do? I wondered. But I found an unexpected solution: a body pillow.

When I fell asleep holding a body pillow, the frequency of nightmares decreased dramatically to once every three days. It seems that the body pillow is most effective when I wrap both my arms and legs around it, holding it firmly while I sleep curled up on my side. I experimented with sleeping without the body pillow again, and I had nightmares, just like before. So I can understand just what an immense effect the body pillow has.

Before, going to bed has always been accompanied by fear and pain, but thanks to the body pillow, I'm now able to sleep normally. I never could have anticipated that this cheap thing I bought casually for just two thousand yen would be so effective. It actually makes me frustrated that I didn't realize the possibilities of the body pillow earlier. If anyone else has a similar issue, I would very much recommend trying a body pillow.

But there is just one thing about this body pillow that rather gets on my nerves. That is, whenever I tell people about it, they always snicker a little at me. Some people will ask, "So which character?" or they'll say, "If you want a pillow case for it, I'll give you one." It seems that society has a very strange view of body pillows. So I'll take this opportunity to be very clear: The one I use does not have a pretty girl on it. It's a plain, normal body pillow. Furthermore, I don't use it to satisfy my sexual desires. I use it because it's a necessary household item for me. I do feel slightly disgruntled that people don't seem to be able to understand this.

It does cause some other problems, as well. For example, I foresee this will cause me trouble when I go traveling, and it's also really embarrassing when people see me sleeping. The travel issue in particular is a difficult one. Obviously, I can't go traveling with my body pillow. Not that I ever go traveling much at all, though.

Well, anyway, body pillows are the best. I believe I will continue to make use of it.

And finally, the acknowledgments:

To my illustrator, Miyagi-san: Thank you very much for your work on this volume, as well. It really helps me out when you point out the inconsistencies in my work, so I'll take this opportunity to offer my most sincere gratitude.

To my editor, T-san: I'm sorry for all the stress I keep causing you. And thank you as well to everyone in the editorial department, the proofreading staff, and the cover designer.

And to all my readers: Thank you very much for your support. It's thanks to you that I can continue the *Rokka: Braves of the Six Flowers* series.

I'll see you again, after the next book.

Best,

Ishio Yamagata